Everyone Is Raving About

UNDEAD AND UNWED

"What can you say about a vampire whose loyalty can be bought by designer shoes? Can we say, outrageous? . . . A hilarious book."
—*The Best Reviews*

"*Undead and Unwed* is an irreverently hilarious, superbly entertaining novel of love, lust, and designer shoes. Betsy Taylor is an unrepentant fiend—about shoes. She is shallow, vain, and immensely entertaining. Her journey from life to death, or the undead, is so amusing I found myself laughing out loud while reading. Between her human friends, vampire allies, and her undead enemies, her first week as the newly undead is never boring."
—*Romance Reviews Today*

"A hilarious book."
—*Paranormal Romance*

"This book is fantastic. These vampires are different from any that I've read about . . . The lead characters are strong and independent, the action fast and furious . . . This is one of the most erotic books that I've read in years."
—*Escape to Romance*

Undead
and
Unwed

MaryJanice Davidson

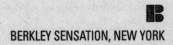
BERKLEY SENSATION, NEW YORK

UNDEAD AND UNWED

A Berkley Sensation Book / published by arrangement with the author

PRINTING HISTORY
Berkley Sensation edition / March 2004

Copyright © 2004 by MaryJanice Davidson Alongi.
Excerpt from *Dead to the World* copyright © 2004 by Charlaine Harris Schulz.
Cover illustration by Chris Long / CWC International, Inc.
Cover design by Pamela Jaber.
Interior text design by Kristin del Rosario.

ISBN: 0-425-19485-X

BERKLEY SENSATION™
Berkley Sensation Books are published by The Berkley Publishing Group, a division of Penguin Group (USA) Inc., 375 Hudson Street, New York, New York 10014.
BERKLEY SENSATION and the "B" design are trademarks belonging to Penguin Group (USA) Inc.

PRINTED IN THE UNITED STATES OF AMERICA

10 9 8 7 6 5 4 3 2 1

This book is dedicated to
Anthony Alongi,
my editor, my partner, my bearded nemesis,
and my friend.
All praise to my darling husband.

Acknowledgments

There's really no need to thank anyone; I did this *all myself*. Okay, that was a rather large lie. While I did the actual writing, many people helped in ways they might not be aware of.

First, thanks to my husband, who edited every word I wrote, and kept the kids out of my hair while I was on deadline. Thanks also to Angela Knight, who was kind enough to mention my work to the fabulous Cindy Hwang; Tina Engler, who gave me the thumbs-up to write an obscure e-book about a dead secretary; and Martha Punches, who edited a rough draft for free.

Thanks also to my book club, the Magic Widows, who often gave me great ideas for dialogue, and special thanks to Cathleen Barkmeier for the information on G.A.D.

I'd also like to thank my friends on the Cape: Curt, Andrea, Guy, Vana, and Jon. Anthony brought a Midwestern redneck around, and they welcomed her from day one.

Finally, I'd like to thank my family: Al, Sharon, Yvonne, Paul, Bill, Elinor, Julie Kathryn, Thomas, Betsy, Scott, and Daniel. They have paid me the ultimate compliment of being unsurprised at my success. Or they've hidden their surprise very well. Either way, I'm grateful.

Chapter 1

THE day I died started out bad and got worse in a hurry.

I hit my snooze alarm a few too many times and was late for work. Who wouldn't hit the snooze to get another nine minutes of sleep? No one, that's who. Subsequently, I almost always oversleep. Stupid snooze button.

I didn't have time for breakfast. Instead, I gobbled a pair of chocolate Pop Tarts while waiting for the bus. Mmmm . . . chocolate. My mom would have approved (who do you think got me hooked on the darned things?), but a nutritionist would have smacked me upside the head with her calorie counter.

The bus was, of course, late. You gotta love the Minnesota Transit system. Six buses for a population area of a quarter million. When they weren't late, they were early— I'd lost count of the number of times I'd stepped outside only to see my bus disappearing down the street. Schedule? What schedule?

When the bus, late again, finally did lumber into sight, I climbed on and sat down . . . in gum.

At a nine A.M. meeting (to which I arrived at 9:20) I found out the recession (the one the economists have been denying for years) had hit me right between the eyes: I had been laid off. Not unexpected—the last time good old Hamton & Sons had been profitable I'd been in high school—but it hurt, just the same. Losing a job is the worst. You know, beyond a shadow of a doubt, that somebody doesn't want you. Doesn't matter if the reasons are personal, financial, or practical. They just don't want you.

Hamton & Son, realizing about a year too late that they had to slash costs, decided administrative layoffs were the way to go as opposed to, say, cutting the six figure salaries of senior management. The clerks and secretaries had been deemed expendable. But vengeance would be ours. Without us, those twits couldn't even send a fax, much less run the company.

With this cheerful thought, I cleaned out my desk, ignored the way my coworkers were avoiding looking at me, and scuttled home. I consoled myself by stopping at Dairy Queen for a blueberry milkshake. Signs of spring: robins, new grass, and Dairy Queen opening for the season.

As I walked through my front door, still slurping, I saw my answering machine light winking at me like a small black dragon. The message was from my stepmonster, and from the racket in the background, she was calling from her salon: "Your father and I won't be able to make it to your party tonight . . . I'm on new medication and I—we—just can't. Sorry." *Sure you are, jerk.* "Have fun without us." *No problem.* "Maybe you'll meet someone tonight." Translation: Maybe some poor slob will marry you.

My stepmonster had, from day one, related to me in only one way: as a rival for her new husband's affections. Worse, she never hesitated to play the depression card to get out of something that was important to me. This ceased bothering me about a week after I met her, so I suppose it was just as well.

I went into the kitchen to feed my cat, and that's when I noticed she'd run away again. Always looking for adventure, my Giselle (although it's more like I'm her Betsy).

I looked at the clock. My, my. Not even noon. Time to do laundry and gouge out my eyes, and the day would be complete.

Happy birthday to me.

AS it turned out, we had a freak April snowstorm, and my party was postponed. Just as well . . . I didn't feel like going out, putting on a happy face, and drinking too many daiquiris. The Mall of America is a terrific place, but I've got to be in the mood for overpriced retail merchandise, rowdy weekend crowds, and six-dollar drinks.

Nick called around eight P.M., and that was my day's sole bright spot. Nick Berry was a superfine detective who worked out of St. Paul. I'd been attacked a couple of months before, and . . .

Okay, well, "attacked" is putting it mildly. Like using the word "unfortunate" to describe World War II. I don't like to talk about it—to *think* about it—but what happened was, a bunch of creeps jumped me as I was leaving Khan's Mongolian Barbecue (all you can eat for $11.95, including salad, dessert, and free refills—quite the bargain if you don't mind your clothes reeking of garlic for hours).

I have no idea what my attackers wanted—they didn't take my purse or try to rape me or even babble about government conspiracies.

They came out of nowhere—literally. One minute I was yawning and fumbling for my keys, the next I was surrounded. They clawed and bit at me like a bunch of rabid squirrels while I fended them off with the toes of my Manolo

Blahniks and screamed for help as loud as I could . . . so loud I couldn't speak above a whisper for three days. They stank—worse than my kitchen that time I went to the Cape for two weeks and forgot to empty my garbage before I left. They all had long hair and funny-colored eyes and they never talked to me.

Help didn't come, but the bad guys ran away. Maybe they were rattled by my voice—when I scream, dogs howl. Or maybe they didn't like the way I stank of garlic. Whatever the reason, they ran away—skittered away, actually. While I leaned against my car, concentrating on not passing out, I glanced back and it looked like a few of them were on all fours. I struggled mightily not to yark up my buffet, ginger tea, and sesame bread—no way was I pissing away that $11.95—and then called 911 on my cell phone.

Detective Nick was assigned to the case, and he interviewed me in the hospital while they were disinfecting the bite marks. All fifteen of them. The intern who took care of me smelled like cilantro and kept humming the theme from *Harry Potter and the Chamber of Secrets*. Off-key. This was actually more annoying than the sting of the antiseptic.

That was last fall. Since then, more and more people— they didn't discriminate between women and men—were being attacked. The last two had turned up dead. So, yeah, I was freaked out by what happened, and I'd sworn off Khan's until the bad guys were caught, but mostly I was grateful it hadn't been worse.

Anyway, Detective Nick called and we chatted and, long story short, I promised to come in to look through the Big Book o' Bad Guys one more time. And I would. For myself, to feel empowered, but mostly to see Nick, who was exactly my height (six feet), with dark blond hair cut regulation-short, light blue eyes, a swimmer's build, and dimples! He looked like an escapee from a Mr. Hardbody calendar. I've broken the law, Officer, take me in.

Making Nick my eye candy would be the closest I'd

gotten to getting laid in . . . what year was it? Not that I'm a prude. I'm just picky. Really, really picky. I treat myself to the nicest, most expensive shoes I can get my hands on, which isn't easy on a secretary's budget, and never mind all the money my dad keeps trying to throw at me. If I used his money, they wouldn't be my shoes. They'd be his. Anyway, I save up for months to buy the dumb things, and they only have to go on my feet.

Yep, that's me in a nutshell: Elizabeth Taylor (don't start! I've heard 'em all), single, dead-end job (well, not anymore), lives with her cat. And I'm so dull, the fucking cat runs away about three times a month just to get a little excitement.

And speaking of the cat . . . was that her telltale *Riaaa-ooowwwww!* from the street? Well, super. Giselle hated the snow. She had probably been looking for a little spring lovin' and got caught in the storm. Now she was outside waiting for rescue. And when I *did* rescue her, she'd be horribly affronted and wouldn't make eye contact for the rest of the week.

I slipped into my boots and headed into the yard. It was still snowing, but I could see Giselle crouched in the middle of the street like a small blob of shadow, one with amber-colored eyes. I wasted ten seconds calling her—*why* do I call cats?—then clomped through my yard into the street.

Normally this wouldn't be a problem, as I live at the end of the block and it's a quiet street. However, in the snow on icy roads, the driver didn't see me in time. When he did, he did the absolute worst thing: slammed on his brakes. That pretty much sealed my doom.

Dying doesn't hurt. I know that sounds like a crock, some touchy-feely nonsense meant to make people feel better about biting the big one. But the fact is, your body is so traumatized by what's happening, it shuts down your nerve endings. Not only did dying not hurt, I didn't even feel the cold. And it was only ten degrees that night.

I handled it badly, I admit. When I saw he was going to

plow into me, I froze like a deer in headlights. A big, dumb, blond deer who had just paid for touch-up highlights. I couldn't move, not even to save my life.

Giselle certainly could; the ungrateful little wretch scampered right the hell out of there. Me, I went flying. The car hit me at forty miles an hour, which was survivable, and knocked me into a tree, which was not.

It didn't hurt, as I said, but there was tremendous pressure, all over my body. I heard things break. I heard my own skull shatter—it sounded like someone was chewing ice in my ear. I felt myself bleed, felt liquid pouring from everywhere. I felt my bladder let go involuntarily for the first time in twenty-six years. In the dark, my blood on the snow looked black.

The last thing I saw was Giselle sitting on my porch, waiting for me to let her in. The last thing I heard was the driver, screaming for help.

Well, not the *last*. But you know what I mean.

Chapter 2

BEING dead really makes you think. Mostly, it makes you think about all the stuff you screwed up, or didn't do.

It's not that I had this tremendously exciting life or anything, but jeez, I would have liked to have lived more than a measly thirty years. And when I thought of the way I wasted the last year . . . the last ten years . . . ugh.

I was never a genius. Strictly C-plus average, which was just fine. Who could worry about Geometry and Civics and Chemistry when I had to work on my talent number for the Miss Burnsville pageant? Not to mention keeping three or four fellas on the hook without them realizing they were on the hook . . . sometimes I was exhausted by lunchtime.

Anyway, I tolerated high school, hated college (just like high school, only with ashtrays and beer kegs), flunked out, modeled for a bit, got bored with *that* . . . people never believed me when I told them modeling was about as interesting as watching dust bunnies. But it was true. The money was okay, but that was the only good thing about it.

Modeling, contrary to the idea projected by the media, wasn't the least bit glamorous. You spend your days going to cattle calls with your portfolio tucked under one arm and a desperate smile on your pretty face. You get maybe one job in ten . . . if you're lucky. Then you get up at 5:30 in the morning to do that job, and often work an eighteen-hour day. Then, maybe five weeks later, you finally get paid. And that's after your agent holds the check for ten days to make sure it clears.

Still, I had some fun in the beginning. Runway shows were made for the strut. It was a kick to tell people what I did for a living—this is America, after all, land of the shallow. Announcing the way I earned my money was always good for a free drink or three. God knows, men were certainly impressed.

Print ads were awful, though . . . shot after shot after shot and smile, smile, smile, and sometimes you were on your feet for ten hours at a stretch. And the attitude—smile big, honey, then sit on Daddy's lap—was worse.

And don't get me started on the male models! Much more vain than the ladies. To this day I can't watch *Zoolander;* it just hits too damned close to home. I'm sure Ben Stiller thought he was making a comedy, but it was really more like a documentary.

It was tough work, dating someone who spent more on hair products than I did. And never being able to catch their eye because they were always checking out their reflection. And a lot of them were hounds—turn your back to get a drink, and you were likely to find your dates du jour chatting up some other bim . . . or feeling her up. Or feeling up the waiter. I hated being the last to know I was a beard. So embarrassing!

About two years into it, I'd had enough. All at once.

I was sitting in a room full of tall blond women with long legs and hair . . . women with my height and coloring. And it occurred to me that the men waiting in the back to interview me didn't care that I loved steak and risotto, and scary movies (with the exception of *Zoolander*) and my mom. They didn't care that I was a member of P.E.T.A. and a registered Republican (contrary to popular belief, the two aren't mutually exclusive). Hell, they didn't care if I was a wanted felon. The *only* thing they cared about was my face and my body.

I remember thinking, *What am I doing here?*

Excellent question. I got up and walked out. Didn't even take my portfolio home with me. My friend Jessica has called me a woman of instant decision and I guess there's some truth in that. Once I make up my mind, that's it.

Anyway, I started temping around the Twin Cities, which, like all the jobs I ever had, was fun until I mastered the situation and got bored. Eventually I had so much experience as a secretary they made me a supersecretary . . . excuse me, an executive assistant.

Which brought me to Hamton & Sons, where my job was fraught with excitement and danger. Excitement because there was rarely enough money to pay the company's bills. Danger because I was often worried I'd succumb to the urge to throttle my boss, and go down for homicide. Triple homicide, if the brokers got in my way.

Most people complain about their bosses—it's the American way—but I was serious: I truly despised him. Worse, I didn't respect him. And there were days when I wondered if he was really crazy.

Last week had been typical. I got to work just in time to be met at the door by wide-eyed brokers who had, in the ten minutes they'd been unsupervised, broken the copy machine. The *brand-new* copy machine. I swear they were like children. Little children whom you cannot turn your back on. Little chain-smoking children.

"It's not working," Todd, the head of the broker posse, informed me. "We'll just have to send it back. I told you we didn't need a new one."

"The old one got so overheated all our copies were brown and smelled like smoke. What'd you do?" I said, hanging up my coat.

"Nothing. I was making copies and then it clanked and then it stopped."

"What. Did. You. Do."

"Well . . . I tried to fix it. I didn't want to bother you," he hurried on at my murderous expression.

He tried to scurry away but I grabbed his arm and tugged him toward the machine, which was making an ominous wheezing sound. I pointed to the poster taped on the wall. "Read it."

"Betsy, I'm really busy, the market just opened and I have to—ow! Okay, okay. Don't pinch. It says 'If anything goes wrong, do not under ANY circumstances fix it yourself . . . find Betsy or Terry.' There, okay?"

"Just wanted to make sure you hadn't forgotten how to read." I let go of his arm before I gave in to the urge to pinch him again. "Go away, I'll fix it."

Twenty minutes and one ruined skirt later (stupid toner!), the machine was up and running. So I started to go through my mail, only to stop dead at the now familiar monthly letter from the I.R.S.

I marched straight into my boss, Tom's, office. He looked up when I shut the door behind me, spearing me with the dead stare of the classic sociopath. Or maybe he learned it in business school.

I shook the letter at him. "The I.R.S. is still—still!—looking for our payroll taxes."

"I can't deal with that right now," Tom said testily. He was of medium height—and resented the hell out of the fact that I was taller—and smoked like cigarettes were going to be outlawed within the week. Despite the strict Minnesota

Clean Indoor Air Act, his office smelled like an ashtray. "Talk to me when the market's closed."

"Tom, we're almost a year behind! That money is our employees', to be paid to the government. You know, state and federal taxes? We can't keep using it to pay our bills. We already owe the government over a hundred thousand dollars!"

"After the market closes," he said, and turned back to his computer. Dismissed. And of course, at 3:01 P.M., he'd be out the door, avoiding any tedious meetings with me.

I stomped out. Not a day went by that Tom didn't try something sneaky. He either lied to his customers, lied to his employees, or used their money without telling them. If caught, he would blame me. And he had the uncanny knack of being able to convince people it wasn't his fault. He was a hell of a salesman, I'd give him that. Even I, who knew him well, could often be fooled by his enthusiasm.

I hated being his enforcer, writing up disciplinary reports for the brokers while he got to do the raises—Tom was strictly a fun-stuff guy. And I hated it when he made me lie to his clients. They were nice people and had no idea they were trusting a sociopath with their money.

But, damn it, the money was great. Even better, I was able to work four ten-hour days, which meant three-day week-ends. Three days was just about long enough to muster the courage to go back to the office on Monday. It was tough to give up. Any other secretarial job and I'd have to save for a lot longer to get my shoes. I guess that meant I was a sellout.

I stayed until 5:00 P.M. and, as usual, I was the only one. The receptionist went home at 4:30, and everyone else left at 3:30, after the markets were closed. But Tom lived in fear of missing a vital phone call, so I stayed until 5:00 every night. Well, it was a good way to catch up on my reading.

I left at 5:00 to meet my date . . . Todd's nephew, of all people. He assured me we'd get along swimmingly. Normally I avoided blind dates like they were split ends, but I was lonesome, and hadn't met anyone new in over a year. I was too old for club-hopping, and too young for bingo. So I went.

Big mistake. Todd's nephew was a foot shorter than I was. This didn't bother me—most men were shorter than I was. But some fellows seemed to take it personally, like I'd gotten tall just to spite them. All part of my diabolical plan.

The nephew, Gerry, was one of these. He kept looking up at me, then would glance away, and then, helplessly, look up at me again. It was like he was dazzled—or horrified—by my long legs.

After he'd made several off-color jokes, regaled me with the tales of how he defeated all the grasping, greedy Jews at his accounting firm with wit and cunning, and informed me that the United States should just blow up all the Third World countries and end terrorism at a stroke (presumably with terrorism), I'd had enough. Soul mates we were not. It served me right. I hated dating.

I submitted to a good night kiss only because I wanted to see how he'd reach. He stood on his tiptoes and I bent down. Soft moist lips hit the area between my cheek and my mouth, and I got a whiff of beer and garlic. I didn't mind the garlic, but I positively hated beer. I practically broke my wrist ramming the key through the lock so I could get into the house.

So, a day in the life. My life. What a waste. And now I was done. I never did anything. Not one thing.

Chapter 3

I opened my eyes to pure darkness. When I was a kid I read a short story about a preacher who went to hell, and when he got there he discovered the dead didn't have eyelids, so they couldn't close their eyes to block out the horror. Right away I knew I wasn't in hell, since I couldn't see a thing.

I wriggled experimentally. I was in a small, closed space. I was lying on something hard, but the sides of my little cage were padded. If this was a hospital room, it was the strangest one ever. And the drugs were spectacular . . . I didn't hurt anywhere. And where was everybody? Why was it so quiet?

I wriggled some more, then had a brainstorm and sat up. My head banged into something firm but yielding, which gave way when I shoved. Then I was sitting up, blinking in the gloom.

At first I thought I was in a large, industrial kitchen.

Then I realized I was sitting in a coffin. A white coffin with gold scrolling on the sides, lined in plush pink satin (ugh!). It had been placed on a large, stainless steel table. The table was in the middle of the room, and there was a row of sinks against the far wall. Not a stove in sight. Just several strange-looking instruments, and an industrial-sized makeup kit. Which meant this wasn't a kitchen, this was—

I nearly broke something scrambling out. As it was, I moved too quickly and the coffin and I tumbled off the table and onto the floor. I felt the shock in my knees as I hit but didn't care. In a flash I shoved the coffin off my back and was on my feet and running.

I burst through the swinging doors and found myself in a large, wood-paneled entryway. It was even gloomier in here; there were no windows that I could see, just rows and rows of coat racks. At the far end of the entry was a tall, wild-eyed blonde dressed in an absurd pink suit. She might have been pretty if she wasn't wearing orange blusher and too much blue eye shadow. Her brownish-rose lipstick was all wrong for her face, too. Just about any makeup would have been wrong for her, as she was so shockingly pale.

The blonde wobbled toward me on cheap shoes—Payless, buy one pair get the second at half price—and I saw her hair was actually quite nice: shoulder length, with a cute flip at the ends and interesting streaky highlights.

Interesting Shade #23 Lush Golden Blonde highlights. Heyyyyyyy . . .

The woman in the awful suit was me. The woman in the *cheap shoes* was me!

I staggered closer to the mirror, wide-eyed. Yes, it was really me, and yes, I looked this awful. I really was in hell!

I forced myself to calm down. When that didn't work, I slapped myself, smearing blush on my palm. Clearly I was wrong; this wasn't hell. Hell wasn't a wood-paneled entryway with a mirror on one end and a coffin on the other. It made sense that I looked so repugnant. I was dead. That silly ass in the Pontiac Aztek, doubtless conspiring with my cat, had killed me. The perfect end to a perfect day.

I was dead but too dumb to lie down. Dead and walking around inside the funeral home in a cheap suit and fake leather shoes. The funeral must be tomorrow . . . later today, I amended, looking at the clock.

Who had picked out this outfit for me? And these shoes? I slipped one of the shoes off, looked at the inside.

Property of Antonia O'Neill Taylor.

I knew it. My stepmother! The bitch meant to bury me wearing her cast-off shoes! This bothered me more than being driven into a tree while my cat watched. I nearly threw the wretched shoe at the mirror but instead reluctantly forced it back onto my foot. It was cold outside and I'd need the protection. But at such a price! If Giselle could see me now—if anyone I had ever known could see me now . . .

My cat! Who was going to look after the little monster? Jessica, probably, or maybe my mother . . . yes, probably my mother.

My mother. She'd have been devastated when she got the news. My father, too . . . he might even take the whole day off work for my funeral. My stepmother—well, I doubted she'd much care. She thought I was a headstrong spoiled brat, and I thought she was a conniving, dishonest, gold-digging bitch. And the fact that we were both right and had been since we laid eyes on each other didn't help at all.

It occurred to me that I should seek out my grieving friends and family and tell them I had no intention of being buried. I had to find a new job, for crying out loud, I couldn't hang out in a coffin six feet under. I had to pay my bills or they'd shut off my cable.

Then sanity returned. I was dead. I'd been zombified or whatever, and needed to finish the job the guy in the Aztek had started. Or maybe this was purgatory, a task set for me, something I had to finish before God opened the gate.

I had the fleeting thought that the doctors in the ER had made a mistake, but shook it off. I remembered, too well, the sound of my skull shattering. If it hadn't killed me, I'd be in an ICU now with more tubes than a chemistry class-room. Not dolled up like a . . .

(dead)

. . . whore wearing cheap castoffs on my . . .

(dead)

. . . feet.

All that aside, to be brutally honest, I couldn't bear for anyone to see me looking the way I did. I would literally rather be dead. Again.

I gave my reflection one final incredulous once-over, then walked to the end of the hallway, found the stairwell, and started climbing. The funeral home was three stories high—and what they needed the other two stories for I was *not* going to think about—which should be high enough, since I planned to go headfirst. My nasty shoes clack-clacked on the stairs. I wouldn't let myself look down at my feet.

At first I thought the door was locked, but with a good hard shove it obligingly opened with a shriek of metal on metal. I stepped outside.

It was a beautiful spring night—all traces of snow from the storm had melted. The air smelled wet and warm, like fertility. I had the oddest feeling that if I were to scatter seeds on the cement rooftop, they would take hold and grow. A night had never, ever smelled so sweetly, not even the day I moved into my own place.

City lights twinkled in the distance, reminding me of Christmas. Reminding me all my Christmases were done. There were a few cars moving on the street below, and, far off, I could hear a woman laughing. Well, at least someone was having a good time.

As I stepped onto the ledge, I ignored the not inconsiderable twinge of apprehension that raced up my spine. Even though I was dead, I didn't like looking down at the street. I stifled the urge to step back to safety.

Safety, ha! What was that?

This wasn't my last night on earth. That had been a couple of days ago. There was nothing to feel sad about. I had been a good girl in life, and now I was going to my reward, damn it. I was *not* going to stumble around like a zombie, scaring the hell out of people and pretending I still had a place in the world.

"God," I said, teetering for balance, "it's me, Betsy. I'm coming to see you now. Make up the guest room."

I dove off the roof, fought the urge to curl into a cannonball, and hit the street below, headfirst, exactly as I had planned. What was *not* in the plan was the smashing, crunching pain in my head when I hit, and how I didn't even lose consciousness, much less see my pal God.

Instead I groaned, clutched my head, then finally stood when the pain abated. Only to get creamed by an early morning garbage truck. I looked up in time to see the horror-struck driver mouthing *"Jesus Christ, lady, look out!"* something, then my forehead made brisk contact with the truck's front grille. I slid down it like road kill and hit the street, ass first. That hurt less than hitting the grille, but not by much.

I lay in the street for a long moment, seriously debating whether or not to get up. Finally I decided I couldn't lie there forever—clearly I was bad at just lying anywhere—and slowly got to my feet.

When I stood, brushing dirt from my cheap skirt and blowing my hair out of my face, the driver slammed the truck in reverse and got the hell out of Dodge. Not that I could blame him—I was probably a gruesome sight. But who ever heard of a hit-and-run garbage truck?

Chapter 4

$\mathcal{L}$ am nothing if not persistent. Flinging myself into the Mississippi didn't work: I found I no longer needed to breathe. I trudged around on the muddy river bottom for half an hour, patiently waiting to drown, before giving up and slogging my way back to shore. Interestingly, I couldn't feel the cold, though it couldn't have been more than forty-five degrees, and I was supersoaked.

Grounding myself while I held onto a live power line didn't work, either (though it did *awful* things to my hair).

I drank a bottle of bleach, and the only consequence was a startling case of dry mouth . . . I was *so* thirsty!

I shoplifted a butcher knife from the nearby Wal-Mart— the place to shop if you're dead, it's three A.M., and you don't have any credit cards—and stabbed myself in the heart: nothing. A small trickle of blood flowed sluggishly and, while I watched in horrified fascination, slowed and stopped. In another few minutes the only sign I'd stabbed myself was the cut in my suit and a modest bloodstain.

I was trudging down Lake Street, trying to figure out how to decapitate myself, when I heard low voices and what sounded like muffled crying. I almost moved on—didn't I have enough problems of my own?—when good sense returned and I walked through the alley and around the corner.

I took in the scene at once: three men hulking around a woman in a sort of sinister half-moon. She was holding hands with a big-eyed girl. The girl looked about six or so. Fear made the woman look about fifty. Her purse was lying on the ground between them. Nobody moved to get it, and I had a quick, clear thought: She tossed it at them, and tried to run, and they cornered her. They don't want her purse. They want—

"Please," she said, almost whispered, and I thought the acoustics must be very good for me to have heard them from almost a block away. "Don't do anything to me in front of my daughter. I'll go with you—I'll do whatever you want, just please, please—"

"Mommy, don't leave me here by myself!" The girl's eyes were light brown, almost whiskey-colored, and when they filled with tears I felt something lurch inside my dead heart. "Just—you go away! Leave my mommy alone, you—you—you stinkers!"

"Shhh, Justine, shhh . . ." The woman was trying to pry her daughter's fingers free and made a ghastly attempt at a laugh. "She's tired—it's late—I'll go with you—"

"Don't want *you,*" one of the men said, his eyes on the girl. Justine burst into fresh tears, but not before kicking the ground, raining pebbles and grit on the man's feet. Even in the midst of my shock at witnessing such a horrid scene, I admired the hell out of the girl.

"I'll take you back to my car—the engine's dead but I could—with all of you, just don't—don't—"

"Hey, assholes!" I said cheerfully. All five of them jumped, which surprised me . . . I wasn't the world's quietest walker. I couldn't believe I was doing this. I wasn't exactly the confrontational type. On the other hand, what did I possibly have to lose? "Er . . . you three assholes. Not the lady and the kid. Fellas, could you come over here and kill me, please?" While they were busy killing me, the two of them could run for it. Everyone wins!

Relieved, Justine smiled at me, revealing the gap where she'd lost one of her baby teeth. Then the men moved forward, and Justine grabbed her mom's hand and started dragging her toward the relative safety of Lake Street.

"I'll—"

"Come *on*, Mommy!"

"—get help!"

"Don't you dare," I snapped. "If you mess up my murder, I'll be furious." One of the men had grabbed my arm and was dragging me back toward Justine and her mom. "Just a minute, pal, I've got to—" He poked me, hard, and without thought I shoved.

The rest of it happened awfully fast. Jerkoff number one hadn't poked me, he'd stabbed me, for all the good it did. And when I shoved, his feet left the ground and he sailed back as if hurricane-force winds had blown him. When he finally touched ground he rolled for a good ten feet before he got to his feet and ran like he'd had one too many chimichangas and needed a bathroom.

While I was staring and making my usual vocalization when I didn't understand ("What . . .?"), the other two moved in. I reached up and grabbed them by the backs of their dirty necks, then banged their heads together. I did this entirely without thinking about it—my usual reaction to stressful situations. There was a sickening crunch, and I heard—yech!—their skulls cave in. It was the sound I'd heard at my cousin's wedding when the bratty ring bearer threw the melon boat on the floor, sort of a muffled squishy sound. The bad guys dropped to the ground, deader than disco. Their faces were frozen in eternal expressions of pissed-off.

I nearly threw up into their staring faces. "Oh, shit!"

"Thank you thank you thank you!" Justine's mom was in my arms, reeking of fear and Tiffany perfume.

Ack, a witness to my felony! "Oh, shit!"

She was clutching me with not inconsiderable strength and babbling into my hair. I wriggled, trying to extricate myself without hurting her. "Ohmygod I thought they were going to rape me kill me hurt Justine kill Justine thank you thank you thank you—"

"I can't believe this! Did you see what I did? I can't believe I did it! How did I do it?"

"—thank you thank you thank you so so so much!" She kissed me on the mouth, a hearty smack.

"Whoa! Ixnay the issing-kay . . . we hardly know each other. Also, I'm so straight I could be a ruler. Leggo now, there's a nice hysteric."

She let go of me, still babbling, staggered a few feet away, and threw up. I couldn't blame her—I sort of felt like it myself, though if I hadn't puked after drinking the bleach, I probably never would. She finished retching, wiped her mouth with the back of one trembling hand, knelt, and started picking up the items that had fallen from her purse.

Weirdly, all of a sudden I wanted to grab her back, pukey breath and all. Something about her—the blood, the—she had scraped herself, or one of the men had cut her, and she was bleeding, the blood was flowing beneath her shirt, on the inside of her upper arm, and it trickled steadily and suddenly I was so thirsty I couldn't breathe. Not that I'd been breathing. But you know what I mean.

Justine was staring up at me. She had sidled close to me while her mother was shouting at the floor, so to speak. Her tears had dried, making her cheeks shine in the moonlight. She looked very, very thoughtful. And about six years older than she'd looked five minutes ago.

She pointed. "Doesn't that hurt like crazy?"

I looked down, then jerked the knife out of my side. Very little blood again. Sluggish flow that was already stopping. Again. Urgh. "No. Thanks. Uh . . . don't be scared. Anymore, I mean."

"Why'd you ask them to kill you?"

Normally I wouldn't share unpleasant confidences with a strange child, but what could I say? It had been one of those nights. Plus, she *had* pointed out the knife sticking out of my ribs; I felt obliged to give her an honest answer. "I'm a zombie," I explained, except I was having trouble talking, all of a sudden. "I'm trying to thtay dead."

"You're not a zombie." She pointed at my mouth. "You're a vampire. A good one, so that's all right," she added.

My hand came up so quickly I actually bit myself. I felt the sharp tips of new fangs, fangs that had come out when I'd smelled her mother's blood, fangs that seemed to be taking up half my mouth.

"A vampire? How ith that pothible? I died in a car ackthident, for God'th thake! Aw, thon of a bith!"

"Are you going to suck our blood?" Justine asked curiously.

"Ugh! Blood maketh me throw up. Even the thight of it—ugh!"

"Not anymore, I bet," she said. This was the most levelheaded first-grader I'd ever met. Maybe I could take her under my wing and make her my evil sidekick. "It's okay. You can if you want to. You saved us. My mom," she said, her tone dropping to turn low, confidential, "was really scared."

She's not the only one, sugar . . . and by the way, I bet you'd taste like electricity, all that youth and energy coursing through your bloodstream.

I clapped both hands over my mouth and started backing away. "Run," I said, but I didn't have to bother; Justine's mama had finished gathering up her things, taken one look at my new dentition, picked up her daughter, and galloped away in the opposite direction. Justine managed a wave while bouncing on her mother's hip.

"There'th a gath thtathion at the end of this block!" I yelled after her. "You can call triple A!" I stuck my fingers in my mouth. My lisp was going away, and so were my fangs. "And what were you thinking, having your daughter out at four o'clock in the morning?" I shouted after her, freshly annoyed. "Dope!"

People think because Minneapolis is in the Midwest, rapes and murders and burglaries don't happen there. They do, just not as often in cold weather. I'd bet a thousand bucks the car that had broken down on them was a rental.

Well, the mystery was solved. I was a vampire. How, I had no idea. Car accident victims did not rise from the dead. So I'd always thought, anyway.

In the movies, some bim was always stalked by a tall, dark creature of the night, and she'd swoon into his arms and wake up ravenous three days later. But nothing like that had happened to me. The last tall, dark creature of the night I'd met had been the janitor at work. And he hadn't bitten me, just told me to use the men's room so he could clean the women's room.

There just wasn't any explanation for what had happened to me. Unless . . . could it have something to do with my attack a few months ago? The attackers had been savage, snarling, barely human. Until tonight, it had been the most surreal thing to happen to me, and that included the tax audit and my parents' divorce. Could the attackers have infected me?

And why was I still me? Now that I was a ravenous member of the undead, I should be sucking little girls dry and then lunching on their mamas. I should be a ruthless predator of the night, caring for nothing but my own unnatural fiendish hunger.

The men in the alley had been asshole predators, but I was still horrified when I accidentally killed two of them.

I'd let Justine and her mom go—had *ordered* them to go. I was thirstier than I'd ever been in my . . . uh . . . life, but it wasn't ruling me. I wasn't an animal. I was still me, Betsy, disgusted with my current footwear and ready to give my eyeteeth (or my new fangs) for Colin Farrell's autograph.

Colin Farrell . . . now *there* was someone who'd make a delightful snack.

Chapter 5

"FATHER," I said, "you have to help me."

"I'll be glad to, but I'm not a priest."

"I'm going to hell, and I didn't do a damned thing to deserve being damned. Except for that whole double homicide thing. But it was an accident! Plus, I should get points for saving Justine and her mom."

"I said I'm not a priest, miss. I'm the janitor. And this isn't a Catholic church—we're Presbyterians."

"Fine, you'll do in a pinch. Can you burn me up with holy water?" I had the man by the shirt and was pulling him up on his toes—he was about three inches shorter than me. "Poke me to death with your crucifix?" I shook him like a rat. "Pelt me with communion wafers?"

He gifted me with a sweet, loopy grin. "You're pretty."

Surprised, I let go of him. He did a shocking thing, then: He flung his arms around me and kissed me. Hard. Really very hard, and he put a lot into it, too; his tongue was poking into my mouth and something hard and firm was poking against my lower belly. He tasted like Wheaties.

"Gluk!" I said, or something like it. I gently pushed him away, but even so he flew over the pew and landed with a jarring thud near the pulpit. The grin didn't waver and neither, unfortunately, did his erection; I could see the small tent in his chinos. "Do it again," he sighed, head lolling back on his shoulders.

"Oh, for—just—sleep it off!" I snapped and, to my surprise, his head dropped onto his shoulder and he started to snore. Drunk, then . . . sure. I should have smelled it on him.

I took another look and cursed myself—of course he was the janitor; he was dressed in tan chinos and a T-shirt that read "D&E Cleaning: We'll Wipe Your Mess!" In my keyed-up panic, I'd grabbed the first person I had seen when I walked into the church. He'd grabbed me back, but that was only fair.

I was still surprised I had managed to get inside the church without bursting into flame. Not that I'd been a rabid churchgoer before I died. I mean, I used to go when I was a kid, but that was mostly to get away from my step-monster for a couple of hours. That, and the free grape juice. But since I'd moved out of my dad's house, I hadn't been except for the occasional religious holiday. I was strictly an Easter-and-Christmas Christian.

And now, a dead Christian. So I was amazed I was able to enter the sanctuary without exploding. But nothing like that had happened. The door had opened easily and the church was the way they all were: forbidding, yet comforting, like a beloved but stern grandparent.

I cautiously sat down on a pew, expecting a severe ass burning. Nothing happened. I touched the Bible in front of me . . . nothing. Rubbed the Bible all over my face—nope.

Damn it! Okay, I was a vampire. Shocking, but I was getting used to it. Except vampire rules weren't applying! I should be a writhing tower of flame, not sitting impatiently in a pew waiting for God to send my soul to hell.

I glanced at the clock on the far wall. It was after four in the morning; the sun would be up soon. Maybe a morning stroll would finish me off.

I sighed and slumped back against the pew. "What's going on, God?" I whined. "Sure, I haven't exactly been a frequent flyer for church, but what'd I do to deserve this? I was a pretty good gal. I was kind to children and dumb animals. I even volunteered at soup kitchens, for Christ's sake! Okay, so, yeah, I was kind of materialistic, but quality costs. I don't think it's a sin to want the best shoes money can buy. For one thing, they last forever. For another—pride of ownership. Am I right? So, come on. If Hitler wasn't a vampire, how come I am? Well?"

"My dear?"

"Yeeeaaaggghhhh!" I shot to my feet and nearly fell out of the pew.

A little late, I smelled starch, old cotton, and aftershave, and spun to see the minister walking down the aisle toward me. He was a man in his early fifties, completely bald on top with a white monk's fringe around the sides and back of his head. He wore black slacks and a black short-sleeved shirt, and there was a small cross pinned to his collar. His cheeks were pink from where he had shaved, and he wore thick glasses and sported a heroic Roman nose. A wedding band gleamed on the third finger of his left hand. He was about twenty pounds too heavy for his height, which meant he probably gave the most excellent hugs.

"You scared me," I said reproachfully. "I thought you were God."

"Not quite, dear." He took in the scene at a glance: Cleaning Guy passed out and snoring on the floor, and Dead Girl standing in the pew looking like baked dog shit.

He smiled at me. "It must be Monday."

I ended up telling him the whole story while he fixed

coffee in the fellowship hall, then sat down across from me and listened patiently.

After the night I'd had, the chairs were sinfully comfortable. I drank three cups of coffee with lots of cream and sugar (no need to worry about the waistline anymore) and finished with, "Then I came here, but none of the doors or Bibles or anything are hurting me." I left out the part about the cleaning guy trying to mack on me in front of the pulpit—no need to get anyone in trouble. "You don't have a cross on you, do you?" I added hopefully.

He unpinned the small silver cross on his collar and handed it to me. I closed my fingers around it, tightly, wincing in anticipation, but nothing happened. I shook it. Was this thing on? Still nothing.

I handed it back. "Thanks, but never mind."

"You can have it," he said.

"No, that's all right."

"No, really! I want you to have it."

His cheeks were flushed, and the color deepened as I grabbed his hand, pressed the cross into it, and folded his fingers closed. "Thanks, but it's yours. You shouldn't give it to a stranger."

"A beautiful stranger."

"What?" First the cleaning guy, now the minister! Hitting on the *dead* girl . . . ewwww!

As if in response to my shocked thought, he blinked and slowly shook his head. "Forgive me. I don't know what's come over me." He touched his wedding ring absently, and that seemed to give him the strength to look me in the eyes. "Please continue."

"There's nothing else. I'm lost," I finished. "I don't have the faintest idea what to do. I'm sure you think I'm nuts, and I sure don't blame you, but could you just pretend to believe me and give me some advice?"

"You're not nuts, and I don't think you're lying," he soothed. He had a faint southern accent which put me in mind of grits and magnolias. "It's obvious you've had a terrible experience and you need—you just need to talk to someone. And maybe rest."

Sure, rest. In the grave? I wish. Instead, now I was looking at a nice long rest in a nice place where you can make nice baskets and potholders, and the walls have nice padding. I was too tired to stab myself in the heart with my coffee spoon to prove my point. I just nodded and stared at my coffee cup. Maybe if I broke it into pieces and ate it . . .?

"As to why the Bible didn't hurt you, that's quite obvious, dear—God still loves you."

"Or the rules don't apply to me," I pointed out, but even as I said it I realized how arrogant and ridiculous that was. God's rules applied to each and every person on the planet . . . except Betsy Taylor! Shyeah. I mean, I was vain, but even *I* couldn't go *that* far. "So you're saying I should stop with the attempts at self-immolation?"

"At once." He was still touching his ring, and his voice was stronger now, less dreamy. "You said yourself you helped that woman and her little girl, and you haven't bitten anybody. You're clearly in possession of your soul." He hesitated, then plunged. "A parishioner of mine works for a—a nice place in downtown Minneapolis. Could I give you her card? If you don't have a car I'll be glad to drive—"

"I'll be glad to take the card," I said, then added the lie: "I'll call her later this morning."

The minister and I—he'd told me his name but I had forgotten it—parted on good terms, and when I left he was shaking the janitor awake.

I headed home. The minister had thought I was a nut-job, but that didn't negate his advice. My old life was over, but I was beginning to see that maybe . . . maybe I could make a new one.

I was a heartless denizen of the realm of the ravenous undead, and the urge to drink blood (ew!) was getting stronger, but there were ways and ways, and I didn't have to be a lamprey on legs if I didn't want to. For one thing, there were at least six blood banks in this city.

And God still loved me. I had it on good authority, because ministers can't lie. It was like a law.

God loved me (and so, apparently, did the janitor and the minister). It seemed pretty obvious to me now, and I wondered why it hadn't occurred to me earlier tonight: When you try to kill yourself nine or ten different ways, and none of them works, obviously you're meant to be around for a while.

Incredibly, amazingly, I'd been given a second chance. Me, of all people! And I had no plans to waste it. Anymore, anyway.

I was able to flag down a taxi not even two blocks from the church. Since this was Minneapolis as opposed to Boston or New York, taxis were a rare and wonderful thing. Like a helpful Neiman Marcus employee!

I spotted the taxi at the end of the block, going away from me, and lifted my hand in a halfhearted wave. I heard the shriek of tires gripping pavement, and then the cab was swinging around in an illegal U-turn and zooming up to the curb. The driver leapt out and wrenched open the passenger door for me.

"Uh . . . thanks. D'you mind driving to Edina?"

Nothing. Not even a nod. He just stared at me. He was an older man, about my dad's age, with a paunch from too much sitting down, and crumbs in his beard. His shirt buttons strained over his belly, but he looked nice. He was smiling, anyway. Actually grinning goofily, but I didn't want to walk twenty miles, and was in no position to be picky.

I climbed in and we were off. And let me tell you something, if I'd still been looking to die a horrible death, I should have flagged the taxi as soon as I left the mortuary. Beyond any cliché, this guy was nuts. It didn't help that he kept staring at me in his rearview mirror. The blare of horns or the cursing of an early pedestrian would usually bring his attention—briefly—back to the road.

After he'd nearly creamed a bread truck, a newspaper van, a station wagon full of early morning commuters, and a bus, I'd had enough. I might be invulnerable (probably) to a hideously mangling car crash, but my intrepid driver likely wasn't.

"Stop looking at me!" I snapped, cringing as the bus driver laid on the horn. The sonorous bellow filled my eardrums, my world. "Pay attention to the road."

He instantly obeyed, snapping his gaze back to the street. And we didn't have any more problems.

I belatedly realized, when he pulled up to my house, that I had no way of paying the fare. What had I been thinking when I flagged this guy down? I'd been thinking about a nap and a drink, not necessarily in that order.

"Um . . . if you'll wait a minute, I can run inside and—" And what? If memory served, I had exactly forty-eight cents in my wallet. And two tokens for a free car wash at Insty-Lube. Since my birthday party had been canceled, I hadn't gone to a cash machine that day. "Will you take a check? Or maybe no charge, out of the goodness of your heart?" I joked.

He gave me a loopy smile. "Yes, ma'am."

Ma'am? The guy was twice my age, damnit! I had a horrible thought: Had being dead given me wrinkles?

"Well, okay, then," I said doubtfully, covertly feeling my face for crow's feet. "Thanks for the ride."

He zoomed off, still looking at me out his window. I winced as he bounced over the curb and knocked over a mailbox, then scurried up my driveway so I wouldn't have to see more carnage. It was amazing how easy it was in this state to get a driver's license.

My house looked exactly the same on the outside, but as soon as I walked in—some boob had left the door unlocked (oh, wait, that was me)—I saw a real mess. Quite a few of my things had been packed into boxes, which were stacked haphazardly all over my living room. The lights had been left on in the kitchen . . . and how much had that cost me while I was being dolled up in the funeral home? I smelled my stepmother's perfume (Dune, and she used too much of it) on the air and had a horrible thought.

I rushed to my bedroom. There were more boxes back here, and several of my dresses were thrown across my bed. A few had fallen off and were crumpled on the floor in puddles of polyester, silk, and cotton.

I flung open the closet door and my worst fears were realized. Some of my clothes were there, and so were my Stride Rites and the cheap flats I'd bought for casual days at the office. But my babies, the Manolo Blahniks, the Pradas, the Ferragamos, the Guccis, and Fendis . . . all gone.

My stepmother had told the mortician to dress me in one of her old suits, slapped a pair of her used knockoffs on my feet, then headed to my house and grabbed my good shoes for herself.

Let me say that again: She slapped a pair of her used knockoffs on my feet, then *headed to my house and grabbed my good shoes for herself.*

While I was still processing this information, I heard a tentative *meow* and looked up in time to see Giselle peeking at me from the doorway. Cool, she made it back okay. I forced a smile and took a step toward her—who knew when she'd been fed last? And what was she still doing here?— only to see her puff up to twice her size and run away so quickly she hit the far wall, bounced off, and kept going.

I sat down on my bed and cried.

CRYING'S okay while it lasts, but you can only do it for so long. Toward the end, you always feel a little silly, like, "Am I still making this noise?" And it's weird to do it when you can't make tears anymore. I could sob, but not a tear in sight. Did this mean I wouldn't pee or sweat, either? I was in no rush to go to the bathroom and find out.

Anyway, eventually you're done, and you have to figure out what to do next. Whether it was to break up with the guy in question, stab the boss, shrug off the stepmother's cattiness, or figure out how to get along as a vampire, something has to come next.

I flopped belly down on my bed, limp as a noodle and completely exhausted. And *thirsty*. But I wasn't going to do anything about that now. Except maybe snack on Giselle—no, I wasn't going to do that, either. I was just going to lie here—my room faced east—and let the sun finish me off.

If I woke up dead again, I'd take it as a sign that I was supposed to move on. If I didn't wake up . . . well, at least that was one problem solved. Hell couldn't be worse than a Wal-Mart after midnight, right?

With that thought in my head, I fell asleep.

Chapter 6

I awakened instantly, as I had in the funeral home. This was a definite departure from the norm; usually it took me an hour, a shower, two cups of coffee, and the morning commute to wake all the way up. Not anymore. One minute I was dead (ha!) to the world, the next I was wide awake and rising from my coffin. Well, my bed with Laura Ashley sheets.

I felt perfectly awake, perfectly clear. You know how when you take a nap in the middle of the afternoon, you're groggy for, like, two hours afterward? There was none of that. I felt like I'd just had three Frappucinos. With extra sugar!

The first thing I saw was Giselle, perched imperiously at the foot of my bed. She had apparently done plenty of corpse-sniffing during the day and had decided I would do. So the first thing I did was feed her. Just that simple action—something I'd done twice a day for years—was incredibly comforting. Then I took a shower, brushed my teeth, changed into clean, comfortable clothes, and slipped into my tennis shoes.

I was here, I was dead, get used to it . . . or however the chant for vampire rights went. No more suicide games. It was time to adjust and deal. How, I had no idea, but it was important to get started. Momentum usually helped me figure out the rest of the plan.

Step one: Get my shoes back.

А few words about my stepmother. I could have forgiven her for marrying my father. I could have forgiven her for seeing me as a rival rather than a member of the family. I could *not* forgive her for chasing my father while he was married, bringing him down like a wounded gazelle, and then marrying the carcass.

My father wasn't a saint—still isn't—but Antonia did everything she could to help him fall from grace. You know how some people are born artists or born accountants? The Ant was a born home-wrecker. She even had the right build: falsely augmented breasts constantly swelling out the v-neck of her too-tight sweaters, black miniskirts, bare legs (even in winter! in Minnesota!), and fuck-me pumps.

To complete the stereotype, she was stupid. And blond. She once asked me if lesbians had periods. I managed to choke back the gales of humiliating laughter that wanted to pour forth and explained. "Well, that doesn't make any sense," she had snapped back.

My mother got the house and the humiliation that comes from your family and friends knowing your husband traded you in for a younger, thinner model. My father got Ant and a promotion—she was the definitive trophy wife, and, I'll give her this much, was a great help to his career. I got a twenty-eight-year-old stepmother, at the tender age of thirteen.

The first thing she ever said to me was, "Be careful of my suit." The second was, "Don't touch that." "That" was one of my mother's antique vases, which she'd given to me before Antonia muscled her out.

Yep, she took prisoners and moved in. As for myself, I'll tell the truth and shame the devil: I made no effort to get to know her. I had zero interest in building a relationship with the woman who had destroyed my mother's marriage. Plus, it's hard to be nice to someone when you instantly realize they don't like you. I was everything that was a threat to her: a smart, moody teenager my father loved with all his tiny heart.

About a week after she moved in, when I overheard her referring to my mother as "that cow from the suburbs," I tossed her gold ingot necklace into the blender. Over the sound of my stepmother's screams, I pressed "puree." This was followed by my first trip to a therapist's office.

The Ant was a big believer in therapists. Professionals paid to listen to every complaint you could think up . . . what bliss! Very early on, she proudly explained to me she had been diagnosed with depression, but it was the oddest mental illness I had seen. Medication didn't help, but jewelry did. She would be too depressed to attend one of my school plays, but could always rally for an expensive night out on the town with my dad.

My father, the drone, just tried to keep his head down. To his credit, he never gave in to the Ant's demands that I live full-time with my mother. He had been granted shared custody, and by God he would share me. Instead he kept her quiet with trinkets, and bought me off with shoes, and went to a *lot* of out-of-town seminars. I took the shoes, and tried to get along. Antonia never insulted Mom in my hearing again, and I never again had to toss precious metals into our KitchenAid. But I had little sympathy for either of them. They had made their choices.

I pulled up outside their absurdly large house. It was three stories high, with a red brick exterior and more skylights than a greenhouse. I stared at it, as always surprised by the sheer size—do two people really need thirty-five hundred square feet?—and hopped out of my car. It was a relief to be driving my own car as opposed to being at the mercy of the public transportation system.

Apparently, neither my house nor my car had been sold; nothing of my estate—pitiful as it was—had been settled yet. Well, heck, I'd only been dead a day or two. My family—well, my mom and dad, at least—were doubtless still in shock.

I pushed open the front door in time to hear my stepmother's dulcet tones: "Godammit, Arnie, you should sue their asses off! *They lost your daughter's body!* Now the funeral's been delayed who knows how long, we're going to have to postpone our vacation—Jesus Christ!"

A clink as my father dropped an ice cube into his glass of Dewar's. "I'm mad, too, Toni, but let's give the funeral place a chance. I know they're doing everything they can. If they haven't found—" Here his voice broke a bit, and I instantly forgave him for most of my adolescence. "—haven't found Betsy by tomorrow, I'll make some phone calls."

"If we cancel, we lose the cruise deposit," the Ant warned. Gads! Trapped on a boat with that woman! What the *hell* was my father thinking? "That's three grand, down the drain."

"That's really not my main concern right now," my dad said, very quietly. Oh, now she was in trouble. I could count on one hand how often I'd heard *that* tone.

The Ant, a creature of pure instinct, had the grace to pause. "Oh. Well. Maybe I'll just go on ahead, and you can stay here and—you know. Take care of things."

"Jesus, Toni! I know you and Betsy didn't get along, but for God's sake, your stepdaughter is *dead*. And all you can think about is that fucking vacation." I heard a few noisy gulps as my dad drained his cocktail. "What's the matter with you?"

"Nothing," the Ant said quickly. "I'm just—in shock, I guess. I wasn't thinking about what I said. I'm sorry, Honey Bear. You look so sad! Poor poor baby. Come here and let Mama fix it."

I gagged and nearly galloped down the hallway before I had to listen to more foreplay. "Stop!" I said, walking into the living room with both hands firmly over my eyes. "You guys aren't naked, are you? Because I've put up with a lot in the last twenty-four hours, but I draw the line at that."

I spread my fingers and looked. My father was slumped in his Laz-E-Boy, and the Ant was frozen in the act of crouching over him and running her fingers through his combover. The look on my stepmother's face was well worth the misery of dying and coming back. "Oh, good, you're still dressed. Anyway. Here I am. Ant, where the *hell* are my shoes?"

Dead (ha!) silence, broken by the crash of breaking glass as the stepmonster's wineglass hit the floor. The color drained from her face all at once, and for the first time I noticed she had a fine network of crow's feet around each eye. She was fifteen years older than me, and right then she looked every minute of it.

"B-Betsy?" My father was trying to smile, but the corners of his mouth trembled and I knew he was afraid. It was awful—my own dad, scared of me!—but I wasn't going to do something about it right that second. I kept walking toward his wife.

"You gave the mortuary a pink suit when you know damn well I hate pink. You gave them your shitty castoffs when you know how much I love designer shoes. Then you snuck in my house and *stole* my good shoes. And then you were going to take a cruise! After seducing my father—again! *On the day of my funeral.*" I was having trouble figuring out what made me the maddest.

She'd backed up all the way to the mantel, and in another few seconds would probably crawl into the fireplace. I didn't stop until we were nose-to-nose. Her breath smelled like lobster. Nice! A celebratory dinner on the day of the stepdaughter's funeral. "Now. Where are they?"

"Toni, you really did that?" my father asked. This was typical. He always overlooked the giant, insurmountable issue (daughter returning from the grave) and focused on something more manageable (bitch wife stealing dead daughter's footwear). "You know how long she saved up to buy—"

"She was *dead,* for Christ's sake!" Even now, my stepmonster managed to sound affronted and harassed.

"Hi, Dad," I said. Then, "Antonia, that is irrelevant!" I heard something break behind me, but didn't turn. "Where are they?"

"Elizabeth—I—you—you aren't—you aren't yourself and that's all there is to it!"

"Ant, you treacherous cow, you've never spoken truer words. Better tell me where my shoes are." I leaned in closer and grinned at her. She blanched and I heard her breathing stop. "You should see what happened to the last two guys who pissed me off."

"Check her bedroom," a voice said softly from behind me. I turned and there was my best friend, Jessica Watkins, standing in the entryway. Her eyes were red-rimmed. She was wearing a long black see-through skirt over black leggings, a black turtleneck, and her hair was skinned back in a bun so tight it forced her eyebrows up into a look of perpetual surprise. She had forgone makeup to show she was in mourning. I hadn't seen Jessica without mascara since seventh grade. "Mrs. Taylor would have wasted no time in putting them away, you know. So, like I said, you should check her closet." Then she burst into noisy tears. "Oh, Liz, I thought you were dead! We all thought you were dead!"

"Don't call me that. You know I hate that. And I sort of am," I said as she rushed toward me. Before she hit my embrace, I put a hand on my stepmonster's face and shoved very, very gently—she flew sideways and her ass hit the

Laz-E-Boy, rapidly vacated by my father. "It's a long story. Prepare to be regaled."

Then my oldest friend wept against my neck while I steered her toward the back bedroom. I glanced back and saw my stepmother staring in stunned silence while my father fumblingly fixed himself another drink.

Chapter 7

"AND then I decided to get my shoes back and here I am. Honey, can you let go of me for a minute?"

Jess had been clutching my hand with both of hers the entire time I told her what had happened, and reluctantly let go. I flexed it to get the feeling back.

"I can't believe it," she kept saying, shaking her head so hard it gave me a headache to watch. "I just can't believe it."

We were on our knees in the Ant's walk-in closet. I was carefully inspecting my shoes for scuffs and putting them inside the skirt of my stepmother's fourteen-hundred-dollar ball gown (what forty-five-year-old woman needs a ball gown?). My father and stepmother were hiding in the living room, too afraid to come back and talk to me, to find out what happened. I could smell their fear and unease—it was like burning plastic—and while not having to face them any longer was a relief, I felt bad all the same.

And what was up with all the smelling? Suddenly I was Super Sniffer. I mean, since when did emotions have scents?

But now I was effortlessly relying on my nose as much as my eyes and ears. I was the Undead Bloodhound! It was weird, but cool.

"I just can't believe it," Jess said again.

"*You* can't believe it? Try waking up dead and attempting to grasp the situation. It's taken me almost two days to get used to the idea. Or at least to start to get used to the idea. And I'm not even sure how it happened, or what I'm supposed to—"

"I don't give a *shit*," Jessica said. "You're alive—sort of—walking and talking, anyway, and that's all I care about." She threw her arms around me again. She weighed about ninety pounds and it was like being grabbed by a bundle of sticks. "Liz, I'm so happy you're here! Today was the worst day of my whole life!"

"What a coincidence!" I cried, and we both got the giggles. I added, "And don't call me Liz, you *know* I hate it."

"Or you'll suck my blood?"

"I'm trying to put that off," I admitted, but couldn't help but dart a glance at her long, ebony neck. "The thought of it makes me want to yark. Repeatedly. Besides, I hate dark meat."

That earned me a sharp poke. I needled Jess whenever I could, because it was a best friend's privilege and also because she was grossly prejudiced. She thought all whites were greedy and treacherous, with the possible exception of yours truly. Admittedly, this could sometimes be a hard case to argue against.

When we met in seventh grade, her first words to me were, "Drop dead twice, you privileged whitemeat schmuck." The fact that she was saying this while clutching a Gucci bag didn't seem to be relevant. My response ("Go cry in a bag of money, sweetie.") startled her into becoming my friend. That's how I made most of my friends: the element of surprise.

"Now that you're undead," Jessica went on, "I expect

you to stop repressing me and others of my racial persuasion," which was as big a laugh as I'd had that day. Jessica was about as repressed as Tipper Gore.

"Noted."

"Are you being driven insane with the unholy urge to feed?" she asked in a "would you like cream with that?" tone of voice.

I couldn't help grinning. "Not insane, but I'm super, super thirsty. Like, jump out of bed and work out for an hour thirsty. Dancing at the club all night thirsty. I woke up that way and it's pretty constant."

"Well, stay the hell away . . . I'd hate to have to pepper-spray my best friend."

"Right. After throwing myself off the roof, getting run over by a garbage truck, electrocuting myself, drinking bleach, and committing a double homicide and felonious assault, I sure wouldn't want to be pepper-sprayed."

She smiled. "You're unkillable now. Good. I don't need another phone call like I got last week. And it sounded like those two asswipes got what was coming to them, messing with a mom and her kid in the middle of the night."

"I'm trying not to think about it," I said guiltily.

"I'm just saying, you don't have anything to feel bad about."

"Believe it or not, my new status as vigilante-murderess is the least of my problems. Now, how long have I been dead? What's been going on? I can't ask *them*," I said, jerking my head toward the living room. "He's in shock and she's useless. More worried about losing the cruise deposit than my untimely demise."

Jessica's eyes went all narrow and squinty, but she didn't say anything. What was the point? She'd known the Ant as long as I had. "Well," she began slowly, folding her legs beneath her and clasping her fingers together. She looked like a black praying mantis. "Your dad called me Thursday night. I reacted to the news of your death by calling him a fucking honky liar and slamming the phone down. FYI, I've never called anyone a honky in my life; it's *so* twentieth century. Then I burst into tears. Also very twentieth century. This lasted about eight hours. I talked to Officer Stud—"

"Nick Berry?"

"He called to ask about funeral information. I guess he found out about the accident because he's a cop and all. He was at the funeral," she added slyly. She'd been teasing me about my nonexistent affair for months.

"Oooh, details, who else?"

"Umm . . . most of the gang from work. And John."

"Eww, the guy who picks his nose and wipes it on the walls of his cube?"

"The same. Don't worry, I kept a close eye on Booger Boy. And your former boss was there! He lays you off, you *die,* and the colossal prick had the nerve to be all sad-eyed at your funeral. *And* ask me if I knew where you'd kept the phone number for the copy machine repair guy, and if I knew if you'd taken care of the Carroll shipment before you died."

I burst out laughing.

"Of course, there wasn't actually a funeral . . . they lost your body!" Jessica was warming to her subject; her eyes had a frightening sparkle. "Picture it: We're all standing around, waiting for things to get started, making small talk with people we absolutely hate—"

"The mind reels."

"—and the head mortician guy comes in and tells us there's been 'a slight problem.' Which I thought was weird until I walked into this house and got a look at what weird really was. And speaking of weird, weren't you embalmed? I mean, did it just not affect you, or did your folks cheap out and skip that step, or what?"

"You're asking *me?* How the hell should I know?" I barely suppressed a shudder. The thought of liposuction creeped me out, to say nothing of tubing and embalming fluid. A riddle I was in no hurry to solve, and that was a fact. "Why are you here, anyway? Not that I mind, because you probably saved me from wringing the Ant's neck. But you hate my parents. Don't tell me—you bought up their mortgage from the bank and came over to foreclose on them."

"I wish. Thanks for the idea, though, maybe I'll do that next weekend."

"Jessica . . ."

"I got a look at Mrs. Taylor's footgear at the funeral is all. I knew those weren't her Pradas. So I figured I'd come over and try to get them back."

"It's so stupid," I complained. "She's a whole size smaller than me! They don't even fit her, and she wants them anyway."

"Trash," Jessica said with a shrug. "Who can fathom?"

I smiled at her. She looked like an Egyptian queen, and fought for her friends like a cobra. She positively despised my father and his wife, but braved Hell House the day of my funeral to get my shoes back. "Oh, Jess . . . why? I was dead, for all you knew. I didn't need them anymore."

"Well, *I* did," she said tartly. Which was a lie; Jessica has feet like Magic Johnson. "Besides, it wasn't right. That jerk had to have swiped your dad's keys, snuck into your house, and stole! I knew you wouldn't have wanted her to have them. I figured I'd donate them to the Foot."

I nodded. In her spare time (which was to say, fifty hours a week), Jessica ran The Right Foot. The Foot gave interviewing tips, advice, résumé assistance, and hand-me-down suits and accessories to disadvantaged women to use for job interviews.

"Awesome idea, and bless your heart for thinking of it." I bundled the rest of my shoes into the ball gown, making a sack out of the dress and slinging it over my shoulder like a vampiric Santa. "Of course, there'll be none of that now that I'm back from the dead. If I ever needed fabulous shoes, it's now. Let's book."

I scooped up Antonia's jewelry box, stopped in the kitchen, and handed the sack of shoes to Jess, who looked on with wide-eyed interest as I dumped the Ant's jewelry into the blender, clapped the top on, and hit "liquefy."

The grinding, jarring, and screeching brought her on the run. My father went to hide in his den, comforted by his proximity to old whiskey and new porn.

After a few seconds, during which we all stared at the mightily vibrating blender, I let the whirling blades groan to a halt. I could hear the Ant grinding her teeth, but she didn't say a single word. Just stared at me with equal parts hate and fear.

I liked that just fine.

"Listen carefully, Ant. Pretend—oh, pretend your life depends on it! Don't you *ever* go into my home again without permission. Touch my things again, whether I'm dead or not, and I'll kick your ass up into your shoulder blades." I said this perfectly pleasantly while I yanked the handle off the fridge and handed it to her. "Got it? Super. See you at Easter."

We left. The sight of Antonia O'Neill Taylor shrinking back from me as I passed her was one I'll treasure forever.

Chapter 8

AFTER some argument, Jessica and I parted ways, and I drove to my mother's house. Now that I had decided to make a new life for myself (not that I had any idea how), I couldn't let another minute go by with Mama thinking I was still dead.

"That's fine," Jessica said, "but you might have explained to Papa and Mrs. Taylor that the reason you're walking around is because you're a vampire." Her voice broke on "vampire" and she smothered a giggle. I couldn't blame her. It did sound ludicrous.

"You saw them," I retorted. "Did they look like they were up for any explanations? Dad wouldn't even come out to say good-bye. And the Ant was busy fishing her mangled jewelry out of the blender."

"Good point."

I had asked Jessica to share the news with whomever she thought needed to hear it, but she was horrified by the idea.

"In the movies, the vampire always goes underground," she argued. "Stays dead to their friends and family."

"A, this isn't the movies, and B, I'm not having my friends and family think I'm dead when I'm walking around. This is not a secret! I'm not skulking around in the shadows like some anemic idiot for the next two hundred years. Give me a break."

"What about the government? Scientists? What if they want to capture you or study you? Plus, you've got a death certificate. So your social security number doesn't work, your credit's no good . . . you can't just pick up where you left off. Betsy, think it over."

Those thoughts hadn't occurred to me. How was I going to make a living? Maybe I could be a clerk on the night shift at a motel, or something. "I—I haven't thought that out yet," I admitted. "Give me a break, forty-eight hours ago I was naked on a slab."

"Ooooh, you finally had a date?"

"Har-de-fucking-har. I'll worry about that stuff later. I've got to get to Mom."

Jessica nodded. "Fair enough. I'll come with you."

"Forget it. It's gonna be hard enough telling her I'm back from the dead without you cracking wise in the background."

"You shouldn't be alone," she protested.

"What could possibly happen to me?"

There was a pause, followed by a grudging, "Good point."

I climbed into my car, slammed the door, and rolled down the window. "Tell or don't tell, it's all the same to me. I'm just saying, I'm not keeping it a deep dark secret. How'd you like it if I hadn't told you?"

"That's different. We're practically sisters."

"People can tell," I said brightly, "by the close family resemblance."

Jessica rolled her eyes. "I'm just saying, you don't have to tell *everybody*. Your family and me, I think. Maybe Officer Nick."

"Detective Nick."

She ignored the correction. "You could invite him over . . . have seductive music playing—something awful by Sade, maybe—and then pounce! He could be your first meal."

I shied away from the thought, even while part of me surged hungrily at the mental image of Detective Nick being my first. "You're ill," I told her. "Also, I hate Sade. Go home and get some sleep."

"I'm not ill. I'm freaked out. Which is a good problem to have, given the alternative. Say hi to Mama Taylor for me. And think it over, blabbermouth. The movies can't be wrong about everything."

Which just goes to show, Jessica hardly ever goes to the movies.

I was parked outside my mom's small, two-story house in Hastings, a small town thirty miles outside St. Paul. Although it was almost midnight, all the lights on the lower level were blazing. My mom suffered from insomnia at the best of times. Which this certainly wasn't.

I bounded up the porch steps, knocked twice, then turned the knob. Unlocked—one of the things I loved about Hastings.

I stepped into the living room and saw an old woman sitting in my mother's chair. She had my mother's curly white hair (Mom had started going gray in high school), and was wearing my mom's black suit, and my mom's pearls—a wedding gift from her parents.

"Who—?" (the hell are you?) I almost asked, but of course it was her. Shock and grief had put twenty years on her face. She'd gotten pregnant with me one month out of high school, and we'd often been mistaken for sisters. Not today.

Mom stared. She tried to speak but her mouth trembled

and made speech impossible. She gripped the arms of her rocking chair so hard I heard her bones creak. I rushed across the room and threw myself at the foot of her chair. She looked so dreadful I was terrified. "Mom, it's me—it's okay! I'm okay!"

"This is the worst dream I've ever had," she remarked to no one in particular. I felt her hand come up and gently touch the top of my head. "Yes indeed."

"It's not a dream, Mom." I grabbed her hand, pressed it to my cheek. "See? It's real." I pinched her leg through the skirt, hard enough to make her yelp. "See?"

"You wretched child, I'm going to have a bruise the size of a plum." I felt her tears dripping down on my face. "You awful, awful child. Such a burden. Such a—" She started to cry in earnest and couldn't finish the familiar, well-loved fake complaints.

We held each other for a long time.

"DON'T be scared," I said about half an hour later, "but I'm a vampire."

"As Jessica would say, I don't give a *shit*. Also, you move faster than the human eye can track."

"What?"

Mom tossed a handful of freshly grated Parmesan into the risotto and stirred. "When you ran to me. I blinked and you were at my feet. You moved faster than I could follow. It was like watching a movie that had been speeded up."

"That's not the least of it—I've got a nose like a bloodhound. I could smell your perfume the second I walked in the house, and it's not like you dump the stuff on." I didn't tell her that I could smell emotions, too. Her relief and joy smelled like tea roses.

"Interesting. Either you've been involved in some sort of secret scientific government-sponsored experiment and never mentioned it—"

"No, but that's a good one. I'll have to remember it."

"Or there's a supernatural explanation."

I blinked. Mom had always had a strong practical streak, but she was adjusting to my undead status with unbelievable aplomb.

She must have read my expression, because she said, "Sweetie, you were dead. I was at the morgue. I saw. And now you're back. Do I care why? Not remotely. My prayers have been answered. Not that I prayed. I've spent the last few days positively furious with God."

I was silent, picturing her agony. The long walk down the sterile-smelling hallway . . . sterile, with a faint whiff of death underneath. Burning fluorescent lights. A professionally sympathetic doctor. Then, the identification: "Yes, that's my daughter. What's left of her."

"Just about every culture has legends about vampires," Mom continued. "I've often thought there must be some truth in the stories . . . else why would there be so many of them?"

"By that logic," I said, "I can assume the Easter Bunny will be stopping by this month?"

"Funny girl. Risotto?"

"Please." Mom had stopped crying, washed her face, changed out of the suit she wore to my funeral, and cooked my favorite meal: pork loin with risotto. Like Jessica, she couldn't stop touching me. Like I minded! "I'm *so* hungry, and that smells terrific."

I wolfed it down in about thirty seconds. Then I spent five minutes in the bathroom throwing it all up. Mom held my hair back from my face and, when I finished and slumped dispiritedly on the bathroom tile, she handed me a damp washcloth.

I started to cry, that odd tearless crying that was now my specialty. "I can't have regular food anymore! No more risotto, shrimp cocktail, lobster, prime rib—"

"Cancer, AIDS, death by mugging, rape, homicide . . ."

I looked up in mid-sniffle. Mom looked down at me

with the combination of compassion and practicality that was her trademark. I'd seen that look when I told her I was going to flunk out of college. She loved me more than she loved herself, but that never stopped her from telling the truth. No matter how little I wanted to hear it.

"I'd like to be more sympathetic," she said kindly, "but I'm so happy to have you back, Elizabeth. As awful as it's been for you, you have no idea what the last three days have been like for me, for your father and your friends—I thought Jessica was going to collapse at the funeral home. I didn't think the girl *could* cry, but she practically melted today. Your father didn't even recognize me, he was in such a daze. Your stepmother was—er—upset."

I shook my head at the truth, and the lie. "Oh . . . Mom."

"But I never have to worry about going to the morgue again, unless you trip on a stake on the way home. As to the rest of it: We'll deal, as the kids say. Haven't we been doing just that since you were thirteen?"

I scowled. "I don't think people who can eat risotto should have an opinion."

"Silly child. It's just fuel. In the big scheme of things, this is a minor one indeed. Brush your fangs, and then we'll talk some more." She turned to leave, but not before I saw the smirk.

"Very funny!" I yelled after her.

Chapter 9

I pulled into my driveway at 4:30 in the morning. I was still feeling vaguely ill after eating real food, but I was immensely cheered by my mom's rah-rah-be-the-best-vamp-you-can-be speech. It had been a long night, but a productive one, and I was ready to drink a gallon of water—not that it would help my thirst—and go to bed.

There was a strange car parked in my driveway, a white Taurus. Sighing, I parked on the street and, as I walked up my driveway, I peeked inside the car and saw the bubble light. Cop. And when I entered my house (lugging the Ant's ball gown and my shoes), I could smell Detective Nick Berry's clean, distinctive scent. Which, by the way, I'd never been able to do before. Whenever I saw him at the station, all I could smell were stale croissants (the doughnut thing is a myth) and old coffee.

He hurried out of my kitchen—what had he been doing, making himself a snack?—and stopped dead when he saw me. His jaw sagged and he made a motion toward the gun in his shoulder holster.

"Oh, *that's* nice," I snapped, slamming the door behind me and dropping the ball gown. "Don't you dare pull a gun on me in my own house. And where's your warrant?"

"I didn't need one, seeing as how you're dead. Also, you didn't lock your front door again."

"I had a few other things on my mind when I left," I grumbled. "Boy, Jessica just couldn't *wait* to tell you, could she?" I'd strangle her the next time I saw her. I said my undeath wasn't a secret, but I didn't mean she should run to the cops first thing. Her matchmaking was going to be the end of me. Well, probably not. "That jerk . . . friends are the quintessential mixed blessing."

He was staring at me like a dog zooming in on a pork chop. "I didn't believe her—figured it was a rotten joke—but promised her I'd check it out."

"The fact that her family owns two thirds of the state probably didn't figure into your decision," I said dryly.

"The chief had me put it pretty high on my list," Nick admitted. He blinked rapidly. "I can't believe I'm discussing this with a dead girl."

"*You* can't?"

"Did you know it's against the law to fake your own death? The D.A.'s gonna be pissed."

"Believe it or not, Nick, that is the least of my problems right now. And I didn't fake anything."

He'd been gaping at me while we talked, and as I kicked off my tennis shoes he crossed the room. To my complete astonishment, he pulled me into his arms like a hero in a romance novel.

"Eh? Leggo."

"God," he said, staring into my eyes. We were exactly the same height, so it was a little unnerving. His eyes were light blue, with gold flecks. His pupils were huge. I could see myself staring in them, mouth hanging open. "You're so beautiful."

I was frozen with amazement. Nick had touched me a few times—mostly to shake my hand, and once our fingers brushed when he handed me a Milky Way—but he'd always been cool, pleasant, and nice. Nice Guy nice. I had sensed zero interest, which is why I'd never pursued him, and why Jessica's hints and intimations were so annoying. But now—

"God," he said again, and kissed me. Except it was more like he was trying to swallow me. His tongue jumped into my mouth—at least that's what it felt like—and suddenly I was breathing his breath. This was startling, but not unpleasant. Then: "Ow!" He jerked back and touched his lower lip, where a tiny drop of blood welled. "You bit me."

"Sorry—you thtartled me. I mean, you took me by thurprithe. Oh, thit." I could *not* look away from that tiny little crimson drop. It gleamed. It beckoned. It begged to be tasted. "Nick, you thould go. Right now."

"But you're so beautiful," he whispered, and kissed me again, more gently. I tasted his blood, and that was that. Had I thought I was thirsty before? The strongest, most compelling craving I had ever known completely took me over.

I kissed him back and sucked on his lower lip, which was plump and tasty. Mmmm, the better to eat you with, my dear! Then he was tearing at my clothes like a horny teenager. I heard the "clunk" of his holster hitting the floor, prayed his gun wouldn't misfire, heard the jingle of the coins in his pockets as his slacks hit the floor in a polyester puddle, heard the riiiiiiip that meant I'd need to buy a new T-shirt. I had no idea what had happened to my leggings. He could have eaten them for all I would have noticed.

I tore my mouth from his, jerked his face to the side, and bit him on the side of the neck. I wasn't remotely horrified. There was no reticence at all, no maidenly shrinking at the thought of drinking his blood like it was a cranberry spritzer. I couldn't wait. I *wouldn't* wait.

I'd been prepared to really bite down, but my fangs slid through his skin like a laser scalpel, and then his blood was flooding my mouth. My knees buckled as my body truly came alive for the first time since that Aztek knocked me into a tree. Everything was suddenly loud and bright and vivid; Nick's heartbeat thundered in my ears and the dim lighting in the room seemed more like a stadium lit up at night. I could smell his lust—like crisp shavings of cedar.

Nick had gone rigid in my fiendish embrace, but given the firm length I could feel against my belly, he didn't seem to find this objectionable at all. Thank God, because I couldn't stop. He was fumbling at his tidy whities, but couldn't seem to get them pulled down—he'd try and then he'd squirm and shudder against me.

Now, I can count the number of sexual partners I've had on one hand. Okay, on three fingers. Madame Slut I was not. And with every one, as with most women, it took time and manipulation to make me come. Not to mention I had to be naked! That whole three strokes and it's time to ride the orgasm train thing is a pure myth, and I feel sorry for women who believe it and then think there's something wrong with them when they need more than a slap and tickle to get off.

That said, when Nick groaned and shuddered against me while his blood was in my mouth, I was instantly jolted into orgasm, and his dick wasn't anywhere near me. It was still swaddled in his cotton Jockeys, and I still had my Friday underpants on (yech! I was pretty sure it was Tuesday).

It was a shallow orgasm, the kind you get when you're diddling with yourself and squeeze your knees together at just the right moment, but a come is a come (I should stitch that on a sampler sometime). Drinking blood had made everything more *there,* all sensations were more intense and opened a vein of sensuality I never dreamed existed.

His broad swimmer's chest was pressed up against mine hard enough to flatten my breasts. He was sweating and panting, and I abruptly realized I didn't need to drink anymore. My thirst was gone and I felt better than I ever had. I felt like jumping over the house. Maybe I even could.

I stopped drinking and pulled back, licking the bite mark to get the last few drops. Nick clutched me with both hands while he fought to keep his feet; his eyes were rolling and there were beads of sweat on his upper lip. I could still hear his heartbeat hammering in my ears—it sounded like his pulse was about one-sixty. I was shocked—I could have run (and won) a marathon, and poor Nick looked half dead.

"Oh, Jesus—"

"Don't," he whispered against my neck.

"Nick, I'm so sorry, I—"

"Don't stop," he managed. "Do more. Bite me. Again."

The full impact of his request hit me, and in my horror I nearly dropped him. I suddenly remembered the church janitor . . .

(you're pretty)

. . . and the minister . . .

(a beautiful stranger)

. . . and how odd they'd seemed; odd but, as I was having such a strange night myself, I'd shrugged off their reactions. Now here was Nick, a perfectly pleasant man who had showed no interest in me except as a witness, Nick with his clothes in ruins and blood on his throat, Nick who wanted me to bite him again. *Again!*

Not only could I live through car crashes and electrocution, not only could I toss grown men like they were magazines, but I could make men want me. Me! I mean, I was cute in high school, and carefully maintained my cuteness as an adult, but the boys certainly never fell all over themselves trying to be with me. They did that to Jessica, usually after they got a look at her checkbook.

But now . . . now they looked at me and wanted me,

didn't care if I drained them dry as long as they could hold onto me while I did it.

I got ready to yowl with horror and frustration, when I got a grip (*you've overreacted enough the last two days*) and instead picked Nick up and carried him to my room like he was a blond male Scarlett and I was an undead Rhett.

"SO it's true."

"What is, Nick?"

"Vampires."

"Yes. It's true. I'm really, really sorry." I threw my arm over my eyes. I couldn't look at him. Now that I had satiated my evil thirst, I was thoroughly embarrassed. Talk about your first date faux pas!

He propped himself up on an elbow and looked down at me. I knew this because I peeked. We'd been lying in bed, side by side, for about five minutes, in silence. I was both relieved and frightened when he started talking.

"Don't be sorry. That was the best of my life. I mean, not that we actually . . . never mind. Did you—" He paused. "Did you get enough to . . . um . . . eat?"

I winced. "Yes. I'm fine. Thank you." And now, the incredible awkwardness that happens between two acquaintances who got too intimate too soon and now have to chat. "Uh . . . are *you* okay?"

He touched his neck. I was amazed to see the bite mark was almost entirely healed. "It hardly even hurts." Then he blushed like a kid. It was really charming—weird to see it perfectly in the dark, but charming. "And I came in my pants. Haven't done that since—"

"Last week?" I asked brightly.

"Very funny." He was still feeling his neck. "This is amazing. I can't even feel where you bit me!"

"Like a dog, I apparently have an enzyme in my saliva that speeds up healing."

He burst out laughing. Oh, thank goodness. Then he was rolling over on top of me and nibbling my throat. "Time for another drink?" he asked, and the naked eagerness in his voice made my heart lurch.

"No." I pushed him, but he immediately settled back on top of me. "Absolutely not."

"I don't mind—"

"Dammit! You do, I bet, way down deep inside you, you probably mind plenty. Nick, I *bit* you! I drank your blood and I didn't even ask."

"You never have to ask," he said quietly. "Besides, I wanted you to. I was grabbing onto you just as much as you were grabbing onto me. You didn't have much choice, the way I see it."

I snorted. "You couldn't have hurt me and you sure as shit can't force me. I think you're having trouble figuring out who the victim is here." Did vampirism encourage Stockholm syndrome?

He was still lying on top of me and I could feel his groin pressing against mine; he was throbbing and hard as a pipe. Amazing! The guy had to be in his forties. "I don't feel like a victim. Come on," he coaxed. "Let me in . . . and I'll let you in."

"No no *no*. Never again, Detective Barry, absolutely not. It'd be like rape. It *is* rape. Also, you have to go home and take a shower. Seriously."

He laughed at me, but stopped when I asked, "How'd you feel about me before I died?"

"Uh . . . I thought you were great. Really cute. I mean, beautiful."

"Ever want to slam me up against a wall and try to screw the bejeezus out of me while I drank your blood?"

"Uh . . ."

"Exactly. But you're ready for all that now, suddenly. You don't even mind if I *drink your blood* while we grope. Hello? This is not normal behavior. It's not me you want.

It's—it's whatever makes me a vampire. A supernatural gift or whatever—but it's not *me*. It's my undead pheromones. And that's why we're done."

He protested, but I turned a deaf ear, helped him reholster his gun, so to speak, reassembled his clothes, and pushed him out my front door. Even so, he hammered on it for fifteen minutes, begging to be let back in.

I fled to my bedroom and put a pillow over my head, but I could still hear him for a long time.

In the movies, vampires are always these all-powerful jerks who use people like Kleenex. Now I could see why. A clean-cut boy next door who lets you drink his blood, then begs for more of the same, will let you do anything.

Anything at all.

Chapter 10

"**D**!**C**, bloodsucking hellspawn!"

My eyes flashed open and I saw the stake descending. Whoever was holding it was probably moving pretty fast, but to me it looked like slow motion. I grabbed the wrist holding the stake and tugged.

The woman flew over my head and sailed across the room. I got a whiff of Chanel No. 5 and steak sauce as she soared through the air with the greatest of ease. She could have been hurt, but she landed on the futon mattress, clearly dragged in while I was sleeping the sleep of the sated animal.

"Dammit, Jessica!"

She crouched on the mattress, almost giggling. "And now," she boomed, her voice artificially deep, "the blood-sucking fiend rises from her grave to mete out harsh punishment to the mere mortal who dared try to end her unnatural life!"

"What the hell is wrong with you?"

She bounced up from the mattress, grinning. "That's the

only thing you've got to worry about now, kiddo. Where there be vampires, there be vampire hunters. *They* don't know you're one of the good guys. I figured we could do some drills." For the first time—I never said I was a genius, or even especially quick—I noticed she was wearing jeans, a heavy sweatshirt, kneepads, elbow pads, and a biker's helmet. She looked like an armadillo. "You know, get your anti-stake reflexes really humming."

"Coffee," I groaned, staggering toward the bathroom. I was perfectly awake—and I certainly didn't need to pee—but I was determined to maintain some sort of routine. "And get lost!"

"No way. Now that you're back from the dead, I'm doing everything I can to keep you from biting the big one again. I'm not going through last week again. Liz, are you prepared to *deal with THIS?*" She yowled that last as she leaped toward my back. I had plenty of time to sidestep her, and she hit the wall like a bug and bounced off, landing on her padded knees in front of my dresser. "Ooh, nice!" she said approvingly. "You didn't even turn. We'll add superhearing to the list."

"Please go away," I begged. "I plan to stay inside and wallow in guilt all day. Night, I mean."

"Why?"

Good question. I couldn't tell her about Nick. I was too embarrassed. Plus, since Nick had—err—finished, in Jessica's mind it would count as a CA (carnal act). She'd probably whip out the Sex Calendar and update it on the spot. As a goad to upping the frequency of my CAs, she had started to keep track. The pitiful number I racked up last year was especially humiliating. "Because I'm now an unnatural creature, that's why. Buzz off."

"No way! We're going to fight crime tonight."

"We are, huh?"

"Yup. Also, you're kind of clammy. I tried to take your

pulse when I got here, and your wrist is chilly. I know! Let's take your temperature."

I shuddered at the thought. Was I room temperature? Cold-blooded like a snake? Ugh. "Let's not."

"You were impossible to wake up. I made plenty of noise coming in, and you never budged. I even shook you a coupla times—nothing. You were sleeping like the dea— like someone really tired out."

"Well, how come I woke up when you were swinging a stake at my head?"

She pointed wordlessly out the window. It was quite dark. "Waited until sunset."

I shrugged. I was in the bathroom by now, staring at the toilet. I had absolutely no urge to sit on it. Time to think up a new use for it. Maybe unhook it, empty the water out, and plant irises in the bowl?

I took a shower, but it didn't do a thing for me. I mean, it got me clean, but I didn't have that oh-this-is-so-refreshing feeling I usually got from a hot shower in the morning. Evening.

I dried off, quickly got dressed, and found Jessica putzing around in the kitchen. I found out Miss Stabs-A-Lot had been busy while I was resting (it was too deep, dreamless and, let's face it, deathlike, to call it sleeping). She'd set up my computer to download all the pertinent news stories of the day, so when I *(rose)* got up I'd see what had been happening in the world during the day. She'd also bought my house.

"My house," I said slowly.

"Yeah, house, it's a noun. As in, the place you live." She must have noticed my expression remained blank, because she elaborated. "Hey, it was going on the market at the end of the month. You're dead, remember? You don't live here anymore, and since you still had eleven years to go on your mortgage, the bank was kind of interested in getting it back." She handed me a thick sheaf of papers. "It's all taken care of."

I blinked down at the paperwork. "Jess . . . I don't know what to say. This was so thoughtful . . . and *smart*. I hadn't even started thinking about stuff like my house and car—"

"Which I also bought," she added helpfully.

"So quickly? I haven't even been dead a week. How could you do all this stuff in a day?"

"It helps to be ridiculously wealthy," she said modestly. "Also, duh, I'm the executor of your estate, remember?"

"I thought you were joking."

"All the paperwork you signed, you thought that was part of the joke?"

"D'you blame me? I mean, *what* estate?"

She snorted. "Anyway. I started the stuff the day you died. It—it gave me something to do. Besides, I didn't want Mrs. Taylor doing something rotten with your things. Figured I'd legally own it all, have plenty of time to sort through everything, then put it back on the market once everything was—you know—settled."

I shook my head. "No wonder you kicked my ass on the SATs. Okay, well, I suppose I can make my house and car payments to you instead of the bank—"

"Uh-oh, no way."

"Jessica—"

"Forget it."

"You can't just spend all that money—"

"You're dead, I can't heeeeear youuuu . . ."

"—and not get anything ba—"

"La la la la la *la la la la!*" Her hands were clapped over her ears and her eyes were squeezed shut.

I kicked her ankle, very very gently. "Fine, fine, *fine!*"

She opened her eyes and smiled at me, then bent and rubbed her ankle. "Good. And ouch! Besides, it's not a gift. You're not going to have much income coming in for a while, but you'll be ambushing bad guys at night—"

"I haven't decided *what* I'm going to be doing at night."

"So it evens out," she finished with trademark stubbornness. "You shouldn't have to worry about house payments on top of everything else."

"Well . . . thanks. I really don't know what to say. You're too good."

"Damn right I am. I'm gonna be your rich anonymous backer while you go out at night and kick ass for the side of goodness and right. And Lord knows you can't do that on what *you* make. Made, I mean."

I knew I should have fought her more, but the fact was, Jessica could have paid off the homes of everyone we went to high school with, and still have about a billion dollars left over. It was stupid to protest when she had the bucks and the inclination. But I'd find a nonmonetary way to make it up to her.

Look her in the eyes and tell her to take your money, a treacherous inner voice whispered. It sounded alarmingly like my stepmother. *Make her bend.*

I shoved the thought away, horrified, and told myself it wouldn't work: Jessica was a woman, and had no interest in seeing what color underpants I had on.

You can make her be interested.

"No!"

"No what? Cracking up already? Heck, it's only 7:30. Way too early for hysterics." My phone started ringing. "I'll get it, dead girl . . . we better figure out the phones, too."

I stared into my fridge and thought about how thirsty I was (and tried not to think about all the pints of yummy blood coursing through my energetic pal). Eggs? No. Leftover pasta salad? No, it had been spoiled *before* I died. An orange? That might not be too bad. I could cut it into quarters and suck out the juice.

Jessica trotted back into the kitchen. "Your mom says howdy and to be careful fighting crime. *Man,* she's cool! If anyone else came back from the dead, their folks'd still be in a rubber room. How'd it go last night?"

"I didn't do anything!"

"To your mom? I should hope not."

"Oh. Right. Uh—she was incredibly cool about it. A real one-eighty from Dad and the Ant. Very 'oh, you're a vampire, that's nice, dear, watch out for holy water' . . . like that. Which was surprising, even for her. I guess she took my death really hard. She was really, really happy to see me, and beyond that, didn't give a fig for the details."

"That's how I feel, too. Plus, I can't help it, I think it's so *neat*."

"Please. You sound like a cheerleader."

"Well, I was one. But I can't get over your mom . . . man, I'd give anything to—" I heard her teeth clack together as she made herself stop talking, and I turned my back on her. It was ostensibly to cut up my orange, but actually, it was to give her a few seconds to collect herself.

Jessica was loyal, loving, and marvelous in nearly all ways, but she had the temper of an Everglades gator whose eggs were threatened. And the thing that made her crazy, made her absolutely nuts, was when people fucked with kids. Because, as a kid, she'd been thoroughly fucked with.

Her father invented some dumb little circuit board that every computer in the world needed to work right, and he owned the patent . . . Mr. Watkins was probably the only person on the planet who'd been able to outsmart Bill Gates. The money poured in. He was one of the richest men in the world; he made more in one year than Oprah made in ten. He contributed generously to charities, political campaigns, and cities (six parks, four schools, and seventeen athletic fields had been named after him in this state alone).

When he wasn't accepting worship from the press and public, he studiously ignored his only child. So they lived under the same roof but never really interacted, until she hit adolescence. Then he took an interest. An extreme one.

Jessica went to her mother first, asking her to please "tell Daddy I don't like all the grabbing and stuff, and he tickles too hard." Mrs. Watkins, a former Vegas showgirl—Jessica wasn't beautiful and scrawny by accident—ignored her. She had no intention of upsetting the gravy train.

She tried her mother again when her father started coming into her room dressed only in his tidy whities. She got slapped for telling lies.

The night Mr. Watkins came to her room wearing his birthday suit, Jessica was waiting for him with a baseball bat—the only weapon she'd been able to smuggle to her room without being noticed.

She nearly killed him. Then she threw the bat out the window, called the police, got dressed, and calmly waited. The police were the ones who called the ambulance for her father.

At the station, Jessica told them everything.

Due to the power of the Watkins name, most of the details were kept out of the newspapers. Months went by, months of painful physical therapy for Mr. Watkins, while neighbors took care of Jessica, who had retained a lawyer and was going about the business of becoming an emancipated minor. Mr. and Mrs. Watkins were served with the papers the day Mr. Watkins had been told it was safe for him to eat solid foods again.

Mr. Watkins was so enraged at the thought of his daughter, his property, getting away from him for good with the help of the courts he had expected to control, he drove too recklessly to his favorite four-star restaurant, and plowed into the south side of the Pillsbury building. Neither he nor his wife were wearing seatbelts. Mrs. Watkins was killed instantly. Mr. Watkins hung on for three weeks through sheer rage, then someone mercifully pulled the plug and it was over.

Jessica, at the age of fourteen, inherited everything.

She didn't go to the funerals.

"So, I'm gonna try an orange, see if I can keep that down," I said, forcing myself out of the unpleasant reverie. Jessica deserved a mom like mine—everyone did. But there was nothing to be done about it. "Did I tell you I throw up solid foods?"

"A fine party trick. Also, breakfast is served." Jessica held out a glass. One whiff and I knew it wasn't brimming with V-8. There was a green leaf stuck artfully to the side of the glass, which had been chilled, and its rim had been dipped in coarse salt. "It's O negative . . . the universal drink."

"You have garnished my glass of blood," I observed, "with basil and margarita salt."

"Sure. This is no drive-thru McDonald's blood. Aquavit closed!"

"Seriously. Where'd you get it?"

"I'll never tell. But we should set up a minibank or something for you here, so you don't have to prowl alleys looking for a fix. I've got a guy working on that right now. He thinks I'm an eccentric heiress who's setting up her own blood storage in case of a national shortage." She chortled. "He's right, of course. Cheers!"

I took the glass with all the enthusiasm I'd have shown if she was offering me a glass of pureed rattlesnake. The smell was making my head swim, and not in a good way. While Jess looked on, I took a tentative sip and nearly gagged. It was like drinking a dead battery, fallen leaves, a candle that had burned down to nothing. That's what it tasted like: nothing. And that's what it was doing for me, too. I was just as thirsty as I had been when I woke up ten minutes ago.

I handed the glass back, shaking my head. "Nope. It's got to be live."

Her face fell. "Nuts. So much for that plan. You really can't—uh—get nutrients out of it, or whatever? Metabolize it?"

"It's like gulping down a vitamin and saying that's supper. You'd starve to death pretty quick. But thanks for going to all the trouble," I added, because she looked so crest-fallen. I had to admit I was pretty disappointed myself. Now I'd have to hunt.

I thought of Nick. *Give him a call, why don't you? He'll be here in a heartbeat.* Then I made the thought go away.

The phone rang again, but I put up a hand to stop Jess from bounding back into the other room. "I'll get it. It's probably my dad, anyway. He's had a day to get over the shock." I walked into my living room, and saw that Jessica had thoughtfully unpacked the boxes and put my things back. She was an exhausting pal, but I was damned lucky to have her on my side. I would do well to keep that in mind. "Hello?"

"Is this Elizabeth Taylor?"

"Yes. And don't joke about my name; I've heard them all."

"Elizabeth Taylor of seven-two-one-seven-five Louis Lane in Apple Valley?"

I yawned and covertly felt my teeth. Nope; fangless. "Yes, and I'm perfectly satisfied with my long-distance service. Thanks anyway."

"Why," the voice—male, sounded like he was in his early twenties—demanded, "are you answering the phone?"

"Because it rang, dope. Now, I'm really very busy, so if—"

"But you're dead!"

I paused. How best to handle this? Who was this guy? Visa? Xcel Energy? "Don't believe everything you read," I said finally. "Also, the checks are in the mail, but since I just got laid off I'd like to make payment arrangements—"

"You're a vampire and you're in your own house answering your phone? Get *out* of there!"

I nearly dropped the receiver. "A, how did you know that, and B, fat chance! Plus, the mortgage is paid off. I'm not going anywhere. Nighty-night."

I hung up, but almost immediately the phone rang again. If a phone could ring angrily, mine was furious. Or maybe I was just picking up the emotions of the person on the other end. Either way, the phone practically jumped into my hand. "Hello?"

"Why are you answering your phone?"

"Because it keeps ringing!" Why, why, *why,* didn't I get caller I.D. when I had the chance? "Now stop bugging me before I star-six-nine your ass."

"Wait! Don't hang up!"

Like I would. Could this be another vampire? Even if he wasn't, he knew I *was.* Maybe he could tell me what's been going on, give me some pointers. Anything was better than spending the next ten years finding things out the hard way. "Well," I said coyly, "I'm very busy."

"Look: Come to the downtown Barnes and Noble . . . you know where that is?"

"Sure." Hard not to; it took up an entire city block.

"After you feed, meet me in the cookbook section . . ."

"That's mean!" I protested.

"Okay, fine, the humor section."

"That's not much better," I grumbled. "What, are you allergic to the romance section? And I don't have to feed. I'll just go right now."

A long pause, so long I thought he'd hung up, when he practically whispered, "You don't need to feed? Have you had time this evening?"

"It's no big deal. I can go a few days. I mean, so what, right?"

"What?"

"Which word didn't you understand? Are you listening to me?"

"What?"

Was this guy hard of hearing, or just dim? "What do you look like? How about a codeword? Or a superduper secret undead handshake we can use?"

"Don't bother," he said, and he sounded incredibly rattled. "I know what you look like, Miss Taylor."

"Now, how d'you know that?"

"Your obituary. Nice picture, by the way. See you in an hour." Click.

"Oooh, now that sounds ominous." I quit speaking to a dead line and hung up. I hoped the Ant hadn't picked a picture for the newspaper that was too heinous.

"What was that about?" Jessica asked.

I just looked at her.

"Helloooo? My lips are moving, can you understand what I'm saying? What. Was. That. About?"

Convincing Jessica I needed to meet a mysterious someone who knew I was dead—alone—wasn't going to be easy. Best to get it over with.

Chapter 11

$\mathscr{L}$ love my cat. She's a pain in the ass, but she's dependable, and has never once told me to change my shirt because I look like a crack whore in periwinkle blue. Heck, the whole reason I was in this fix was, in part, because of Giselle, but I hadn't gotten rid of her, or even snacked on her. I was definitely a cat person.

Which was why it was unbelievably annoying to discover dogs now found me irresistible. Before I woke up in the funeral home, I had ignored dogs, and they had ignored me, and we'd gone about our separate business. No longer.

By the time I'd gotten out of my car and walked a block, nearly a dozen dogs were following me. They were relentless in their adoration. When I turned to kick them away, they darted closer and licked my ankles and grinned big goofy doggy grins. I don't know why it hadn't happened the other night when I was prowling around Lake Street trying to kill myself in a variety of ways. Maybe my vampire pheromones took time to kick in. Maybe there were more dogs in this neighborhood. Maybe I'd gone insane.

As if the slobbering pack wasn't bad enough, my ears were still ringing from the scolding Jessica had given me. To sum up, she thought going out alone to meet a stranger who knew I was a vampire was (a) crazy, and (b) stupid, and if I was going to do such a thing, I was (c) crazy and stupid. I pointed out that it'd be even nuttier to bring my fragile, mortal pal along for the ride.

When she threatened to follow me, I went out to my driveway and tipped her car over. It was so easy . . . I'd had more trouble, in my old life, opening a garage door. Jessica was impressed, but pissed. I'd never smelled a mixed emotion before, and it was weird as hell—chocolate pudding on fire.

When I left she was willfully messing up my cupboards. She knows it makes me nuts when I can't find things.

I had parked my car in a prohibitively expensive ramp and was getting close to Barnes and Noble when a filthy, mud-spattered black limousine screeched up beside me. The dogs (there were eight: three black labs, a corgi, a golden retriever, two fat poodles, and a mutt; they all had collars and were trailing leashes) were startled by the noise, and I took advantage of that to hiss, "Get lost!"

All the limo's doors popped open.

"Huh?"

And several pairs of hard hands grabbed me.

"Hey!"

And stuffed me inside. The door slammed shut, and off we went.

"I knew this would happen," I informed my captors. "Just so you know. I mean, that phone call was so obviously a trap." My captors—there were four seated across from me (whoa, big seats!) and they made The Rock look puny—were all holding large wooden crosses at arm's length to ward me off. One of them was agitating a small, stoppered bottle, which I took to be holy water. They were a little tense, but hardly stinking of fear. They'd done this before. "Which one of you fellas called me?"

Dead silence.

"Well, okay, be that way, but I'm not scared, y'know. Actually, this is sort of bringing me back to prom night. The rough handling, the over-the-top limo, the sullen expressions . . . ah, it all comes roaring back."

The one opposite me snorted, but the other three remained sphinxlike. They all looked like vague clones of one another: broad through the chest, well over six feet tall, with big hands and big smelly feet. They all needed a shave, they all had dirty-blond hair and brown eyes, and they all smelled like Old Spice mixed with cherry cough syrup.

"Are you guys brothers?" I asked. Nothing. "Well, then, do you all have cocker spaniels? Because you know that saying, about how people start to look like their pets after a while? Because you guys look like cocker spaniels, if spaniels could walk erect and shave most of the hair off of their bodies. And talk. Assuming you guys talk. Which I shouldn't assume, because none of you has said a word. It's just me doing all the chatting. Which is fine, I don't mind carrying the burden of conversation, though it's just this sort of thing that drives my stepmother up a tree. It—"

"Shut up," the one on the end said.

"Really is unbelievable, I mean, *she* can talk about clothes and dinner parties and pool maintenance ad nauseam but God forbid anybody else get a word in edgewise, it's really—"

"Shut up," they said in sullen unison.

I folded my arms across my chest. "Make me," I said, fearlessly if immaturely.

The spaniel on the end leaned and shoved his cross closer to me. I toyed with the idea of grabbing it, breaking it into a thousand toothpicks, and using one of the toothpicks to clean my teeth, but (a) there wasn't anything in my teeth; (b) it seemed vaguely disrespectful, and (c) I didn't want to tip my hand. They were holding crosses and holy water and they felt safe. I was in no hurry to disabuse them of their quaint notions about vampires.

Which was something to think about, so I thought about it. I assumed if crosses and Bibles didn't work on me, they didn't work on any vampires. But I must be wrong about that, else why the crucifix brigade?

What else didn't work on me, but worked on "normal" vampires? I would have to keep my eyes and ears open, and that was a fact.

As I decided this, I realized the spaniel was still brandishing his cross about four inches from the end of my nose. "No, ah, no, please, it burns," I said politely. And stopped talking, which is what they seemed to prefer. Well, it was nothing to me. I decided to enjoy the scenery.

I groaned when we pulled up outside . . . a cemetery! *Mwah-hah-hah!* Who knows . . . what evil . . . *lurks* . . . in the hearts . . . of men. Oh, puke.

"Come on, you guys," I complained as they prodded me from the limousine. "Must we live out every stereotype? If you're taking me to see a guy in a cape with a high collar, I'll be very upset."

We tromped through the sufficiently spooky cemetery, complete with de rigueur moonlit tombstones, eerie owl hoots (in Minneapolis?), and large, spooky, utterly silent mausoleums. We paused outside the largest and spookiest. According to the six-inch-high letters, this was the CARLSON family mausoleum, a pretty typical name for a region settled by Norwegians.

"Ooooh, the CARLSON mausoleum," I mocked, as the Cocker Boys struggled with the heavy door. "How sinister! What's next, a plate of lutefisk and square dancing? Need a hand with that?" They did not; the door was finally swinging open. "What, no scary creaking sound from rusty hinges? Better get that looked into, it totally ruins the spooky mood thing you've got going here—jeez, don't *shove,* I'm *going.*"

I plodded down several steps, past the big stone (yuck!) coffins, through a stone archway, and down another dozen or so steps. Obviously underground, this room was well lit by— of course—torches. There were several people milling about the room, but my gaze went to one right away.

He was unbelievable. Easily the most amazing-looking man I'd ever seen outside of *Playgirl.* Not that I read such trash. Well, hardly ever.

Tall, very tall—at least four inches taller than me, and I'm not petite. He had thick, inky black hair that swept back from his face in lush waves. Not many men could have pulled off the Elvis hair swirl thing, but this guy had it. His features were classically handsome: strong nose, good chin, nice broad forehead. His eyes were beautiful and frighten- ing: deepest black, with a hard glitter to them, like stars shining in the dark winter sky. And his mouth was saved from being tender by a cruel twist of the upper lip. He looked mean and he looked *bad*.

And his body! He was so broad through the shoulders I wondered how he'd fit through the door, and his arms looked thick and powerful. The charcoal suit superbly set off his long frame, and speaking of long, his fingers were slim and straight; they looked deft and capable. Pianist's hands. Surgeon's hands. His shoes were—whoa! Were those Ferragamos? It was a rare and wonderful thing to see a properly shod man in an underground mausoleum. Inter- estingly, the tips were wet, like he'd rushed through the dewy grass to get here. Which was weird, because he didn't look like the sort of guy who rushed any place.

I started to edge toward him to get another look, when I glanced at his face again. Almost as interesting as his incred- ible good looks was the fact that he looked as annoyed to be there as I was.

There were other people in the room, too. I guess. Who the hell cared?

"Ah, gentlemen, you bring our newest acolyte!"

The overly booming voice—not, sad to say, from the fella I was admiring—brought me back to myself in a hurry. Yes, there were other people in the room. Other pale people, in fact. Pale, with glittery eyes and white, sharp teeth. They were standing perfectly still, like they were all playing statues. Except they looked ill. Too pale, even for vampires (I guessed . . . what did I know?), and thin, and cold, and ragged. Every one of them had at least one stain on their clothing. That was just sad—being dead was no excuse to get sloppy.

They huddled together and stared at the speaker, and I kind of felt sorry for them. They would have been scary if they hadn't looked so pathetic.

"Now, Miss Taylor, as our newest supplicant, you will be allowed to feed in just a moment. All of you will, in fact."

At this, the horde looked absurdly grateful.

The speaker was approaching me from the far side of the chilly stone room. He wasn't nearly as impressive as the other guy: medium height for a guy, about a head shorter than me, slightly chubby around the middle, a cleft chin (what Jessica would call, with unfailing tact, an "ass face"), watery blue eyes. And—(*groan!*)—dressed in a black tuxedo. Not a cape, but almost as bad.

"Uh, hi," I said, staring at the walking stereotype. In the books and movies, all the vampires were righteously good-looking, even the villains. Guess this guy hadn't read any of the books.

He took one of my hands in his and gripped it tightly. His hand was cold—colder than mine. Then he kissed it with his icky cold lips. I managed not to vomit on top of his bent, balding head. Finally—thank God!—he straightened up and let go of my hand, which I instantly wiped on my leg. Rude, but I just couldn't help it. Being kissed by Bald Boy was like being kissed by a dead fish.

"First, however—and I require this of all new Undead Children—" That's just how he said it, too. You could hear the capital letters. "—You must get down on those dimpled knees of yours and swear fealty to me. Then we will feast, and you will rest at my side, our newest undead child, and my current favorite."

"Dimpled knees?" Who *was* this guy?

I didn't mean to. I didn't want to. But I started to laugh and just couldn't stop. Everyone else in the room stopped rustling and murmuring, and turned shocked gazes in my direction. Except Mr. Gorgeous in the corner. His eyebrows arched and his lips twisted, but he didn't smile. He just studied me with that perfect, icy gaze.

"Stop it!"

"I can't," I giggled.

"I command you to stop laughing! You will not be allowed to drink at the sacred throats of our—"

"Stop, stop, you're killing me!" I giggled and snorted and leaned against the stone bust of a Carlson so I wouldn't fall down. "Next you'll tell me there will be dire consequences for daring to mock your august self."

He pointed a finger at me. Nothing happened. This seemed to surprise him (had he expected me to turn to dust?), and it also pissed him off. "Gentlemen! Punish her!"

This set me off into gales of laughter again. The Cocker Boys approached me, brandishing crosses, and one of them hurled water into my face. I must have sucked some in from laughing, because I started to sneeze. And laugh. And sneeze. And laugh. When I finally had control of myself the Cocker Boys were backed in the far corner, behind Bald Tux Boy, and all the other vampires—except one—were wedged as far from me as I could get.

"Oh, dear," I said. I wiped my eyes. I hadn't actually cried, of course, but my face was wet with holy water. "Oh, that was really great. Well worth the price of parking downtown. And hardly anything is, you know. Except maybe dinner at the Oceanaire."

"You're a vampire," Tux Boy said, except he didn't thunder it majestically this time. It sort of squeaked out.

"Thanks for the news flash, but I figured that out when I woke up dead a couple of days ago."

"But . . . but you . . ."

"Yeah. Well! This has been superfun, not, but I think I'll be going now."

"But . . . but you . . ."

"But . . . but I was curious so I came along for the ride. I mean, if somebody calls you up and knows you're a vampire, and *you* only knew for a couple of days, wouldn't you take a ride?"

"Called you? I—"

"So here I am, and excuse me, but yuck! It's filthy down here. And boring, which is worse. If hanging with other vamps means I have to go the whole movie cliché route, then forget it. Cemeteries? Acolytes? Partying in chilly mausoleums? Pass."

"You—"

"Also, nobody wears a tux this time of year unless they're going to a wedding. You look like an escapee from the set of *Dracula Does Doris*."

I paused for rebuttal, but nobody said anything. They were all just staring at me with their big glittery eyes. I'd been stared at more in the last three days than in the last thirty years, and I couldn't decide if it was cool or annoying.

I shrugged and walked out of the room, climbed the steps, and was back outside in a jiffy. The evening had been mildly educational, but ultimately disappointing. I couldn't believe vampires were so boring and uncool. I had set trends when I was alive . . . apparently it was up to me to carry the coolness torch when I was dead, too. There was no rest for the fashionable.

"Wait." It wasn't a shout; it was a cool command. And, weirdly, my feet stopped moving like they'd been spiked to the ground. I looked down at them in annoyance. Traitors!

I turned. Tall, Dark, and Sinister was rapidly approaching. He'd been the only one not to cringe before me in the mausoleum. At the time, I'd kind of liked it. Now I wasn't so sure.

"What is it? I have to go; I've wasted enough time in this pit."

He ignored me and grabbed my face with both hands, pulling me toward him until our mouths were millimeters apart. I squeaked angrily and tried to pull away, but it was like trying to pull free of cement. I had thought my undead strength was spectacular, but this guy was easily twice my strength.

He was touching my face, examining me like I was a really fascinating specimen, touching my lips, peeling my upper lip back and looking at my teeth.

I snapped at his fingers, which made the corner of his mouth twitch. "Let go! Jeez! I knew I shouldn't have gotten up this morning. This evening, I mean." I kicked him in the shin, which hurt like hell. It was like kicking a boulder. And his reaction was about as animated. "You don't get a lot of second dates, do you, pal?"

"You *are* a vampire," he said. It wasn't a question. He released his grip, and I backed up so fast I fell down.

He blinked down at me, then extended a hand. I smacked it away as I jumped to my feet. "What do you want, a prize for figuring it out? Jeez. Trust me, being dead—"

"Undead."

"—is the only way I would have been hanging around a bunch of too-pale, poorly dressed weirdos. But that is *not* my scene and I'm outta here. Sooo nice to meet you," I added sarcastically.

His hand shot out and grabbed me above the elbow. "I am also taking my leave, but you'll accompany me, I think." The stone face cracked and he almost smiled. "I insist on the pleasure of your company. We have much to talk about."

"My ass!"

"If you wish, although I'd have to see it first to truly comment. If it's anything like the rest of you, I'm sure it's quite nice. Also . . ." He yanked me up against his chest with about as much trouble as I'd have tossing a tissue. That icy black gaze bored into me. I felt everything inside me turn cold. It was like being glared at by an evil yeti.

"You haven't fed tonight, and yet you're energetic. You don't look at all hungry. In fact, you look . . . quite nice. However did you manage that?"

I cleared my throat to work up some spit (tough work, when you don't make much in the way of bodily fluids anymore) and said, "First of all, mind your own business, and second, it's none of your damned business! Now." My voice went hard and cold. I'd never heard it sound like that before, not even when I told the Ant she couldn't send me to military school. "Remove the hand, while you can still count to five with it."

He stared at me for another second, then laughed. I'd never heard chuckles sound so humorless.

"Quit that," I snapped, trying not to show how unnerved I was.

"Yes," he said, almost purred, and my arm was numb from the strength of his grip, "you'll come to my home. And we'll talk. About all kinds of things. And really, girl, it's for your own safety."

"Sorry, but I already promised the Wolfman I'd be his girl. Now let go!" I tugged, furious that my strength, one of the few good things about being a vampire, was useless here.

His other hand was on my face again; his fingers forced my teeth apart and he stroked one of my canines with a thumb. Then he pushed, hard, and I felt a drop of blood hit my tongue. This was shocking, for several reasons: it was delicious—five times better than Nick's—it was cool to the taste, and I didn't think vampires bled.

"I wonder," he said in a low voice, more breath than words, and his thumb was pushing, forcing its way into my mouth, an odd kind of rape and as infuriating as it was exciting. "I wonder what you'll taste like?"

Well, why don't you find out? Wait. What the hell am I thinking? This is a very bad man.

"That'th it. For the latht time, *get off me!*" I shoved as hard as I ever had in my life. And I could hardly believe what happened next.

Although the whole thing took little more than a second, I saw it in slow motion. Tall, Dark, and Psychotic flew away from me like he'd been fired out of a cannon. He crashed back into a monument—a large cross—and *through* it. Stone flew everywhere, because as soon as he hit the cross it blew up and the back of his suit began to smolder. But he kept going, until he smashed into the side of the mausoleum and collapsed to the ground like a sack of dirt.

I didn't wait around to find out if he was dead (again), or pissed, or what. I ran.

Chapter 12

WHEN I finally slowed and looked around, I saw with amazement I'd trotted sixteen blocks in about three minutes. Summer Olympics, here I come. Assuming they held the races at night.

I was on one of the side streets behind Minneapolis General Hospital, and figured I should go inside and call a cab. Maybe I'd luck out and get a woman cab driver.

I sure as hell wasn't going back to the cemetery—I wasn't meeting up with any of those losers again. And if I *ever* saw that rat bastard Elvis wanna-be sociopath again, I'd have his eyeballs for . . . for something disgusting you'd use eyeballs for.

Every time I thought of his hands on me, his thumb in my mouth, I got hot. No, dammit, I got pissed. Really pissed. I should shove my fingers in *his* mouth, see how he likes it. I should shove my fingers into his windpipe! Up his ass! Around his—

By now I was really stomping down the street, and

when a pair of dogs slunk out of the alley, they took one look at me and ran the other way. Well, good! Canines beware! I was not one to fuck with, by God. How dare that gorgeous creep put his hands on me? *Me?* I hardly ever kissed on the first date, much less allowed strange vampires to shove their digits into my mouth.

I was almost relieved when a dull voice cut through the light traffic and the other night noises: "See ya, world." Yes! Something to distract me from the unsettling events of the last hour.

I looked up. Six stories above, a guy a few years younger than me was standing on the ledge. I could see him as clearly as if he was standing six feet away. He was looking down, straight at me. In a romance novel, it'd be something like "our gaze met and sparks jumped" or something silly, but in fact he looked tired and resolved, and I was gaping up at him with my mouth hanging open like a rube enjoying her first night in the big city.

I knew at once he was waiting until I got out of the way so he could jump without taking the chance of splattering himself all over me. I stopped walking.

The building he was standing on was an old one, built of rough brick, and as I put my hands on the wall, testing the texture, I had a thought—a brainstorm, really. They really are like storms for me—it's like there's this *crash* and then I've got a brand new idea from nowhere. Anyway, I pulled myself up and started to climb. In no time I was skittering up the side of the building like a big blond bug. I was still pissed about what had happened in the cemetery, and worried for the guy on the roof, but couldn't help also being elated at what I was doing. I was climbing *six stories* of vertical wall . . . me! I couldn't even climb that damned rope in gym class, not even the easy one with the rubber grips.

But this was easy. It was wonderful! It required about as much effort as opening a can of Pringles. I was fast, I was strong, I was . . . I was *SpiderVamp!*

I got to the top and gave a little jump, which sent me soaring a few feet in the air, then I landed on the roof and bowed. "Ta-da!"

He was really cute. Dressed in scrubs which—mmmm—smelled like dried blood (ewww! Did I just think *mmm*?). Here was another guy with deep black hair. Except while Finger Boy gave off an air of understated menace, this fella was throwing off vibes of exhausted despair.

His hair was cut so brutally short I could see the pale gleam of his skull. His eyes were dark green, and he had a goatee that made him look like a tired devil. He was almost as pale as I was and thin, almost too thin. He stared at me with eyes gone huge.

"What have you been eating?" he said at last.

I sat on the ledge beside him. "Let's not go there. It's a long story and you wouldn't believe me anyway."

"I must really be tired," he said, more to himself than to me.

"Nice try, but I'm no illusion. Although in these second-rate tennis shoes, I ought to be. You look like hell, if you'll pardon my saying so."

"Well," he said reasonably, "that makes sense, because I feel like hell."

"It's none of my business, but why d'you want to jump? What happened?"

He blinked at me and shifted his weight. He wasn't nervous to be talking to me, not at all. Probably thought he could jump long before I got to him. And he was *so* sad and unhappy; nothing was surprising him tonight. "I'm sick of kids dying; I'm in debt up to my tits for medical school; my dad's got cancer; I haven't had sex in two months; I'm being kicked out of my apartment because the owner sold his house; I have G.A.D. and my Valium has stopped working for me."

"What's gad?"

"G.A.D. General Anxiety Disorder."

"That's pretty bad," I admitted. "I mean, I don't know what G.A.D. means exactly, but that's a pretty impressive shit list. Except for the sex thing. Typical man, wanting to jump because you haven't dipped your wick in a measly eight weeks. I once went two years."

He pondered that for a minute, then shook his head. "What about you? What happened to you?"

I crossed my legs and got comfy. "Well, I died earlier this week, found out I can't die *again*, my stepmother stole all my good shoes, I can't eat any kind of food, I practically raped a perfectly nice guy last night, met a bunch of vampires who turned out to be every bad movie stereotype imaginable, threw a persistent date through a stone cross, and found out I'm now one of the fastest creatures on the planet. Then I saw you."

"So you're a vampire?"

"Yes. But don't be scared. I'm still a nice person."

"When you're not raping men."

"Right." I gave him my friendliest, most winning smile, the one that had cinched the Miss Congeniality sash for me in high school. Luckily the blood on his scrubs was dry and didn't smell too yummy, or there'd be fangs poking through my pageant smile. "How about we go get a cup of coffee, talk about why our lives suck?"

He hesitated. The wind riffled his scrubs, but his hair was too short and didn't move. He glanced down at the street, then back at me, then down at the street again.

"You know, once I make up my mind, I usually try to follow through . . ."

"Come on," I coaxed. "Vampires exist and you never had the faintest clue, right?"

"Well—"

"Right! Shoot, I know I didn't. I mean, come on! Vampires? Hello, are we trapped in a bad movie? But if we do exist, think of all the other amazing things out there you don't know about. What if—what if there's werewolves and fairies and witches and stuff like that? It's a little early to shut the book on your whole life, don't you think? What are you, twenty-five?"

"Twenty-seven. Are you just luring me down so you can feed on me to quench your unholy thirst?"

Why were people always asking me this sort of thing? "Noooo, I just don't want you to jump. I can wait a while for my next meal."

"I'll get down," he said slowly, "if you'll make *me* your next meal."

I nearly swooned at the excitement that simple statement brought. "What have you been smoking? You just met me! I'm a ghoulish member of the undead!"

"You're also too cute to be scary, and the last two minutes have been the most interesting in the last three years. So . . .?"

Still inwardly preening over being called cute, I had to force myself to address the issue at hand. "Pal, you have no idea what you're asking." I tried to sound tough and cool, but since I gasped out the whole sentence I sounded more like a horny cheerleader.

"Sure I do. Part of the reason I'm up here is—"

"You're really, really bummed about your sex life?"

For that I got a ghost of a smile. "Among other things. You were right, I figured there's nothing new in the world except death and people being shitty to each other. I never should have been a doctor. Never wanted to be. But my dad—anyway, it's just death and paperwork and more death. And it feeds my anxiety, which makes work hard, which feeds my anxiety." He trailed off and I saw his eyes shine with unshed tears. He blinked them back. "Anyway. Sorry. So, prove me wrong. Prove a few more things, besides. I want to feel what it's like. I want to feel something besides—besides nothing."

I bit my lip. The poor guy! "Forget it." But I was sidling toward him. I was thirsty, and here was a perfectly sane specimen (or as sane as a clinically depressed suicidal man could be) offering to be my dinner. I was nuts to turn it down. The alternative was taking it by force from some poor jerk.

Why in the world would I hurt or scare someone, when there was a willing guy standing right in front of me? At least he wasn't all goo-goo-eyed and mumbling about my beauty. He was perfectly clear, and curious, and willing, and what was the harm? And why was I trying to convince myself? I had to eat, right? Why was I still talking to myself?

"Okay . . . if I do this, . . . you promise not to jump?" I did a fairly good imitation of a reluctant night stalker.

"Yes."

"Or leap in front of a truck or take a bath with your toaster or comb your hair with a chainsaw?"

He laughed. He looked years younger when he did that. He wasn't afraid at all. And that made up my mind for me. "I promise. Now do it, cutie, before I come to my senses."

I jumped down from the ledge, pulled him down to me, gently. Brought him to me like a lover. His scrubs top had a v-neck, so I just tugged him toward me and bit him. He gasped and went rigid in my arms, then his arms came around me in a strangler's grip.

He went up on his toes and his hips pistoned toward mine. His blood was slowly spilling into my mouth and it tasted like the lushest, most potent wine ever made. My unbearable thirst became—if possible—even more unbearable for a split second, then abruptly abated. Sounds were sharper, the light—such as it was—became brighter. His heartbeat pounded in my ears and he was breathing in ragged gasps. I could smell his sex, hard and urgent and pressing against me, the smell of musk, the smell of life.

I pulled away. Another thing the movies got wrong. Vampires didn't have to drain a person dry . . . heck, I'd probably had half a cup, if that much. And it would last me the rest of the night, easily. I could drink more, of course, but it would be for pure pleasure, not need. I bet that creep from the cemetery drank ten times a night, just because he could.

"No," my dinner gasped.

"Yes, that's all I need."

"Oh, no . . . more, please God, more."

"Thanks, but I don't think you're exactly yourself right now."

He proved me right by grabbing my elbows and glaring into my eyes. "Do it again."

"Don't be greedy. Uh—what are you—?"

He had let go of me and was fumbling at the drawstring of his pants, tugging, and then his pants were around his ankles and his erection filled his hand. He gripped himself so hard his knuckles went white and, while I watched in total stupefaction, pumped once, twice, three times, and then he was coming and I leapt out of the way.

We stared at each other for a long moment, then he hurriedly put away his dick and pulled up his pants, and tied the drawstring waist with fingers that trembled. He was breathing hard, almost gasping. I felt like doing some gasping myself.

I blinked. "As God is my witness, I have no idea what to say to you."

"Me? What the hell did you *do*?" He asked the question in a tone of total admiration. "One minute I was miserable as hell, the next all I could think of was—uh—the exact opposite of dying." He colored, the blood rushing to his cheeks. I could almost hear it. "I've never done that before in front of—I'm sorry. You have no idea how weird that is for me."

"Pal, you should walk in my Beverly Feldmans for a day. Hey, I'm not complaining. Now that I'm recovering from the shock, I mean. It's no worse than what I did to you. Thanks for taking matters into your own hands, as opposed to trying to plant your dick in me."

"You didn't practically rape that man," he insisted. His gaze was direct and scarily earnest; I found I couldn't look away. "If you bit someone and they wanted more . . . it wasn't rape. He wanted to. In fact, it was probably like he had to."

I didn't want to talk about that. Being overwhelmed by a bloodsucker and needing to boink them didn't mean the bloodsucker wasn't the bad guy. Right? Right. "Never mind. Let's get off this roof, what do you say, Doctor . . . um . . . ?"

"Marc."

"I'm Betsy."

"Betsy?"

"Don't start. I can't help it if I've got unholy powers and a boring first name."

"I'm sorry, it's just—you know, the list is sort of surreal."

"List?"

"Vampire, undead, wicked denizen of the night, unholy thirst, man-raper, and—Betsy?"

"You're right," I admitted. "The whole thing does sound pretty ludicrous. What can I say? I didn't choose any of this. I'm just sort of stuck with it. I guess you could call me Elizabeth if you wanted, except no one does."

"Elizabeth . . ."

"Forget it."

"Oh, come on."

"Nope."

"How bad can it be?"

"Taylor. Elizabeth Taylor."

He laughed, as everyone does when they hear my name. It was the laugh that made us friends, which I thought was just fine.

Chapter 13

"**You** need a sidekick," Marc announced. He'd just finished his second plateful of steak and eggs. I was sticking with tea and honey.

"I've already got one," I said gloomily. "My friend Jessica."

"I mean a badass, not someone from the secretarial pool."

I stuck a finger in his face. "First of all, do not mock secretaries, nor their pools. They're as badass as can be—you think *management* runs a company?"

"You know a lot about it?"

"I was a secretary until last week."

"Then you died?"

"No, I was laid off. *Then* I died. In fact, I should take a drive by the place . . . it's probably gone up in flames by now." I giggled evilly. "When they laid off the admin staff, they lost the capability to call their clients, make their computers work, make the sorter on the copy machine work, place orders for office supplies, update the database, cut checks, figure out the postage machine, calculate payroll, send overnight packages . . . oh, the humanity." I grinned at the mental image, then got back to business. "Second, Jessica is at least twice as smart as anyone sitting at this table. Third—cripes, how much are you going to eat?" During my scolding he'd again flagged down the waitress.

"I've been a little too depressed to eat lately," he said defensively. "And after what happened on the roof, I'm *starving*. Besides, you're just jealous."

"You're right about that." I moodily stirred my tea. "My mom fixed my favorite meal the other night and I threw it up all over her bathroom."

"But you can drink . . . ?" He nodded toward my tea.

"Apparently. Doesn't do a thing for me . . . sure doesn't make me less thirsty. But it's familiar, you know?"

"Sure. That's why I stay in the ER. It's depressing as hell and you get no closure, but at least I know where everything is."

"If you're so unhappy in that job, why not leave? Go work in a nice family clinic somewhere."

"In this economy?"

"Oh, come on. It's not like you're a bricklayer. You're a doctor, and people always need doctors."

He shrugged and looked down at his plate. "Yeah, well . . ."

"I mean, it must be hard. Working in a children's hospital."

"It's unbelievably awful," he said gloomily. "You would not *believe* the evil shit people do to children."

"I don't want to hear it," I said hurriedly.

"Actually, I want to talk to *you* about it. You've got to— to feed, right? Well, I could get you a list of abusive parents, the ones who like to use their babies for ashtrays, the ones who decide to press a hot iron to the kid's back because she slammed the door a little too hard. And you could—you know. Fix things."

"A blood-sucking vigilante?" I was horrified. And intrigued. But mostly horrified. "Did you not hear me? About how until last week I was a secretary?"

"Not anymore," Marc said smugly. Now that he'd thought he'd found a purpose, his entire demeanor—even his smell!—was different. Gone was the slump-shouldered sad-eyed boy. In his place was the Cisco Kid. "You told me you thought you'd fight crime to atone for your feeding habits, right? Well, where better to start?"

I just shook my head and stirred my tea.

"Well, what's your alternative? You don't seem the type to skulk in the shadows and lure the unwary into your fiendish embrace."

The mental image made me chuckle.

"And another thing—vampires don't giggle."

"This one does. And before I forget . . ." My hand shot out. I pulled him toward me and looked deeply into his eyes. Time to use my unholy sex appeal, for good instead of evil. "I'm glad you're feeling better, but if you should relapse, you won't. Kill. Yourself." I paused, then added for good measure, "I command it."

He stared back. His pupils were dots; the lights in the all-night café were ferocious. "I'll do . . . whatever. The hell. I want. But thanks. Anyway."

I stared harder. *Come on, vampire mojo. Do your thing.* "Don't. Kill. Yourself."

"Why. Are you. Talking. Like this?"

I dropped his hands in disgust. "Dammit! I've been able to make men do my bidding since I woke up dead. And more than a few did my bidding in high school, thank you very much. What's so special about *you?*"

"Thanks for sounding so disgusted. And I have no idea. I—uh—" His jaw sagged and I could practically hear his

I.Q. dropping. He stared dreamily over my shoulder. I looked—and nearly fell out of the booth. The psychopath from the cemetery was standing in the doorway of the café, looking straight at me. Ack! His hair was a mess, I was happy to see. I couldn't see his back, but he smelled like burned cotton. Good!

"Oh my God," Marc rhapsodized. "Who is *that?*"

"An asshole," I mumbled, turning back to him and picking up my tea. I was so rattled I sloshed some of the hot liquid on my hand, but I didn't feel a thing.

"He's coming over here!" Marc squealed. "Oh my God, oh my God, ohmyGod!"

"Will you get a hold of yourself?" I hissed. "You sound like a girl with a crush. Ah-ha!" Realization hit, a little slowly as usual. "You're *gay!*" I realized I'd shouted it and everyone in the café was staring at us. Or maybe they were staring at Danger Boy, who was rapidly approaching.

"Duh."

"What, 'duh'? How was I supposed to know? I just assumed you were straight."

"Because you are." He was still staring over my shoulder, hurriedly trying to fix his hair which was so incredibly short it could never be mussed. "*I* always assume everyone is gay."

"Well, statistically that's pretty dumb."

"I don't have to take criticism from an undead breeder . . . helloooo," he cooed. I felt a weight drop on my shoulder: Jerkoff's hand. I shrugged it off and resisted the urge to bite him like a rabid coyote.

"Good evening," Jerkoff said. On top of everything else, he had a killer baritone.

"Fuck off," I said warmly.

He slid into the booth beside Marc. I heard a muffled gasp and thought Marc was going to swoon. "We meet again."

"Yippee fucking skippy."

"I don't believe we've been formally introduced."

"I was just about to take care of that when you stuck your finger in my mouth." I thought about throwing my tea in his face, but the jerk would probably use Marc as a living shield.

"Ah. Yes. Well, my name is Sinclair. And you are . . . ?"

"Really pissed at you."

"Is that a family name?"

Marc burst out laughing. Sinclair favored him with a warm smile. "Is this a friend of yours?"

"None of your fucking business."

"She talked me out of jumping to a grisly death," Marc informed my new archenemy. "Then we came here to plot about all the abusive parents we're going to put an end to."

"We did *not.*"

"Did too!"

Sinclair's nostrils flared, he leaned in close for a good look at Marc's neck (a bruise was rapidly forming, but there were no signs of teeth marks), then he looked at me. "You have fed on this man?"

I blushed. Or at least, I felt like I blushed—who knew if I still could? "Again: none of your fucking business."

He drummed his fingers on the table. I tried not to stare. They were sooo long and slim, and I had a vague idea of the power in them. "Interesting. And here you both are now. Hmm."

"Want to join us?" Marc piped up. I groaned, but they both ignored me. "Have a cup of coffee or something?"

"I don't drink . . . coffee."

"Oh, very funny," I snapped. "What are you doing here, Sink Lair? If it's about the bill for your coat, too damned bad—you brought that on yourself."

"Indeed." His gaze was cool. Black eyes bored into mine. It was about as pleasant as it sounds. "A matter I will bring up with you shortly, but as to your question, I am here for your benefit, my dear."

"Don't call me that."

"You can call *me* that," Marc chirped helpfully.

"Nostro wants you dead for your actions tonight. The vampire who brings him your head will be richly rewarded."

"Who the hell is Noseo?"

"Nostro. He's—I suppose you would call him a tribal chief. Sometimes—often—vampires band together, and the strongest is in charge."

"Why in the hell do they do that?" I griped. "Why don't they just go about their own business like they did before they died?"

"Because they are not allowed to. Vampires are usually forced to take sides."

"Nobody's forced me."

"We will attend to that later—"

"What?"

"—but to answer your question, the undead band together for protection. For a sense of security."

"So this guy Notso is torqued off because I didn't play the game?"

'That, and because of your peals of hysterical laughter when he challenged you."

Marc had been following the conversation closely, and now he stared at me. "The head vamp wanted you do to something, and you laughed at him?"

"For quite some time," Sink Lair added helpfully.

"Betsy, jeez! Didn't he try to off you or something? You're lucky to be here."

"He visited upon her the worst punishment a vampire can endure . . . and she laughed at that, as well." Then, *"Betsy?"*

"Yeah, Betsy, wanna make something of it?"

"Indeed, no." Was the asshole actually hiding a smirk? I looked, and he stared back, expressionless. Must have been my imagination.

"So you're here to try to bring Notso my head?"

"Nostro. And no, I am not. You're far too pretty to behead."

"Barf. Is Nostro short for Nostrodamus? Is the tubby twit that unimaginative?"

Sink Lair looked pained. "Yes, and yes."

"Ugh."

"I quite agree."

"So why *are* you here, Sink Lair?"

"It's SIN-clair, and I should think that would be obvious, even to you—"

"Hey!"

"You are newly undead and clearly a menace to yourself. You don't know any of the rules, and there is now a bounty on your head not seventy-two hours after you first rose . . . well done, by the way. I will take you under my protection."

"And in return . . .?" I didn't mean to sound like there was a bug in my mouth, but I couldn't help it. I didn't trust this guy as far as I could throw him. Hmm . . . better come up with a new cliché. I already proved I could throw him pretty far. "I mean, there's no way you're doing this out of the kindness of your rock."

"In return, we will discover why you are so different from the rest of us. You should have been in agony when they flung holy water on you. Instead it gave you the sneezes. Once I deduce—"

"No thanks."

There was a long pause. Clearly he had expected just about any response but refusal. Awwww, poor baby.

"Really. I insist."

"I don't care! You're not my father—although you're probably old enough to be, creep, and—"

"How old are you?" Marc asked breathlessly.

Sinclair spared him a glance. "I was born the year World War II began."

I gasped in horror. To think I was attracted to this fossil! Well, it wasn't entirely my fault . . . Sinclair looked like he was in his early thirties. There wasn't so much as a speck of gray in his inky black hair, no wrinkles bracketing his fathomless dark eyes. "Ewwwww! So you're, like, ninety years old? Yuck! Do you have a truss under that suit?"

"You are the most ignorant, prideful, vainglorious—"

"It's more like he's in his early sixties," Marc interrupted hurriedly. "And both of you, mellow out. I don't want to be in the middle of a vampire fistfight."

"Indeed. Go to sleep."

"But I'm ggggzzzzzz . . ."

I shoved my hand out, so Marc's head connected with my palm instead of colliding with the table. I slowly pulled away and gave Sinclair a good glare. "What'd you do that for?" And *how* did you do that? I'd have to try that on the stepmonster sometime.

He looked back, cool as a baby lying on a pile of ice cubes. "It was inappropriate for him to hear so much about us. Which is another matter I mean to take up with you. Is it true that you have told your family you are still alive?"

"I'm not still alive, it's none of your business, how'd you find out?"

He ignored my questions. "You must not do such things. You endanger the very ones you would seek to protect."

"Yeah? What do you know about it?"

"Well, I—"

"I don't actually want an answer," I explained. "I'm starting a rant, here."

"Sorry."

"And another thing: Has anyone ever told you, you don't use contractions? Everything is 'you are' and 'I am' and 'you would'. Is this the way they talked during Dubya-Dubya-two?"

"Has anyone ever told you that you lack focus?"

"Sure," I said. I drained my tea and set it down, hard. Marc snored on, oblivious. "Now listen up. I don't appreciate being grabbed, I sure as shit didn't care for your greasy fingers in my mouth—"

"I am tempted to put something else in your mouth this minute," he said silkily.

"Shut up! And I don't like you following me and I don't like you putting my friends to sleep."

"He is not your friend. You only met this evening."

"He's a friend I haven't known very long, all right? Again: *not that it's any of your business.* Now buzz off. I can take care of myself, I don't need you, I don't want you—"

"All lies."

I felt my stomach tighten at his insinuation, but plunged ahead. "And I don't want your stupid vampire tribes, either. Just because I'm dead doesn't mean I can't have a life."

Sinclair blinked at that one, and I hurried on before he could interrupt again. "Yeah, I told my family I wasn't dead . . . why the hell not? They're not going to stake me in the middle of the night—well, my real parents won't. I'm coping as well as I can, and I don't plan on hooking up with any of you undead losers. So stop following me and stop bugging me."

"Finished?"

"Uh . . . let's see . . . can take care of myself . . . it's my business who I tell . . . undead losers . . . stop bugging me . . . yeah."

"We will speak again. There will come a time, Miss Rogue, when you will badly need my help. I will gladly give it. I hold no grudges." He grinned at me. It was terrifying . . . all white teeth and glowing eyes. His canines looked half an inch long. How'd he do that? No one was bleeding that *I* could smell. "Provided you let me put something in your mouth again."

"Ewwwww!"

"Good night."

Poof! Vanished. Or he moved so quickly I couldn't track him. Either way, the undead Houdini was gone, I was shaking with rage and—oh, no!—lust, and Marc was drooling on the formica.

Chapter 14

A few days passed without incident, which was apparently too much for my old pain in the ass, Jessica, and my new pain, Marc. The excitement of my return from the dead had died down, no vampire baddies had come knocking, my relationship with my stepmother and father remained the same (she ignored me, he sent checks), and that was just too darned staid for my pals. Never mind that *I* was perfectly happy with the status quo.

I introduced them and, after they bristled at each other for an hour, they decided to share me. I stayed out of it. As long as they weren't fighting, I didn't care what the arrangements were.

Jessica was always threatened when I made a new friend. I'd tried to explain that, no, I did not love all my friends equally, that she was my absolute favorite and would be forever, amen, but it usually fell on deaf ears. And it was strictly a one-way street: Jessica had loads of society friends who wouldn't know me if I slapped them in the face. Which was just the way I liked it. As Michael Crichton wrote in *Jurassic Park,* "You know what assholes congenitally rich people are."

Dr. Marc Spangler, on the other hand, for all his renewed sense of purpose (and proposed conspiracy to assault child abusers), was still fragile and I wanted nothing said or done to him that might send him back up on the roof. He was staying with me while he looked for a new place, an arrangement that suited us nicely: I wanted a roomie who could move around during the day, and he needed a bed.

Before I'd died I never would have done such a thing. Not because I didn't care, but because I wouldn't dare. You just couldn't know about people, what was really in their hearts and what hid behind a smile. But along with an endless thirst for blood, I now had a pretty good radar. I just knew Marc was an all right guy.

And frankly, I had never cared for living alone, which is why I had rescued Giselle from the animal shelter. I'd watch too many scary movies and stay awake all night in terror, flinching at every creak. The thing that terrified me the most were zombie movies. After watching *Resident Evil* I had nightmares for a week. It was ironic, because now I was one of the unkillable monsters. Still didn't like living by myself, though.

Jessica grumbled a bit, but dropped it when I explained about Vamp Radar. And I laid it out for Marc his first night in my house.

"I gotta tell you, I'm kind of worried about you."

"Me? How come?" He was buttering a croissant—ugh! Like there's not enough butter in one already. "I'd think you would have plenty of other stuff on your mind than little old me." He blinked at me exaggeratedly and sucked down the croissant in one gulp.

"I have surprisingly little on my mind. That was not an invitation to slam me," I added when he opened his bread-filled mouth. "It's just—I'm afraid if I turn my back on you, I'll find you up on another roof."

"Never happen," he replied confidently, lightly spraying me.

I brushed croissant crumbs out of my bangs. "How come?"

"Because I have an anxiety disorder, not suicidal ideation. And people like me almost never kill themselves. We're too anxious about death."

The absurdity of that statement struck me all at once and I burst out laughing. Marc just grinned at me and wolfed down the rest of the croissants.

The three of us were adjusting, but there was a kind of balancing act for me to maintain between Jess and Marc. And so, because I wanted to keep the two neurotics happy, midnight found me in a private exam room at Minneapolis General, instead of checking out the "Midnight Madness Shoe Sale" at Neiman Marcus. "Only for you," I had said to Jessica. "And I guess you," I'd added to Marc.

There was one thing they both agreed upon: I was not your garden-variety vampire, and the more we knew about my abilities, the better. Marc wanted to get a "baseline," whatever the hell that was, and Jessica was just plain curious, so Marc got us a room at the hospital and the exam began.

"I'm not taking off any of my clothes," I warned him.

Marc rolled his eyes. "Aw, gee, I guess no big thrill for me tonight."

"For any of us," Jessica said dryly. "The girl's the color of a toad's belly and she needs her roots done."

"I do not!" I said, shocked. "I had them done two weeks before I died. My roots are fine."

"I wonder what would happen if you cut your hair?" Marc asked thoughtfully, slipping a thermometer under my tongue. "Would it stay short forever? Would it grow back? *Could* it grow back? Would it magically reappear the next night?" He was staring so thoughtfully at my hair I leaned as far away from him as I could without falling off the table.

"So this Sinclair fella . . . he wants to take you under his wing?" Jessica asked. She was rocketing around the exam room on the doctor's stool. She'd zoom up to a wall, kick off, and careen to the other side. Marc was obviously used to odd antics during an exam, but it was making me claustrophobic as hell. She had officially given up mourning colors for me, and tonight she was sporting green leggings, a buttercup yellow T-shirt, a salmon-colored raincoat, and green flats. "Teach you the vamp ropes?"

"God, he is so *hot*," Marc muttered. By contrast, he was a moving pile of rags in torn jeans and a faded T-shirt with the logo "Drop Dead, Fred" . . . an alarming choice for a physician. "Unbelievably yummy. Hoo, boy, I—hmm."

He peered at the thermometer, cleared it, then promptly stuck it in my mouth again. "By the way, I tested all the equipment on myself before you guys got here, so we know it works . . ."

"This assumes *you* work," Jessica pointed out with a smirk.

"No one hit your buzzer, Rich Girl. Now what were we talking about? Oh, yeah—Sinclair. You should see this guy, Jessica. He looks like the prince of darkness and he moves like a matador. I was sweating just looking at him."

"Yum," Jessica said, impressed. "White boy, I suppose."

"You suppose right, and don't forget, he's a hundred years old," I sneered.

"More like sixty-three, so he's got a lifetime of wisdom and street smarts, not to mention years of experience fucking every which way a guy can think up, to go with a nice, hard, powerful, eternally young body. Jesus, I'm gonna have to quit talking about this before I need to sit down."

"Please," I said thinly. I hadn't thought about the experience factor minus the ick factor of a wrinkled, decrepit body. Which was probably hiding under those superbly tailored suits. "Besides, it doesn't matter a purple crap what

Sinclair wants. I'm not playing vamp politics. I'm minding my own business, and he sure as shit better mind his."

"Or you'll throw him through a concrete cross again," Jessica added. "I wish I could have seen it!"

"No you don't," I said glumly. "The whole thing was alternately stupid and frightening. If that's what I can expect from being in a vamp tribe, count me out. I haven't been back and I don't plan to *go* back. It was lame *and* scary, a dreadful combo."

Meanwhile, Marc was holding out a plastic cup. "Fill this."

I stared at it. "Um. I can't."

"Don't worry, you'll have privacy in the—"

"No, I mean, I literally can't. I haven't needed to use a bathroom since I woke up dead."

"Oh. Well, that's fine." But clearly it wasn't; Marc seemed rattled and hurried onto the next part of the exam.

"Think of what you'll save on toilet paper," Jessica said brightly.

"Oh, yeah, that makes it all worthwhile."

Marc slipped the bell of his stethoscope under my shirt. "Deep breath."

"Uh . . ."

"Try," he said, exasperated.

"Hey, watch the attitude, pal! This isn't my idea of fun, you know."

"Both of you be nice. Marc's never done an exam on a talking dead girl before, give him a break."

"Puh-leeze."

"Try," Marc said again.

I did, and I got so dizzy I nearly passed out. And when my breath whooshed out of my dead lungs I nearly threw up.

"Easy, easy."

"*You* take it easy." I slumped over and crossed my arms protectively over my tits. "I'm not breathing again, so I hope you got what you needed."

He was already shining a light in my eye. "Uh-huh," he said, sounding exactly like every other doctor in the world. He shined it in my other eye. "Uh-*huh*."

He backed away from me, shut the light off—not that it made much difference to me; I could still see perfectly well—and looked at my pupils again.

"Jesus!"

I heard the clang as he dropped his eye-thingie. "What? What's wrong?"

"Nothing." He felt around the floor for a second. Because there were no windows in this little antechamber of hell, I guessed it was pretty dark. Jessica was standing stock-still, afraid to move lest she bang a knee into a drawer, and Marc kept groping. If I didn't say anything and they ran into each other, it could get interesting.

"It's about four inches from your left hand," I said.

Marc's fingers brushed the end of the eye-thingie and he grabbed it. Then he got the lights back on and the exam commenced. "Open wide," he said with forced cheer, and I obliged. Then, "Let's see 'em."

"What?"

"Your fangs. Come on, out with them."

I blinked at him. Jessica was edging closer, obviously interested in getting a look-see herself. "I can't."

"Sure you can. You're a restless nightstalker of the night."

"Nightstalker of the night?"

"You hush," he said to Jessica. "Come on, Bets. I want to compare them to your other teeth."

I strained. I even grunted a little. Nothing. "It's no good, I can't."

"Try harder. Think of blood!"

"*You* think of blood," I said, annoyed. "I'm telling you, I can't just make them come out. Maybe when I have a little more experience my teeth will do my bidding, but not this week." I seized his wrist before he could step away from the table. I knew exactly what he was thinking.

Wait, let me clarify. It's not like I read his mind, more like I read his body language and knew what he was going to do next. Another swell vampire trick I found pretty handy. "And don't cut yourself to make my teeth come out, either. There's only so much of this I'm gonna put up with," I warned.

"Okay, okay. Ease up." I let go and could see the finger-marks where I'd grabbed him. They were dead white. He massaged his wrist and glared at me. "Jesus, you've got a grip like an anaconda. Can we please finish this?"

"Oh, like this was my idea?"

Twenty minutes later, after much bitching on both our parts, Marc was finished. He was looking at me a little strangely, which I pretended not to notice. He had watched me climb a building with little surprise, handled being my dinner well enough, and insinuated himself into my home with no fuss, but the scientist in him was finally facing black-and-white facts, and apparently that was a little daunting.

"So, will she live?" Jessica laughed.

"Well." He cleared his throat. "Your blood pressure is ten over five, your Babinski reflex is nonexistent, your temperature is eighty—which is why your handshake is so darned clammy—respirations are three, and your pulse is six. All incompatible with life."

"Wow," Jessica said, impressed. "Girlfriend, you're incompatible with life!"

"And here I thought I was just incompatible with pink."

"Which means you have to watch your ass, Bets," he warned. "If you're found during the day and somebody freaks and calls an ambulance, a doctor is going to pronounce you at the scene, and then you'll be back in the morgue."

Jessica was now staring at me. "You only take a breath three times a minute?"

"I guess," I said defensively. "I don't think about it. I mean, c'mon . . . do you think about your breathing, unless you've got a cold or something?"

"And she's not clammy," she said loyally. "Touching her is—is like lying in a cool shade."

"Clammy," I said glumly. "Nice save on the shade thing, though."

"*But.* Although your vitals are incompatible with life, you're superstrong, inhumanly agile, and on a liquid diet. Also, you still have a PERRLA—"

"English, white boy," Jessica commanded.

"Pupils are Even, Round, and React to Light and Accommodation."

"I could have gone to medical school," I said. "Except for all the math and stuff."

"In fact, your pupils now have a field almost twice as large as ordinary people. I've never seen anything like it."

"What can I say," I said modestly. "I was always special."

"Yes," Jessica said sweetly, "you even have your own Olympics."

He ignored us. "There's very little activity at a cellular level—so you've stopped aging. Not to mention excreting. You say you haven't taken a piss since you died—which makes no sense, because you drink liquids all day long— you don't sweat, and you don't cry."

"She's a very freaky girl," Jessica sang off-key. "The kind you don't take home to muthuh . . ."

"Jessica said you can't drink canned blood." He was tapping the bell of his stethoscope against his teeth while he thought out loud. Yuck! I hope he doused it in rubbing alcohol before he clapped it against some other unsuspecting patient's chest. "So there must be something about fresh—living—blood that keeps you going. Is it the electrolytes? The pure energy found in living cells . . .? I wonder if you harness the—"

"You can't use science to explain everything," Jessica broke in. "There's probably some mystical shit going on, too."

I laughed. "Mystical shit? Is that a technical term?"

We were shrugging into our coats, shutting off the lights, and heading out the side door as quietly as possible. Marc wasn't scheduled to work tonight, and he didn't feel up to answering awkward questions about the talking dead girl on the exam table.

"I don't know. I've never believed in this stuff. Not ever . . . shit, I don't even read science fiction. But some of the stuff I've seen at the hospital . . . as a species, we're incredibly adaptable. We can survive a lot of stuff that would kill just about anything else."

"Yeah?" I asked, impressed.

"Believe it. I've seen kids come into the ER with poles sticking out of their skulls. And the next day they have a huge breakfast and want candy for lunch. It's unbelievable and completely unpredictable. So there's an explanation for—for what you are now. Maybe you're a mutation. Maybe a vampire is just another word for—"

"Mutant freak. Very comforting."

"Man, oh man, the paper I could write about this," he said, eyes glowing with scary fanaticism. "I'd be famous . . . right before they checked me into the psych ward for a pleasant year of pureed apricots and finger painting."

That gave all of us the giggles. The door slammed behind us and we started walking through the alley toward the street, when all hell broke loose.

I sensed the problem before Jessica and Marc did—those two didn't have a clue until the bitch was on us—but I wasn't fast enough. There was a blur and then a small, dark-haired woman with the bluest eyes I'd ever seen had Marc. She'd locked a forearm across his neck and was bending him back so his throat was at the level of her mouth. Jessica was facedown in the snow—while grabbing Marc, Shorty had shoved her into the wall, knocking her out.

"The infamous Betsy," Shorty purred. She was small, probably about five feet tall. Maybe ninety pounds. And clearly as strong as an ox on steroids. Her face was unremarkable, even plain—average nose, bare bump of a chin, narrow forehead—but her eyes were astonishing and lovely. Large and the color of a spring sky, they were fringed with dark, sooty lashes. Her canines were growing while I watched. "At last we meet." Annoyingly, she did not lisp.

"Friend of yours?" Marc gurgled. Half of his air was being cut off and he was bent so far back he was staring at the stars. I could see all the little hairs on his forearms were standing straight up. He was scared shitless, but his tone was just right: casual, unconcerned. I was very, very proud of him. Frankly, I hadn't known he was brave until just then. "Maybe an old school—glkk!—chum?"

"I've never seen her before. Listen, Tootsie Roll, you want to let go of my friend before I jam a cross up your ass?"

She laughed and tightened her grip. Marc gasped, but didn't say anything. She licked the side of his throat and he shuddered, while at the same time he leaned into her. "Oh-ho, this one's had a taste, yes? No wonder you're keeping him close."

"He's *my* lunch. Go grab your own." I took a casual step forward, and she bit him. Savagely—there was none of my tentativeness or care. She ripped off an inch-wide swath of skin, spit it out, then gulped back the blood like a dog sucked down water on a hot day.

Marc screamed, a lost sound in the dark.

I did a little screaming of my own. "Stop it!" I was reeling from the suddenness of the confrontation. A minute earlier we were just stepping outside, for God's sake. Even the cemetery meeting hadn't been this alarming. "Just—quit it, okay? What do you want?"

She stopped drinking. Her pupils were huge. Was that what Marc meant? I shoved the thought away and tried to stay focused as she replied, "You, of course. Your presence is requested by my master."

"Nosehair?"

Her nostrils flared. Blood gleamed on her chin. I actually wanted to lick it off, how's that for sick and disgusting? I could feel my teeth growing, seeming to fill my mouth. I was so embarrassed I couldn't look at Marc. "Nosehair? Is that supposed to be a joke?"

"No! I'm jutht really bad at nameth."

"What's wrong with your voice?"

"Never mind. You were thaying about your mathter . . . ?"

"Nostro desires your company. He told me to use any means to persuade you. Now, I will . . ."

"Okay."

She paused. "What?"

"Okay, I'll go with you. We can go right now. Just let go of him, all right?"

"Don't you dare," Marc said to the sky.

"Marc, shut up."

"Do *not* disappear with this bitch, Betsy. Bad, bad plan."

"Marc."

"Yes, Marc." She gave him a squeeze and I heard his ribs groan under the pressure. Or maybe that was Marc groaning. "Shut up." She considered for a long moment. Obviously she'd expected more resistance. "Well, then."

After what seemed like half an hour, she released Marc, who just about broke something scrambling away from her. He went immediately to Jessica, knelt, and fumbled at her neck for a pulse. "Very well. Come with me now."

"Marc." My fangs were retracting . . . thank God. "You find a pulse?"

He looked up at me, shivering from the adrenaline rush. His eyes were huge, and all the color had fallen out of his face. "Yes, I think she's all right—just knocked out."

Congratulations, Short Stuff, maybe you'll live through the next hour. "Okay. Take her to the ER. Get her looked at, and have somebody take a look at your neck. I'm sorry."

"It's not your fault. I'll make up something good. I'll tell the attending we were mugged, or something."

"I'm sorry." I started walking out of the alley. Shorty watched, a look of amused scorn on her nasty little face. "I'll be back later."

"Not necessarily," Short Stuff tittered.

"Shut the fuck up, you cunt." I'd never used the C word before tonight, but she seemed an ideal representation of it. And the shocked look on her face—as if I'd slapped her, which I sort of had, only with a word instead of my hand— was almost worth how awful I felt about what she had done to my friends. *And oh, sweetie, you want to watch out if I catch you with your guard down . . .*

But she was a spear carrier, a soldier. Nostro had sent her to me, had told her to do whatever she could to gain my attendance. His was the hash I had to settle first.

Chapter 15

"MY master will—"

"Shut the fuck up."

"You cannot speak to—"

"Shut the fuck up."

She leaned forward and her eyes went the color of the sky right before sunset. "You don't wish to fight with *me* ... Betsy."

Ooooh, eyes that change color when she's in a snit. Now I was *really* scared. "You bet I do, Tootsie Roll. Bring it, you cow! Let's see how you do when you're not hiding behind one of my friends."

I must have sounded almost as angry as I felt, because she hesitated. Then she crossed her arms over her chest, doing an admirable impression of someone who hadn't been momentarily frightened, sat back, and stared out the limo window.

Yep, I was back in one of Noseo's limos. It had been waiting at the mouth of the alley like a big black gas-guzzling omen of death. I snapped the antenna off, just for fun, and threw it at Tootsie Roll's head. She ducked—barely. The driver didn't say a word, just held the door for me.

"I am Shanara."

"Shut the fuck up." I fumbled with my pocket—stupid linen trousers, they were going to wrinkle like hell—and tossed her a five dollar bill. "And go buy yourself a real name."

She let the bill bounce off her nonexistent chest, unfolded her arms, and started tapping her long red fingernails on the armrest. She was starting to get pretty pissed but, interestingly, wasn't doing anything. Did Nostril's edict give her permission to hurt my friends, but not me?

Time to find out. "Long red slut nails are so five minutes ago," I informed her. "In fact, it's more like five years ago. Just because you're dead doesn't mean you have to be a fashion eyesore."

"*Un*dead," she snapped.

"Dead," I said implacably. "When was the last time you had a nice steak? Or even a salad? Shit, a piece of toast? Dead people don't eat. We don't eat. *Ergo,* we are dead."

"We have more power than mere mortals can—"

"Blah, blah, blah. Save it for the recruitment center. So, when did you die? You don't look a day over sixty."

Her flat bosom heaved in indignation. "I became gloriously transformed in 1972."

"That explains the nails and the bell bottoms."

"These are in again!" she nearly screamed, pointing to her Gap knockoffs.

"Nope, sorry. I know, I know, it can be hard to keep up. Most people aren't smart enough to pull it off." From the front I could hear a curiously muffled sound, almost like someone was strangling on their own laughter.

Shaloser turned and, quick as thought, slammed her palm against the partition separating us from the driver. The glass cracked but didn't break. "Just drive, oaf!"

"Touchy," I commented. "By the way, Shamu, if you

ever touch one of my friends again, I'll bite off all your fingers and stick them up your nose." I smiled pleasantly. "And that goes for ol' Nostril, too."

I was all talk, of course . . . shit, I was a secretary, not an avenger. An out-of-work secretary, I might add. I could type like a son of a bitch, but I'd never thrown a punch.

But I could talk. I could yak until Judgment Day, if I had to.

"You'll pay," she said stonily. "You won't be like this tomorrow."

"Bored and pissed off? God, I hope not."

She flinched like I'd poked a fork toward one of her eyes. Odd, very odd. I quickly thought about what I'd just said: bored? Pissed? God?

"God," I said. Another flinch. "Jesus Christ. Lord. 'Our Father, who art in Heaven . . .' "

"Stop it, *stop it!*" She was practically climbing the door, trying to get away from me. "Don't say it, don't say *Those Words!*"

"Stop talking in capital letters and I won't."

"What? I don't understand you."

"No one with your footwear," I said with a meaningful glance at her Prada knockoffs, "ever could."

"ARE we there yet?"

"No."

"Are we there yet?"

"No."

"Are we there yet?"

"No."

"Are we there yet?"

"Shut up! I had to bring you to him but I should not have to listen to another word out of your stupid sheep's mouth! Stop it, stop it, *stop it!*"

"Okay, okay. Say it, don't spray it, bee-yatch." I waited a few seconds, then asked brightly, "Are we there yet?"

"Mercifully," she said through gritted fangs, "we are."

"Hey, neat trick, you're all toothy. Why? Hungry?"

She probably was. She looked ghastly. Too white, too thin, and sort of haggard. Of course, that could just be the residual effect of being trapped with me in a closed space for thirty minutes.

The Ant, my father, and I went on one cross-country trip by car when I was a teen.

One.

"Don't even think about snacking on *me*."

"You wish," she snapped. The limo came to a smooth stop, the door popped open, and Shanara grabbed my elbow and practically shoved me out of the car. "Come along."

"What, no cemetery?" We were standing outside a gigantic house on Lake Minnetonka. It was three stories high, dark green, with four white pillars. It looked like Tara gone bad. All the lights were out, of course. "I thought your boss really went for the stereotypes."

No answer. She just grabbed my elbow again and jerked me along. I could tell she really, really wanted to hurt me. A sensible, intelligent person would use this opportunity to keep quiet and look for escape.

"So, Shanockers, are you this guy's retriever or what? 'I want Betsy, bring me Betsy . . . fetch!' Is it like that? Or are you just such a loser you don't have a life of your own, so you hang onto this guy's coattails? Hey, watch the suit!" I was wearing a tan linen Anne Klein pantsuit and last year's Helene Arpel flats. I was glad I wasn't more dressed up, or wearing my good Arpels. I'd hate for these assholes to think I was trying to look nice for them.

She was pulling me through the house, which, although dark, seemed well lit to me. She brought me (well, dragged me) through a set of French doors, which opened to a ballroom. I looked up warily for the disco ball and was relieved not to see one.

The room was full of about twenty people, all dressed (natch) in black. The women all wore lipsticks in various shades of red, and the men were all in tuxedos. Ugh! Rented suits! Is there anything worse?

"Ahhhhhh, Elizabeth." Nostro stood up from a (groan!) throne. An actual throne at the far side of the ballroom. Really ugly, too, all gold-plated and shiny and gauche, with a big gold fan where his head would rest. At least he wasn't wearing a crown. "Thank you for bringing her, Shanara."

"Arf arf, good dog, that's a good little bitch," I muttered under my breath.

Sounding like my mom's teakettle, she actually hissed at me before replying. "Your slightest wish is my most urgent command, Master."

I snorted. Sha-na-na shot me a look of purest venom. Which I pointedly ignored. "Listen, why am I here? Why'd you set your dog on me?"

"You left too quickly last time," Nostro said pleasantly. As he got closer I was again struck by his nondescript looks. In the books, the vampire villain is always some superurbane, gorgeous guy (or stunningly beautiful woman), but old Nostro looked like a mean-spirited monk, the kind who tortured mice when the other monks were praying. "I'm very glad you've chosen to return."

"You're so full of shit," I said. There were several gasps, but no one moved, or said anything.

Nostro forced a smile and went on as if I hadn't said anything. "Now we can complete the ceremony, and you can join my family." He swept his arm around, indicating the others in the room. "They are most anxious to greet you."

"Yeah, they look like they'd be a laugh a minute. Listen, Nostro, I don't appreciate any of this. I didn't choose to come back and you know it. Your knockoff-wearing hench-whore here hurt a friend of mine to get me here. And I'm not participating in any ceremony. And I want you to *leave me alone.*"

More gasps. Nostro looked around slowly, a cobra watching for careless mice, but nobody made eye contact. They were all staring at the floor. Except for me, of course. Too dumb to be scared, I guess. Or too mad.

Nostro turned back to me and forced yet another smile; I was amazed to see it. His pupils, I noticed for the first time, were rimmed in red. It was quite a bit scarier than the big spooky house, the dumb tux, the stupid throne, and the fake courteous mannerisms. That stuff just made me want to laugh. The thing he couldn't help—his creepy, creepy eyes—that was really scary.

"I must insist," he said silkily. "I require your participation in the ceremony and I will *not . . .*" "Not" was screamed, actually screamed; I jumped. He continued in a perfectly mild voice. ". . . tolerate you siding with Sinclair."

(Note to self: Either being undead drove this guy crazy, or he was crazy first.)

"Sinclair?" I was ready to swoon with relief. Not that I was the swooning type. "You're worried about me siding with *that* rat bastard? Don't sweat it, chief. I wouldn't go near him on a bet. Yuck!"

Nostro blinked slowly, like a frog. A fat, mean, dead frog. "You do not wish allegiance with my clan or Sinclair?"

"By jove, I think he's got it!" I said this too brightly, hoping for a laugh, and was rewarded with silence. I coughed and elaborated. "No, I don't want to hang out with any of you. I don't want ceremonies or vamp politics or my friends getting ambushed because someone's really hot to talk to me . . . I don't want any of it. No offense," I added, seeing his expression darken.

"None taken," he said with completely fake sincerity.

I tried really hard to keep the sarcasm out of my tone as I continued. "I just want to live my death the way I lived my life." I looked around the room, trying to make eye contact with somebody . . . anybody. "Oh, come on!" I said loudly. "I can't be the only one who feels like this. Don't you guys want to see your friends? Maybe find your old boss and scare the shit out of him? Show your parents you're not taking a dirt nap? Why do we have to huddle together in little undead covens?"

"For protection, for—"

"For bullshit. The stories aren't all true—we've managed to hang onto our souls. Why can't we stay individuals? Why can't we turn the goddamned lights on? Why are you all wearing black? Why do you all look like extras from a B-movie vampire set? Seriously, what's *wrong* with all of you?"

Nostro flinched at "God," just like Shanara had, but other than that, he was completely unmoved by my rallying cry.

"Enough," he said, because a few of the others were looking at me with surprise and not a little curiosity. "I hate to use a cliché . . ."

"*You* do?"

". . . but you're either with us, or with Sinclair. Which is it?"

"Neither! I think you're both creeps with ridiculous names."

"Ridiculous names?"

"Nostro? Come on. I'll bet you a hundred bucks that's not the name on your birth certificate. What's your real name? George? Fred? I bet it's something really mundane. Because boy, oh boy, you are *really* overcompensating."

As soon as it was out of my mouth I knew I'd gone too far. He lunged for me, crossing the six or seven feet between us in a blink, his hands going to my throat, closing off my air. Which would have been a huge problem if I'd needed to breathe more than a few times a minute.

"Join me!" he screamed up into my face.

"Glkk!" I said, or something like it. I knew I should be more frightened than I was, but it was *so* hard to take this yahoo seriously. In the movies, at least, the villain was tall and towering and good-looking and sinister—like Sinclair! Being assaulted by Nostro was like being assaulted by a storefront Santa on a bad day.

He shook me like a maraca and, on cue, the horde descended on us. There were too many of them to do me much damage; all I really saw (and felt) was a flurry of fists. Nostro released his grip and I heard him say, "The pit for her!"

"The pit for me?" I croaked. "Puh-leeze. Do you hear yourself? Oh, wait, I get it, it's not the pit, it's The Pit! DUM-de-DUM-dum."

The mumbling horde bore me away. I didn't try to fight—why bother? The odds were twenty to one. Instead I focused on keeping my footing, which was tough because they were sweeping me along so fast and furiously my toes were barely skimming the floor.

Down, down, down the stairs we went, and before I could so much as get a look at the room they'd swept me into, I was flying through the air, from darkness to more darkness. And someone came down into the darkness with me.

Chapter 16

THE someone was a girl. Well, she could have been a hundred years old for all I knew, but she looked as if she'd be carded for buying cigarettes. Although it was quite dark in the pit, my undead eyeballs were working just fine, and I could make out her delicate, pale features: blond hair, sharp chin, high cheekbones, and big dark eyes, even more impressive than Shaknocker's. Pansy eyes, I think they're called, large and pretty and fringed with beautifully sooty lashes. Me, I had to pile on the L'Oreal Luscious Lash to prove I even had eyelashes.

We stood in the pit and stared at each other. She looked so young, so fresh; if she'd whipped out a pair of pompoms and started cheering I wouldn't have been surprised.

Instead, she dropped to her knees and bowed so low her forehead was scraping the pit's bottom. "Majesty, I beg your forgiveness . . . I couldn't help you upstairs, there were too many of them."

"Get up, don't call me that, and don't sweat it. Jeez, will

you get up? This floor is disgusting." I shifted tentatively; yup. My shoes were definitely sticking. It was like being in a movie theater after a midnight showing of *The Rocky Horror Picture Show*. "Seriously, get up." I bent, seized her arm, pulled her upright.

"Majesty—"

"Betsy."

"Queen Betsy—"

"Bet. See."

She looked away from me, then shyly glanced back. "I can't. Could you call Elizabeth the Second *Betsy?*"

"Well, no," I admitted, "although someone probably should. And I'm not the queen."

"Not yet," she said mysteriously.

I let that pass. She was a cutie, if obviously deranged. "Where are we? I mean, why am I down here? Is this like the dungeon?"

"If only, Majesty."

"Stop calling—if only? What's that supposed to mean?"

"The Master keeps his Fiends down here."

"I don't suppose Fiends is his code name for bunnies, is it?"

"Even now he is rushing to pull the lever."

"There's a lever, huh? Figures. Is it just me, or are we stuck in yet another bad movie?"

She blinked at me, obviously rattled by all the interruptions. What can I say, I talk a lot more when I'm nervous. "The cage doors will go up," she explained as if talking to a very small, very retarded child, "and the Fiends will be upon us."

"Well, that's a helluva note." I was nervous, but not out-and-out terrified. Not yet. I found the cheerleader extremely interesting. Why did she jump in with me? And why did she have the idea in her head that I was a queen? I wasn't even a Leo. "The walls are pretty steep in here . . . I'm betting this is so we don't have time to climb out. Any suggestions?"

"Yes." The cheerleader was digging in her jeans pocket and came up with a small, thickly padded envelope, the kind you mail computer disks in. She practically threw it at me, so anxious was she to get rid of it. "For you. Only you can wield this."

"Uh . . . thanks. Gee, I don't have anything for you . . ." I opened the envelope and peeped inside. And smiled. I upended the envelope and felt the cool gold chain slide into my hand. It was a beautiful gold cross on a chain so fine even I, with my superorbs, had trouble seeing it in the gloom of the pit. Excuse me, The Pit. I put it on, feeling the teensy clasp with my fingers and getting it hooked around my neck after a few seconds of fumbling. "Thanks a lot. I left mine at home."

"This is why you're the queen. Or you will be. You were foretold, you know."

"No I don't know . . . and who are you, anyway?"

"I'm Tina."

"Thank goodness!" I said so loudly she stepped back. "No silly-ass overdone names for you, m'girl."

"It's short for Christina Caresse Chavelle."

"Well, you did the best you could."

I heard a creaking noise just then, a really obnoxious one. Hinges clotted with dirt were turning with torturous slowness. The sound made me want to clap both hands over my ears. I didn't, though. No need to start losing coolness points with Tina who had, after all, jumped into a pitch-dark pit with me and brought me a present. "What the heck is that?"

"The gate is going up. The Fiends are out." Tina said this in a perfectly placid tone, but she was nibbling at her lower lip. "Don't be afraid."

"Are you talking to me, or yourself?"

"Both," she admitted.

"I s'pose we should have done less chatting and more

climbing, and now it's too late. You know, if this was a movie, I'd be throwing popcorn at the screen and yelling at the dumbass heroine."

"I had to answer your questions, Majesty."

"Oh, so this is *my* fault? Sure, blame the monarch for everything," I cracked.

She glanced up at me—boy, she was tiny. Barely up to my shoulder, and just as cute as a bug. "They will come at you but over my body, Majesty."

I tried not to laugh. "Thank you, Tina, but that's not very Queen-ey, is it? Cowering behind someone smaller? I mean you're, what? Ninety pounds?"

There was a rushing noise, like wind through capes, and I saw their eyes in the dark, little sullen coals. I counted ten coals. Clearly The Pit had an entrance, other than the top. But the other end was blocked, or the Fiends would be gamboling out in the moonlight like big evil puppies. If we dealt with them (big freaking if), we'd probably have time to climb out, but what then?

Tina stepped in front of me just as the first Fiend reached us. For once I was sorry I could see so well in the dark. They were vaguely human—like the devil is vaguely human. Although they had two legs, they scrabbled about on all fours. Their hair was, to a man (or a woman . . . their sex was indistinguishable), long and lank and kept flopping into their eyes. Their mouths were all fangs: toothy and sharp and terrifying to contemplate. Their cheeks were so hollow they'd be the envy of any supermodel. They were wearing rags, unbelievably filthy and pitiful rags, and though they were there to put the hurt on me, I felt a stab of sympathy all the same. These things were Nostro's pets, and he wasn't taking good care of them.

"Back off, boys," I said, my voice booming around the small walls. "You don't want to mess with an out-of-work secretary. We're real testy."

The Fiends cringed away from me, but I doubt it was because of my threat. And I suddenly realized I could see a lot better than a few seconds ago.

The cross. The cross around my neck was glowing.

Not much. Not blazing with a pure white light like in the movies. The glow was feeble and yellowish and the cross wasn't burning me, wasn't even warm, but the Fiends couldn't bear it. Neither could Tina; she'd thrown her arms over her face.

"Wait a minute!" The hair . . . the scrabbling motions . . . the way they were more animal than human . . . I knew these things. "You attacked me! You guys attacked me outside Khan's last fall!" I wanted to fall down. I wanted to kick them in their evil ribs. It was a shocking idea, unbelievable, but I suddenly knew how I'd come to be a vampire. These . . . *things* . . . had infected me. Then along came the Aztek a few months later, and whatever the Fiends had put into my bloodstream from the scratches and nips had become active.

Was that why most anti-vamp things didn't work on me? Because I didn't die by a vampire's hand, I'd only been infected by one? Or five?

I shook myself like a dog to get my head clear—I'd been standing there like a dummy, my mouth sprung ajar, but this wasn't the time. The Fiends were still cringing away from me, from the cross. I knew now why Nostro had thrown me down here—these ornery little fellows would have torn a regular newborn vamp to pieces. There but for the bravery of Tina would I be kibble for the Fiends.

"Get out of here," I said softly, and took a step forward. They scuttled back, then turned and fled.

"Come on, shortcake," I said. "Let's get out of this fucking hole. And I've got a few choice words for your boss."

"Nostro isn't my boss," Tina said, sounding mortally offended. I tucked the cross into my shirt and she slowly lowered her arms. "You are."

"We'll talk about it later. Come on."

It was short work for us to climb out of The Pit. The walls were made of brick, and there were plenty of vampire-friendly crevices. Nobody was standing guard—Nostro was pretty confident, then, we'd been chomped. Overconfident asshole—didn't he watch any James Bond movies? You never, *ever* take your eyes off the good guys.

Tina knew the back way out, and I followed her. A few people spotted us, but they were too scared to make a peep. Instead, they shrank back from us and looked everywhere but our faces. Interesting.

Though she'd saved my bacon and I was feeling warm and friendly toward her, I had a rather large problem with Tina's next suggestion.

"No fucking way!"

"Please, Majesty—"

"Betsy, dammit!"

"It's for your safety. Sinclair must know what Nostro tried to do. And what he could not do. This is the chance to band together and defeat him once and for all. If you join Sinclair, Nostro will be destroyed."

"I hate that creep."

"Which one?"

"Both, frankly, but especially that snooty jerkoff, Sink Lair."

"Well." I had the sense Tina was choosing her words carefully. "If you help us defeat Nostro, you will be the reigning queen. You could order the jerkoff to leave town."

"Now that's a little more like it," I said approvingly. "Although I have no queen qualifications."

"Untrue," she said quietly. "I saw. You were foretold."

Some fool had left his keys in a handy unlocked Lexus, so we climbed in and off we went. We drove steadily south. I didn't feel terribly bad—served him right for living in a vampire neighborhood, anyway. Probably *was* a vampire. Besides, I'd leave the car in a safe place. After what I'd been through this week, it was tough to break a sweat over a little grand theft auto.

"Foretold," I said, clutching the armrest as Tina took the turn nearly on two wheels. "You said that before."

"There's a book. We—vampires—call it the *Tabla Morto*. A thousand years ago, vampires knew you were coming. '*A Queen shall ryse, who has power beyond that of the vampyre. The thyrst shall not consume her, and the cross never will harm her, and the beasts will befryend her, and she will rule the dead.*'" Tina nodded in satisfaction.

"My!" I coughed. That bit about the beasts . . . it explained the dogs. During the short walk to the car, every dog in the neighborhood had broken free and come to see me. Tina was wide-eyed while I swore and scolded and tried gently to boot them away. When we drove off they were barking enthusiastically at our taillights. Real subtle getaway. "What a lovely story."

Tina didn't crack a smile. "That's you, Majesty. You're the first vampire in a thousand years who could hold a cross without screaming or throwing up or being burned."

"You should see my other party tricks."

"Nostro threw holy water in your face and you laughed. You laughed." She said this in a tone of complete admiration. "The dogs do your will—"

"The hell they do. They never leave when I tell them to. Just lick my ankles and slobber on my shoes. *My shoes!*"

She quirked a little smile at me. "They don't leave because they know you're not truly angry with them. They just want to be near you. Best get used to it."

"Super." And here I figured I'd had a lot to think about *before* I went in the pit! Tonight was blowing all my circuits. "If that's true, if I'm the foretold SuperVamp, how come you're the only one who knows it? Why were you the only one who came in the pit with me? And thank you, by the way. That was really brave. I didn't know what I was getting into, but you did, and you came down anyway." I touched her shoulder. "If you need a favor, sunshine, you come and see me first."

She gave me the biggest smile I'd ever seen. "Oh, Majesty, it was nothing! It was the very least I could do for you! If I could have gone in the pit alone, I would have." The smile disappeared as quickly as it had shown up. "As to your question, the reason I was the only one to come with you is because Nostro's followers are a pack of fucking cowards."

"Tina!" Not that I'd never heard the F word before, but it sounded especially bad coming out of that cute mouth, that sweet face. Plus, the way she switched from formal English to twenty-first-century jargon was jarring, to put it mildly.

"They won't fight," she said stubbornly. "They do only what he says. Even if it means hurting innocents. Also, you're more myth than reality. Like the second coming of You-Know-Who."

"Christ?"

She shuddered and the car swerved, and then she nodded. "Yes. Him. Everyone knows about it, but how many people really truly believe it? Or would recognize that person if He were to return? They talk about miracles, about walking on water and turning water into wine, but if I ever saw someone doing it, I'd be so afraid. So would a lot of people, I think. Well, that's like you, Majesty."

"Um . . . I don't think you should run around comparing me to Christ. No offense. That's, y'know, not too cool. I mean, people got pretty pissed when the Beatles did it."

She ignored that. "Every vampire knows about you . . . but hardly anyone believes."

"What about Sinclair?"

"He was the first to suspect who you could be. One of his men called you, asked you to come to the bookstore . . . remember, the night you were kidnapped?"

"Which night?" I grumbled. "Getting hard to keep track." But I remembered. So Sinclair's henchman had called me, not Nostro's. But there was obviously a spy in camp, because Nostro's men got to me first. Sinclair must have busted a gut to get to the mausoleum before I did. I remembered noticing his shoes, trying to get a closer look at them. He'd been leaving wet tracks, as though he'd plowed through the dew and arrived only seconds before I did. "So you work for Sinclair?"

"Yes."

Hmm. That was interesting, if icky. Still, I couldn't help being a bit suspicious of Miss Tina—she knew the back way out of the bad guy's house? She knew how to get out of the pit? But she wasn't *with* the bad guy?

"So," I said encouragingly. "What's the deal with you and Captain Grabby?"

She didn't crack a smile. "Sinclair saved me from Nostro," she said simply. "If not for him, I'd be one of those spiritless creatures."

"I gotta tell you, Tina, it creeps me out that you work for ol' jerkoff. What, you're like his runner or something?"

"I'm his servant, yes."

Ah-ha! "So he's like Nostro."

"No."

Oh.

"I'm with him because I choose to be with him," she continued. "If I wanted to leave tomorrow and live in France and never do another thing for him, he wouldn't demur. I made him, you see."

The car seemed to shrink, suddenly. I stared at her, slowly freaking out, and she stared through the windshield. "You made Sinclair a vampire?" I practically squeaked it.

"Yes. I was desperate. Nostro hardly ever lets us feed, it's his way of controlling us, making sure no one gets stronger than him."

"Creep," I commented.

"Indeed. I found Sinclair in a cemetery at night. His parents had died that week. Murdered. He was alone in the world. He saw me . . . I was too hungry for stealth and he saw me."

Tina's voice was getting softer; she could hardly get the words out. It was as if she was desperately ashamed of her actions that night, so long ago. "He opened his arms. He invited me to him. He knew I was one of the monsters and he didn't care. And I—I took him. I killed him."

"Well . . . uh . . . that's what you guys do, right?"

She shook her head. "That's another thing forbidden . . . we're only allowed to make more vampires if we have Nostro's permission, but I was starving and I didn't care. He—Nostro—fancies himself a scientist, and that's why he's making the Fiends—never mind, I'm getting off track. To sum up, I was careless, and Sinclair paid for it. I was waiting for him when he rose."

I digested that one for a while. I didn't like the story for a number of reasons, and big number one was because it made me feel sorry for Sinclair. I could picture the scene—him in a black suit, pale with grief, alone, not caring about anything anymore. And Tina coming up to him, stick-thin and ghastly white and shaking with hunger. And how he took her in at a glance and opened his arms to her, welcomed her. Because he had lost everything, and nothing else mattered, not even death by vampire. "Wow. That's . . . that's really something. And he got you away from Nostro."

"Sinclair was strong the moment he awoke. Some—a very few—are like that."

"How come?"

"Nobody knows. Why are some people born great painters or great mathematicians?"

"Got me . . . I flunked trig."

"Sinclair's will . . . it's incredible. Nostro didn't want to mess with him, nobody did. So he let Sinclair go—"

"Why not just kill him?"

"Among other things, Nostro's quite mad, which I'm sure you could not help noticing," Tina said dryly, "and his judgment is open to question. Perhaps he was curious. Perhaps he was afraid."

"Perhaps he's a flaming dumbass. This guy's *got* to watch more James Bond movies. They're like Bad Guy 101. So he let Sinclair go, and—"

"—Sinclair took me with him, yes. And that's how it's been, for years and years."

"How old are you?"

"I was born," she said, taking a sharp left and driving down a dirt road—when had we left the city?—"the month and year the Civil War began."

"Wuh . . . hmm. Okay, my mom's really into the Civil War and she'll have about a thousand questions for you later, but meanwhile—how old is Nosehair?"

She giggled at that, but abruptly snapped off the sound, as if it was dangerous to laugh at him, even miles away from his lakeside lair. "No one knows. From his strength, I would guess at least four hundred years. Maybe more."

"Unbelievable." I shook my head. "He's a supreme bad-ass, but I can't look at him without wanting to crack up."

"That has been a problem," Tina said dryly.

"Oh, come on! Don't tell me you're afraid of him."

"I've seen him at work. I watched him slaughter an entire first-grade class while I was too hungry and weak—all of us were—to stop him. I saw him crack their bones and suck out the marrow. I saw—"

"Okay, okay! Jeez, enough of that." I managed to overcome the urge to yark all over the fine leather upholstery. "Um, you said from his strength he must be really old—still can't get my head around that one—what did you mean by that?"

"I told you Sinclair was born strong, but for most vampires, strength is acquired. The longer you feed, the more you learn, and the stronger you become. An eighty-year-old man has more life experience than you, yes? They've—uh—been around the block? Now: Picture the old man in a young body that never gets tired, with limitless strength and speed."

"Gotcha." Unlike most of what had happened to me lately, this made perfect sense.

"So a three-hundred-year-old vampire is much, much stronger than the vampire who rose for the first time yesterday. I suspect Sinclair was an extraordinary man when he was alive, because he was strong so quickly after death."

"Ooooh, Tina! Sounds like you've got the hots for the boss."

She smiled at me. "No, Majesty. I admire him a great deal, but as for the rest . . . I gave that up a hundred years ago."

"That may be the most depressing thing I've heard this week, cutie. Uh . . . sorry." The woman was old enough to be my great-great-great-great grandma, even if she looked like she just made the pep squad. Time to eighty-six the condescending nicknames.

"Majesty, you may call me Mistress Retch if you prefer. It's a pure pleasure to just be in your company."

"That's enough of that." If I'd been able to blush, I would have. "And I still haven't agreed to go to Sinclair's house."

"We're here," she said apologetically, as the gates swung open. We scooted through, fast enough to press me back into my seat, but when I heard the gates crash closed I knew why.

"Damn! The guy doesn't leave the front door open very long, does he?"

"He's a careful man," was all she said.

I mumbled something in reply, and I'm pretty sure Tina caught the word "jackass," but she was too polite to comment.

We pulled right up to the front of the house—it was a gorgeous red Victorian, but after Nostro's palace and, of course, growing up with a zillionaire pal, I was getting pretty bored with grand beautiful manors. Why didn't any of these people live in tract housing?

Tina shut off the car, scooted around the front, then held my door open for me before I'd even realized we'd stopped. "Quit that," I said, stepping out.

"Like the dogs," she said with a smile, "I know you don't entirely mean it. Shall I carry you up the steps, Majesty?"

"Only if you want to feel my foot up your ass," I warned, and she grinned. I was glad to see it. Tina was a little intimidating. And old! Sure, Nostro was old, too, ditto Sinclair, but the difference was, I kind of liked Tina.

The door opened as she approached, and we were ushered inside by a man who was maybe an inch taller than Tina. He had a small, sleek head and a pencil-thin mustache. His eyes were small and set close together, and his features were almost delicate . . . he looked like a clever whippet. He was wearing a billowy white shirt, black tailored pants, and small leather boots. Superdapper. "Hi," I said to the top of his head, because when he saw me he went into a deep bow. "I'm Betsy."

That straightened him up in a hurry. "Betsy?"

"Dennis . . ." Tina warned.

"You mean the future queen of the undead—*my* future queen?—is named Betsy?"

"Hey, it's a family name," I said defensively. "Short for Elizabeth, but don't call me that, I don't like it."

"Elizabeth is eminently more suitable to your station."

"Who cares? And I'm not going to be the queen of anything; I've got enough problems of my own without taking responsibility for a bunch of two-legged parasites. And will somebody get these dogs away from me?" To add to Sinclair's odious qualities, he apparently kept a hundred dogs. On closer inspection, it was more like six, all big fat black Labs. All slobbery. Thank God I was wearing last year's shoes!

"It's just a shock, that's all," Dennis said, looking me up and down. "You're—different from what I expected." Then, "Did you just call me a two-legged parasite?"

"Hey, I know your voice! You're the guy who called me to get me to the bookstore."

He bowed again. "It was my pleasure to be of service."

"Yeah, nice work—I got snatched by Noseo's henchmen, the Cocker Spaniel Boys."

"Er—what?"

"So thanks for *nothing*," I finished triumphantly.

"Dennis, help me with the dogs," Tina ordered. She looked stern, but as soon as she hustled the dogs into the other room I heard her laughing. At me, Dennis, or the big stupid dogs, I had no idea. Probably all three.

I looked around the entryway. It was a room unto itself, with soaring ceilings and a glorious staircase that looked like it had been lifted from one of the houses in *Gone with the Wind*. God, I loved that book. How could I not? The heroine was a trendy, acquisitive, vain jerk. I read *GWTW* about ten times the year I stumbled across it in high school, and twice a year since then. Sinclair's staircase looked like the one at Twelve Oaks.

Tina came hurrying out, dogless. "If you'll stay here, Maj-Miss Taylor, I'll let Sinclair know you're here. Dennis will get you anything you need."

"Yes, I surely will." Dennis had finally remembered his manners. "Tea? Coffee? Wine?"

"I'd love a glass of plum wine," I admitted.

He blinked, then smiled. "Of course. The boss likes that stuff, too. Not me, though. It's like drinking sugar syrup out of a wineglass."

I followed him to the wet bar in the corner. "That's why I like it. Most wines taste like sour grape juice to me. Plum's the only stuff that's sweet enough." I glanced up at the ceiling and saw the mirror over the wet bar. "Jeez, that mirror's bigger than my whole bedroom."

Dennis followed my gaze and lowered his voice. "I'll tell you, Miss Betsy, I was shocked when I rose and found out I still cast a reflection. It took me days to get over it. I felt like all those movies had betrayed me."

"Why wouldn't we cast reflections?" He cracked a brand-new bottle for me, poured, and handed me the glass. I sniffed—yum! It smelled like sugar and dark purple plums bursting with ripeness. Unfortunately, like coffee and gasoline (don't ask), wine never tasted as good as it smelled.

"Well. Because of not having a soul."

"We have souls. Sure we do. Otherwise we'd do bad things all the time. You know, like politicians."

He dropped the trendy butler attitude and stared at me with what looked a lot like hope. It made him seem much younger. "Do you really think so?"

"I know so." I said this with complete conviction, and added, "Besides, a minister told me."

"A minister? When?"

"Right after I woke up dead. I went to a church to blow myself up, but nothing worked."

If Dennis's eyes got any wider, they were going to fall right out of his head. "You were standing in a—a holy place? You were able to get past the steps?"

"Yeah, yeah, but listen, that's not the point. That whole 'vampires don't cast reflections because they have no soul' makes no sense. I mean, look up." He obeyed. "D'you see the bar? How about the bottles? And the floor? And the chair in the corner? We can see those in the mirror. And dogs and cats. And babies and frogs. They all cast reflections."

"True. But that doesn't exactly make your case about vampires keeping their souls."

"*You* make my case. And so do I. I mean, you probably hated blue jeans before you died, right?"

He actually shuddered.

"Right, easy, don't barf all over the bar. Well, you're not sporting any now, right? You don't have a pile of Levi's squirreled away in the back of your closet, do you? The stuff that made you *you* . . . it's all still there. You're just on a liquid diet now." I took a gulp of my wine. "Like me!"

"You know, there's something there," he said thoughtfully, but he wasn't looking up at the mirror anymore, he was looking at me. He topped off my glass. "Some sort of odd charisma. Even when you're being a pill, I like listening to you."

"Uh . . . thank you?"

"Frankly, Sinclair and Tina are about the only vampires I can stand."

I thought about that for a minute. "I haven't been one very long. Maybe that's what it is."

"No, it's not," he said seriously, "because young vampires are the worst. All they can think about is how hungry they are. You can't have a civilized conversation with them for at least five years."

"Bummer! That's all they do? Eat?"

"And sleep, yes."

"So, they're like newborn babies, except with fangs and rotten tempers?"

"Exactly."

"Well, I'm glad that didn't happen to *me*."

"And that's the question, isn't it?" Dennis was looking at me very closely. "Why aren't you like them?"

"Um . . . clean living?" I guessed.

"No, it's something more."

Uncomfortable with the turn this conversation was taking—not to mention the way Dennis was staring at me like I was an amazing bug—I changed the subject. "Listen, what's taking Tina so long? Where's Sinclair?"

"I think he's feeding with his ladyfriends." He said it just like that, all one word. "I'll see if I can give Tina a hand." He put the bottle away, then hurried up the stairs. "Excuse me, I'll be right back," he said over his shoulder, then got to the top and disappeared around a corner.

I let a minute go by, then said, "Well, screw this." I drained my glass, put it down . . . and then I heard the scream.

I bolted up the stairs after Dennis.

Chapter 17

$\mathcal{I}$ T wasn't a bad scream. It was a good scream. It was, in fact, a scream of ecstasy, like when I find out Gucci is having a shoe sale. Sinclair's "ladyfriends"? Try harem.

It didn't take long to find the room, even in a palace like this. I just followed the gasps and groans. By now I was pretty sure whoever had screamed wasn't in trouble, but I was curious. And annoyed—if I was such a vampiric big shot, how come Sinclair the Fink was keeping me waiting?

I opened the door at the end of the hall and saw Tina standing before a large window. She turned, saw me, and spread her hands in apology. "They're very busy," she explained. "I didn't have much luck getting his attention. It should only be a few more minutes."

Curious, I walked over and stood beside her. The window was clear—it was like one of those rooms within a room you saw in police stations. And through the window I could see Sinclair and two—whoops, there was another set of tits—three women. They were writhing and groaning and purring in the middle of a bed that was, if possible, bigger than king-sized. I mean, that bed looked like a satin-covered acre.

It was a four-poster, and each poster was as big around as a tree trunk. The bed was covered in chocolate-colored satin sheets (well, at least they weren't red . . . soooooo last year's *Cosmo*), but the pillows—all nine—had been knocked to the floor.

Sinclair looked happy. He was almost smiling! And he ought to be, in the middle of a brunette nest like he was. The three women all had elbow-length dark hair and sturdy limbs . . . no anorexic models for this guy. One of them even had a gently rounded belly. Two of them were fair-skinned, and the third was the color of milk chocolate, with the high cheekbones of Egyptian royalty.

They were human. I was a little surprised at how easily I could tell. They had a glow, a vitality that Sinclair and Tina and I lacked. Maybe it was because their hearts had to beat so much faster, they had to take so many breaths.

I coughed. "Uh . . . should we be, like, spying on them?"

Tina looked surprised. "They can't hear us. This glass is three inches thick. Besides, Sinclair doesn't mind. This room usually has a watcher."

"That's sick!"

"No, that's common sense."

"Um, you know, I have a totally different definition of common sense."

"Do you know how many men of power have been killed between the sheets?"

"I can safely say that I have no idea."

"Well, it's a lot. I told you he was a careful man. He never lets his guard down. Not even during times like these."

I was (uncharacteristically) silent. That was one of the worst things I'd ever heard. If you couldn't relax during sex—particularly during a *Penthouse*-inspired fantasy like this—well, that didn't sound like much of a life. Being careful was one thing. Being buried alive was something else.

"Why can't he stop?" I grumbled, folding my arms across my chest. Uncomfortable? Me? Naw. "I mean, I don't mind being kept waiting if it's—you know—business you can conduct while fully clothed. But why do we have to hang around while he gets his undead jollies? I had the impression this was important."

"This is," Tina said seriously. "We're not like you, Betsy. We *have* to feed. We can't put it off for a day or two. Sometimes not even an hour or two. For Sinclair, this is vital. It's . . . it's as close to life-affirming as we can ever get. Nothing else takes precedence."

One of the women squealed.

"Life affirming?" I asked dryly. I glanced away before I saw something unfit for Christian eyes. Then, like Lot's wife, I looked back just in time to see Sinclair position himself behind one of the women. Though it pained me on several levels to admit it, the man had the best ass I had ever seen. Taut, muscular, and sweetly rounded in exactly the right places. Yum.

"How come we can hear them?" I croaked, and realized just how dry my mouth was.

Tina pointed wordlessly to our left; I looked and saw the speaker on the wall. "That's sick," I said again, and looked back at the scene to assure myself that the depravity was continuing. I mean, somebody had to pay attention to this stuff, be aware of just what a pig Sinclair was.

"They're so beautiful," Tina said softly. She rested her hand on the glass, palm down. "So alive and fresh and young."

Young? Tina was right, not a single woman in that room was hard on the eyes, but they were in their late thirties, early forties, at the least. They were beautiful but they looked like real women: soft bellies, heavy thighs, laugh lines. No nineteen-year-olds for Sinclair.

I sort of liked him for that.

After a minute, Sinclair pulled away, bent, and said something to one of the women, too low for me to hear. She gifted him with a sated smile and her eyes slipped to half-mast. Then he turned his attention to another woman.

It was really something to watch. Part of me was ordering myself to leave the room, give them some privacy. I mean, in life I didn't even like watching late-night Cinemax—not even with the sound off—much less real people doing the sweaty mambo.

But it was hard to look away. For one thing, it was really hot. Unbelievably hot. Part of it was Sinclair's stamina, but another was his three companions. There was no jealousy, no cattiness; they were happy just to be there, to take turns. It was unlike anything I'd ever imagined. I figured in a ménage a—shit, what was the French word for four? Well, anyway, I figured in any sort of ménage there were bound to be hurt feelings. Not here.

"You've got the best ass I've seen in fifty years," Sinclair told his partner of the moment. He wasn't out of breath. In fact, he sounded amused, and his tone instantly made my hackles rise. It wasn't like he was detached; it was more like any three women could have been in there with him. Any three at all. "At least fifty."

"A thousand years!" the one with the great ass declared, and the three women giggled in unison.

Sinclair snorted and pulled out. I gasped. I don't know why I was surprised. Sinclair was huge—big, broad shoulders, powerful arms and legs—well over six feet, easily two hundred pounds, and not a scrap of flab on him. I should have expected—err—other parts of him to be—uhh—larger than average. All the same, I couldn't help being shocked.

"Jesus Christ," I said. "No wonder he doesn't go for the nineteen-year-olds!" If some little club bunny saw *that* coming at her, she'd go for the whip and chair.

Tina, my little sex tour narrator, nodded. "Sinclair prefers older bed partners. If they're not . . . experienced . . . he could hurt them. He wouldn't mean to, and he'd be sorry later, but they'd be hurt, just the same."

Meanwhile, back in Sodom, Sinclair was still hungry. He was gentle enough, but firm; one minute one of the women was almost asleep, and the next Sinclair was gripping her arms, holding her easily, while he bit her on the side of the neck.

She convulsed against him, crying out, "Ah, God, again, again!" while he drank from her throat, while her head rolled back on her shoulders in ecstasy.

Sinclair stopped drinking. A small rill of blood ran down his chin, which he caught with his tongue. His dick wagged in the air, momentarily friendless. "Don't stop," he said. Then, when he saw his partner of the second had to stop, was in fact in a near-faint, he said, "Someone else."

Another woman was instantly kneeling in front of him, but he grabbed her hair and pulled her toward him, pushed her on her back, leaned in, spread her thighs with his big hands, and bit her in her femoral artery.

"These guys," I commented dryly, "are in great shape." I tried to sound cool and detached because, the fact was, I'd never been as turned on in my life. I could have watched them all day. Which explained why Tina had been so reluctant to separate them and tell Sinclair he had a visitor.

The new partner was moaning while Sinclair's mouth was busy on her plump thigh. She was stroking her breasts, squeezing them hard enough to leave white marks in her flesh, screaming "More, more, more, *more!*" at the ceiling.

What are you doing?

Dead or not, vamp or not, I was standing in a strange mansion watching a creep and his harem *have sex*. This wasn't me! Betsy Taylor did not watch soft porn, much less act like some icky voyeur.

"I-I have to go." I said this with a complete lack of conviction. "I mean, they'll finish up soon."

"Yes, Majesty."

"And then we can tell Sinclair what happened tonight."

"Yes."

"And figure out where to go from there."

"All right." Tina said this with all the animation of a store mannequin.

"You okay?"

"It's just that I have to kiss you now." She turned and pulled me toward her. Her pupils were huge. I looked down at her pretty, pretty face and tried to feel a little more shocked. I'd never kissed a woman in my life. Never even been curious. My stance on homosexuality was exactly the same as my stance on heterosexuality: If you were having sex with a consenting adult, it was none of my business. Just keep it out of my face.

"I must beg your indulgence," Tina was saying. She went up—up, up!—on her tiptoes. Her mouth was dark red, with matching lip liner (I approved; clashing lip liners were so twentieth century), and her top lip looked like a little bow. The mouth of an enchantress . . . hopefully a good one. "Just . . . one . . . kiss."

"Forget it!" I said loudly, breaking the spell. She had—it was like I'd been hypnotized for a few seconds. First a voyeur, now a lesbian? Don't think so! "My God, you people are sick, sick! Does he do this every night? *Don't answer that!* And you! You keep your hands to yourself, missy!"

I shoved her away. She had let go the second I resisted, so my shove sent her reeling across the room.

"I thought," I said numbly, because even though I'd been right, I felt bad, "I thought you gave that stuff up a hundred years ago."

"Men," she said, watching me sadly with her big dark eyes. "I gave up men. I'm very sorry. I couldn't help it. I haven't fed tonight and you're so beautiful. But I'm very sorry."

"Well . . ." Being called beautiful momentarily distracted

me, and I fought the urge to bask. *Focus, damn you, focus!*
"Being dead is one thing, but having to watch Finklair romp
in his bed o' babes . . . and then you decide to bring my latent
lesbian tendencies to the surface—real latent, by the way,
because when I was alive the thought of lip locking with
another woman never crossed my mind, although there was
that one time at summer camp when Cheryl Cooper dared
me to French kiss her because we were playing Truth or Dare
and like a moron I picked Dare and I-I—where was I going
with this?"

"I have no idea, Majesty."

"Forget it. Forget it! I'm out of here."

"Please don't go. It's my fault. All my fault. I'm so
sorry." To my horror, she was sinking to her knees, and
actually—was she? She was! She was kissing the toes of
my shoes! "Please, Majesty, forgive my impertinence.
Please!"

"Stop that!" I hissed, hopping back so her lips weren't
touching my shoes, then jerking her to her feet. She wouldn't
look at me, was cringing away from my anger. Which made
me feel bad. Which made me even angrier. "Don't kiss my
shoes ever again! Jesus Christ—" She moaned and flinched
away. "—why do vampires have to be so *weird* about everything? Why am I the only one who wants to live a normal
goddamned life?"

She cringed at goddamned. I gave way completely to
the anger and worry that had been plaguing me since I
woke up dead. "God! God! God!" I screamed into her face,
taking grim pleasure in the way she cowered. "Enough of
this weird shit, I've had enough! Do you realize I haven't
even been dead a week?" I let go of her arm and stormed
out. I practically knocked Dennis to the floor as I stomped
down the stairs.

He jumped out of my way in a hurry. Lucky for him.
"What's wrong, Miss Betsy?"

"Nothing. Everything. I gotta go."

"Please don't!" Tina cried from the top of the stairs. "Please stay! We need you!"

"Well, I don't need you," I said, practically running across the marble floor. "And I've never been more grateful for anything in my life."

I heard a swish, and suddenly Sinclair was standing in front of me, which efficiently scared the bejeezus out of me. "Aaggghhh!" I looked up. He'd obviously jumped from the floor above and landed in my path. "And *you*. Get out of my—hey!" He gripped my elbow and dragged me toward a door across the room. I set my feet, but it was no good. At least he'd wrapped a sheet around his waist.

He slammed the door, plunging us into near darkness (well, more like twilight since I had undead eyesight) and shutting Tina and Dennis on the other side. "Elizabeth," he said calmly, as if we'd met on the street. "So good of you to drop by."

"Ugh, ugh, *ugh!*" I hissed. I was trying to pry his fingers off my arm, with no luck. "Let go, you perv. I want out of this—this house of sin!"

"But I don't want you to leave," he said reasonably. "Not now."

"Too damned bad! I don't want anything to do with you! You—you slut!"

"Now, Elizabeth," he said, and he had the nerve to sound reproachful, "I don't come to your house and criticize your lifestyle, do I?"

"Eeewwwwww! Lifestyle? God, I can still smell them on you!"

"Jealous?"

I gagged. "Not hardly. Now let go; I'm out of here."

"You've upset Tina dreadfully."

"Get it through your head: You're disgusting, I don't care what you think, I could care less how upset Tina is, let the fuck go."

"In a minute," he said carelessly, and then, with that

infuriating strength he'd shown in the cemetery, he pulled me to him and pressed his mouth to mine.

I opened my mouth to yell—or bite—which proved to be a tactical error, as he used it as an excuse to shove his tongue into my mouth. I made fists and hammered at his chest as hard as I could, and I actually heard something snap. He shrugged off the blows and deepened the kiss. My knees went weak, which was annoying beyond belief. I'd never been so attracted to someone I absolutely despised, and it was infuriating.

I could feel his hand on the small of my back, pressing me close to him, could feel his hard length against my stomach—how could he want anyone after what just went on upstairs? Didn't he need a nap? Or a shower?

He pulled back, so abruptly I staggered. "There," he said, sounding indecently satisfied. "Now you'll stay, and we'll chat."

The crack of my slap was very loud, and I was savagely thrilled to see him rock back on his heels.

"If you touch me again, I'll kill you." I was practically crying, I was so angry. I turned and fumbled for the door-knob, and practically ran out of the room.

I ignored Dennis's stare, Tina's anguished "Wait!" and yanked open the front door. "Take a good look," I said grimly, "because you'll never see me again."

Tina burst into tears, and I slammed the door on her dry sobs. And I didn't feel bad. Not one bit. Nope. Not at all.

No.

Damn you, Sinclair.

Chapter 18

I got home, after committing grand theft auto. Again. Once out the front door I'd circled around to the side and found Finklair's garage. It was full of at least half a dozen shiny cars, and the keys were conveniently numbered and hanging from a board by the door. I grabbed the set for the Jaguar and off I went. Nobody tried to stop me. Lucky for them.

I drove like a madwoman, and disdained my seatbelt. Who cared? Like a car crash could do anything to me anyway. Like a trip through the windshield wouldn't be a vacation after the day I'd had. And the car was choice—black, with a sweet-smelling leather interior and a gas pedal that went all the way to the floor just as easy as you please. I made the forty mile trip in about twenty minutes.

I screeched into my driveway and hopped out, after leaving the keys in the ignition. Childish, but I really hoped someone would steal it. The thought of Sinclair sitting in a police station filling out report after report was immensely cheering.

I saw my door had a giant crack running through the middle, like someone had been kicking it for an hour or more, and stopped short on my front stoop.

I'll admit it—I wasn't much interested in finding out who had broken in. Nope, forget it, I'd had enough. Whoever it was, they were welcome to my cotton sheets, dirty dishes, and fluffy magenta bath mats.

I was turning away, possibly to go find my mom and cry on her shoulder for three or four hours, when . . .

"Bets! Is that you?" Jessica's voice.

"Get in here quick!" Marc's.

What fresh hell was this? I pushed the door open and slowly walked inside. At least Jess was okay—sounded okay, anyway. Shanara couldn't have hurt her too badly. Jeez, had she bushwhacked us in that alley only three hours ago? It felt like three years.

My friends were kneeling beside a big pile of rags in the middle of my bedroom floor. Marc had a neat white bandage on his neck and was still wearing the bracelet they'd given him at the hospital. Jessica looked perfectly fine. I felt so bad I'd forgotten about them, even for a few moments. "Are you guys okay?"

"Yeah. Are you, girlfriend? You look a little white around the gills. More so than usual," Jessica chortled. Then she sobered up and pointed to the rag pile. "You got problems, Betsy. I mean, besides the ones we've already been dealing with."

Marc gently prodded the pile . . . and it was Nick! He looked unbelievably bad—like he hadn't eaten in three days, slept in five, bathed in ten. His hair was a mess of greasy tangles. His eyes rolled toward mine. They were so deeply bloodshot they were more red than white. "More," he husked. "Moremoremore."

"No, oh no!" I rushed to him. "Jesus, Nick, what happened?"

"Um . . . we were sort of hoping *you'd* know," Marc said, fingering his bandage. "I mean, he doesn't exactly look like he's been through a garden-variety bad day. And he can't stop saying your name."

"Oh, shit, shit . . ." I trailed off and buried my face in my hands. "I can't deal with this, you guys. *I can't deal with this!* Not being able to eat and being dead and my dad scared of me and bad guy vamps throwing me into pits and Sinclair being a slut and a great kisser and Nick being traumatized and me being a car thief again—I've had enough!"

Jessica's eyebrows arched. "Err . . . who's a great kisser?"

"Who threw you into a pit?" Marc asked, interested. Then, "Car thief *again?*"

"More," Nick whispered. His lips were dry, cracked. He smelled like a garbage truck on fire. "Betsy. More. Betsy."

"Jesus, I was just hungry, I didn't mean—"

"This is fucked up," Marc said. "I mean, you chowed on me, too, but you don't see me turning into a puddle of yearning lust."

"No," Jessica said slowly, and there was a funny look on her face I didn't much like, "but you sure moved in just as quick as you could."

Marc blinked. Nick moaned. I stared. "What's that got to do with anything?" he asked, honestly puzzled.

"Well . . . don't you think it's kind of strange, seeing as how you're same-sex oriented, and—"

"Not now, you guys! We've got bigger problems. One great big problem lying in the middle of the floor." I covered my eyes with my palms. "Oh, shit, Nick—I didn't mean—what did I do? What did I do?"

"Exactly the opposite," Sinclair said thoughtfully, "of what I do."

I whirled and dropped my hands. Sinclair, Tina, and Dennis were standing just inside my bedroom. I'd never heard them come in. Never sensed their presence, never so much as heard the pitter-patter of their little vampire feet. Neither had Jessica and Marc, because they both let out little screams and practically leapt into each other's arms.

Nick was oblivious. He'd started rocking back and forth on the floor in an effort to soothe himself, and never looked away from my face. It was unbelievably horrible—like watching a crippled dog crawl after his master. You didn't know whether to shoot the dog out of kindness, or pet him out of pity.

"You *gotta* be Sink Lair," Jessica practically gasped. She was annoyingly wide-eyed.

"Hi, Mr. Sinclair!" Marc trilled. He even waved. "You guys drop by for a snack?"

"You three get out of here!" I snapped. "I've got enough problems right now, thanks."

Sinclair pointed to Nick. "That one is of your own making, I think . . . I can smell you on him. Under about six layers of dirt, that is." He said it so carelessly I wanted to kill him. My hand went to the cross Tina had given me. Would he sound so cool and detached if I jammed this little trinket in his ear?

But Sinclair was already striding toward us. "Tina," he said quietly, kneeling beside Nick, "help me." His actions were the diametric opposite of his words, which was really confusing.

"What's wrong with him?" I cried. "Is he becoming a vampire?"

"No. He craves you. He's an addict, now."

Tina was wide-eyed. "How many times did you feed off this one?"

"It was only one time."

"You *dog*." From Jessica, naturally. "And you never said a word, you bad girl."

"Once," Sinclair repeated.

"Yeah. Just once. I swear!"

"But you only fed on me once, too," Marc said. "I mean, don't get me wrong, it was great—really different and cool and sexy and weird and all—but that was it. Why's this guy such a wreck?"

"Once?" Tina said, pointing to Nick.

"Do I have to paint it on my forehead? Yeah, once, just the one time."

Skeptical silence, broken when Sinclair said, "You can't just have them and release them, Elizabeth. You fled my home after you saw a—a certain aspect of the vampire lifestyle. But I would never do to mine what you did to yours."

That stung. A lot. "He's not *mine*. I barely even know him!"

"Well." Dennis cleared his throat. He was crouching over us, resting his hands on his thighs. He looked like an undead umpire. "That's worse, you know."

"But I didn't know!"

"I warned you," Sinclair said. He was shrugging out of his topcoat and putting it over Nick's shivering form. "You don't know the rules. Most vampires would learn or die. But you were born strong, and you have few of our weaknesses. So while you're learning, the innocent are being hurt."

"Hey, leave her alone. *I* wasn't hurt." Bless Dr. Marc! "I mean, sure, I feel sort of lonely and vulnerable sometimes . . ."

"Shut up," Jessica said, biting her lip, hard, so she wouldn't smile.

Sinclair ignored them completely. "Is my offer of help still so completely unacceptable?"

Jessica and Marc looked at me. Despite their attempts to make me feel better, I felt the weight of their judgment.

"Okay, okay . . . tell me what to do. How to help Nick. And I'll—I'll take your Vampire 101 class, Sinclair. But only after Nick is better."

"Your word on it, Elizabeth."

"She already told you she'd let you help," Jessica said, her voice like ice. She might think Sinclair was yummier than a triple fudge sundae, but nobody was going to question her best friend's honor in her own home. "If that's not enough, Sink Lair, don't let the door hit you in your big white ass on the way out."

"Please don't pronounce my name like that," he sighed. He lifted Nick easily into his arms. Then, "Big white ass?"

"Bring him to the bathroom," Tina said. "Dennis and I can take care of him."

"But—" I closed my mouth with a snap. Nick was almost as tall as Sinclair, which made him two heads taller than Tina and Dennis. Never mind. They could probably muscle a Volkswagen into my bathroom if they had to.

Sinclair carried Nick to my bathroom and carefully laid him on the floor. Dennis stripped him, grimacing at the smell, while Tina started the shower. Meanwhile, Sinclair put a hand on my shoulder, turned me around, and marched me out. Of my own bathroom!

"Hands to yourself, buster," I warned.

"You—uh—want something to drink?" Jessica was standing in the bedroom doorway. She blushed, which isn't easy to tell with her. "I mean, like tea or something, Mr. Sinclair?"

I was shocked. That was a quick reversal, especially for Jessica "I can hold a grudge until the end of time" Watkins. Sinclair's undead sex appeal must work on women like mine did on men.

"Please call me Eric," the undead skunk was saying with convincing warmth. "After all, you're a friend of Elizabeth's."

"He likes plum wine, get him a glass of that," I said irritably.

"I'll get it!" Marc said. He'd gone to throw Nick's rags into my washing machine, but leapt for the doorway the instant Jessica did. They became jammed at the shoulder, Three Stooges style.

"No, I'll get it!"

"Fuck you, getting drinks should be beneath you, honey."

"Fuck *you,* this is my house. I paid for it, didn't I?"

They struggled, then both popped free of the doorframe. I heard pounding footsteps as they raced each other to the kitchen, and put a hand over my eyes. Friends . . . the ultimate mixed blessing.

"A pity you are not as fond of me as your companions are," Sinclair teased.

"They don't know what a creep you are," I said sourly. I was annoyed to see Giselle purring in his arms as he absently tickled her under the chin. Fickle feline tramp! I snatched her away and tossed her in the direction of the doorway. With a snooty backward glance, she went. "If they had the slightest clue how wretched and nasty and despicable you are . . ."

"Now, Elizabeth, how can you say that?" He blinked at me with innocent Bambi eyes. Cold, glittering Bambi eyes. "You know I tried to help you at the mausoleum, and I sent Tina to help you at Nostro's home tonight. If she hadn't given you my gift the Fiends would have torn you to pieces."

"Your gift?"

"The cross belonged to my sister."

My fingers went instantly to the necklace, fumbling to take it off, but he stopped me with a shake of his head. "Keep it. I certainly can't wear it, and it might help you again."

Shocked, I said, "Yeah, but . . . it was your sister's."

"Yes, I know that. And now it's yours."

"Well . . . thank you. But—and it's not that I'm not grateful—"

"Not that, never that," he said mockingly.

"—but if you're so concerned, why didn't you come yourself tonight?"

"I did come," he said innocently. "More than once, in fact. I thought you were watching."

I felt my face get red, a good trick, since I was dead. "Very funny! You know what I mean."

"Alas, too well. Unfortunately, one of the conditions of Tina's release from Nostro was that I never set foot in his territory."

"Okay, well, this probably isn't the time to play Q and A, but some stuff has really been bugging me. Like that—why did he even let Tina on his property? He must have known she'd tell you everything she could."

"He likes to flaunt his power," he replied simply. "Thus, although I can send envoys, I myself must stay clear, unless he violates my territory. And he relishes showing off for my people. You might say he lives for it. However, the mausoleum where you first met Nostro is neutral ground . . . any vampire, from any city in the world, is welcome there. There are such neutral territories all over the planet."

"So you could come to the mausoleum for the—the party, I guess it was?" Lamest party *ever*, but oh well.

"I had no intention of coming, until I heard you were going to be there."

"Oh." Dammit! Hearing more details about how he got Tina away from Noseo—and how he wanted to meet me—made me start to hate him not so much. Which was not a good way to feel about a character as slippery as this guy. My hand went instinctively to the cross again. "Well, I'd thank you—"

"My heart! Can it stand the strain?"

"—except I know you've got some sneaky motive for helping me out."

"My anti-Nostro, pro-Elizabeth stance has been clear for a few days, there's nothing sneaky about it."

"Sneaky's your middle name—"

"Actually, it's Astor."

"—which reminds me, what are you doing here, anyway?" And wasn't an astor a kind of flower? I made a note to look that one up ASAP.

"You have my car," he pointed out. "I must insist upon its return. You don't strike me as a sensible and sane driver. And you were certainly in a dangerous rush to leave."

"Let's not talk about it."

"A prude born in the late twentieth century? I hadn't thought such creatures existed."

"Just because I don't think you should be gaily boinking multiple partners—at the same time!—doesn't mean I'm a prude."

He gestured toward the bathroom, where poor Nick was being ministered to by Tina and Dennis. "I don't think you're in any position to question my judgment. My ladyfriends know what they're getting into."

"You're still a pig," I said bitterly. "I saw you. It didn't matter which three women were there—you didn't care. They were for you to *use*. That's not how you treat a friend."

"Well." His brows arched in thought. "Perhaps I simply haven't met the right woman."

"Or perhaps you're a pig!" I threw my hands in the air. "Did you really *need* three of them? I mean, come on. Realistically. *Three?*"

"Well." He smiled slowly, and I felt my stomach tighten. "Does anyone ever really *need* a banana split, when a single scoop sundae would do?"

"These. Are. Human. Beings." I was pushing the words out past gritted teeth; I was so pissed my eyes were crossed. "Not. Ice cream. Sundaes. *Pig*."

"Your tiresome preaching has made me see the light. I have the bargain of the century for you, Elizabeth. I will give up their friendship at once, and all others for all time. Tonight. *If* you take their place in my bed. For all time."

My mouth fell open and I gaped at him. A zillion

emotions—outrage, curiosity, fear, lust, shock—screamed through my head in half a second, and before I knew I was going to do it, my hand leaped to his face and slapped him hard enough to snap his head back.

He felt his jaw and looked at me. His black eyes glittered and I swallowed the phrase, *I take it back!* that wanted to come out.

"Nice," was all he said. "I didn't see that one coming. Though I suppose I should have. You have, after all, done this before."

I tried to say something appropriately haughty and scathing, but couldn't think of a thing.

"Thank you," he said, so polite, and took the glass Jessica was offering him. Marc was right behind her with a tray of cocktail accessories: maraschino cherries, lemon slices, olives. They hadn't seen the slap. Heck, I had barely seen it—it was like my hand had moved quicker than thought.

"What was that noise?" Jessica asked.

"Never mind. All that stuff for wine?" I sighed, rolling my eyes and rubbing my palm. Smacking Sinclair had been like smacking a chunk of granite.

For spite, Sinclair carefully selected a lemon slice and dropped it into his wine.

Jessica peeked into the bathroom, then hurried back to report. "They got that boy stripped mother naked and they're scrubbing him with your brand-new loofah."

I winced. Thirty-seven ninety-nine at The Body Shop, kaput. "Fair enough. It's my fault he's in this mess. What happens after he's clean, Sinclair?"

"Eric."

"Errrrrrric . . ." Jessica and Marc repeated in dreamy chorus.

"Don't you two have *anything* else to do?" I practically screamed.

"This is the most interesting week of my entire life,"

Marc pointed out. "Vampires! Alliances! Gorgeous good guys. Sneaky bad guys. Fighting the good fight! Now we're scrubbing a delirious cop in your bathroom. What's next? Who knows? And why in the world would we go find something else to do?"

"Possibly because the events happening here are none of your business?" Sinclair asked smoothly.

Marc snorted. "I live here, pal. That makes it my business. Besides, what else am I going to do? Fight red tape at the hospital, beg HMOs to do the right thing while a kid dies? And what's Jess going to do—count her money?"

"Besides, we're the sidekicks. Part of the team. Anything that involves Liz here involves all of us," Jessica added.

"I shall endeavor to keep that in mind. To answer your question, Liz—"

"Don't you dare."

"Then no more Sink Lair, yes?"

Dammit! "Yes."

"Very good. As I was saying, once Detective Berry has been purified, Tina or Dennis will relieve his immediate need by feeding on him. Then we will make him forget he ever knew you as a vampire. He'll wake up in his own bed, with a week's worth of stubble, feeling like he's recovered from the flu."

"But I don't want this to happen to anyone ever again," I said. "I mean, your plan sounds like a good one, and God knows you've had a lot of years to perfect your sinister ways, but I'm looking to treat the disease, not the symptoms."

Sinclair had winced at "God," but answered smoothly enough. "Then pick one—or two—or three lovers who don't mind sharing blood along with their bodies, and use them as often as you must. Or they wish."

"Don't even think of glancing in my direction, girlfriend," Jessica ordered.

"Seriously," Marc added. "Unless you've managed to grow a penis in the last couple days."

"Thanks for nothing, creeps. Listen, Sinclair, even if I did such a yucky thing—and don't hold your breath—how do I know they won't become like Nick?"

"Because they'll have access to you. You won't have fed once and then turned your back on them."

"It wasn't like that," I said quietly.

"As you say." He was practically sneering, the big creep.

"It's probably not as bad as he's making out," Marc said, comforting me. "I mean, *I'm* not a wreck. About this, anyway."

"He is a homosexual. He is affected differently."

" 'He' is also standing right here, hello?"

"And," Sinclair went on, "as Jessica pointed out, he lives here. With you."

"Hey, somebody's got to defrost the freezer."

I laughed. Sinclair ignored us and continued lecturing. "Pick two. Or three. And feed on them, and let them have their way with you. You will find it's quite a satisfactory arrangement."

I wasn't laughing anymore. "Well, that's one of the big differences between thee and me, Sinclair, because I disagree!"

"She's a poet," Marc informed us, "and she didn't know it."

I glared at him, but Marc smiled back and didn't budge. I turned back to Sinclair. "It's like—it's like making a human being your—your pet or something." I'd never forget the coolly amused look on his face while he took one of his ladyfriends, then the other, then the other. They could have been anyone—he absolutely didn't care who was in his bed. I'd never do that to a person, make them feel like they were interchangeable parts of someone's machine.

Never.

"Did you not eat meat before your accident?" he asked. "You were strong and to keep yourself strong, you used the weak. That's what predators do. That's what vampires do.

Otherwise, you are like those fools in P.E.T.A., who think we should all nibble grass and drink nectar."

"Uh-oh, here we go," Jessica muttered. "Every dead guy for himself."

"*I'm* a member of P.E.T.A.," I said. "I ate meat, sure, but I don't think we should pour shaving cream down a rabbit's throat, or rub eye makeup onto a dog's eyeball so American women can have lush lashes. It's one thing if you need the protein, but it's another if you want to hang a big dead stuffed head on your wall, or design a deodorant that makes your armpit smell like a flower patch."

"A vampiric P.E.T.A. member." Sinclair couldn't quite keep the smile off his face.

"You're one of *them?*" Marc said, horrified. "Oh, cripes! I had no idea. Jesus, I feel dirty! Why didn't you tell me?"

I blinked. "My being a vampire doesn't bother you, but my giving money to P.E.T.A. does?"

"Hey, it was one thing when you were a soulless underling of Satan, I could work with that, but a tree-hugging marmoset lover . . . ugh! I've got my pride, dude."

Jessica got the giggles, then started to laugh. Before long she was having one of her gut-busters and hanging onto the wall to keep from falling over.

Sinclair smirked, watching me. I noticed he was careful to keep his teeth covered, probably so that Jessica and Marc wouldn't run screaming from the room.

"I'd better go check on the others," I said at last. I passed them on my way to the bathroom and ignored the evil-eye sign Marc forked at me.

Marc was still freaking out. "P.E.T.A.! Man, I'm gonna have to sit down and think this one over. Didn't mind being the sidekick of a bride of Satan, but a tree-hugger who, like, blows up labs and stuff . . ."

"Perhaps you *should* sit down," Sinclair suggested solicitously.

I passed Dennis on my way in. "We'll need some clothes for your Nick," he said over his shoulder. "Something he can wear home, that he can't trace back to you."

"I've got some old sweatsuits I never wear anymore—bottom drawer on the left. They don't have my name on them or anything. They'll be a little small, but they'll get the job done." Then I was stepping into the bathroom.

Nick was looking a little livelier, and well he should, since his head was pillowed on Tina's breasts and she was slowly, luxuriously working soapy lather over the muscles in his back. He was, as a matter of fact, extremely happy to see her. This was a great relief to me. When I saw the wreck that was the former Detective Nick Berry on my bedroom floor, I was afraid he'd never be happy to see anyone again.

"How's it going in here?" I asked. Squeaked, actually—I was a little nervous to be talking to Tina. What if she lost control and tried to molest me with the soap on a rope?

"He'll be all right. Do you think you could help me? I would ask Sinclair or Dennis, but—"

"It's my mess. Yeah, I'll help." I slipped out of my clothes, then slid the shower door aside and stepped in. "What—uh—what do we do now?"

"Now I fall upon you with ravenous hunger and hump your brains out."

I burst out laughing. I *was* scooched as far away from her as I could get, and that was a fact. I also felt a little weird about being naked in front of a lesbian. I probably had been before, at one time or another—public showers, that sort of thing—but you don't know for sure, right? You just assume everyone else is straight, and if someone's staring at your tits you figure she's working up the nerve to ask who did your boob job. "Very funny. Sorry."

"I'm the one who's sorry. I abused your trust and put everything in jeopardy." Her voice was so bitter it shocked me. "All because I couldn't keep myself to myself."

"Hey, whoa, calm down, sunshine. You just wanted a kiss, it's not like you tried to knife my kitty. Besides, I owed you a favor, right? From the pit?"

She shifted Nick as easily as a grown woman shifted a baby. "So," she said, straight-faced, "I risked my life and faced the prospect of a horrible death to save you, and in return you rebuffed my advances, and now we're even."

"Right." I smirked.

She rolled her eyes. "The devil help us if you really are the queen." But she said it with a smile, and I knew she was teasing to make me feel better. "Very well, then. To business. If you'll drink from his throat, I'll take him inside me. He'll have relief and then we'll be able to plant the suggestions we need to."

"Take him—oh. Oh! Ack! Right here? Now?" How how *how* did I get myself in these situations?

"He is dying," she said seriously.

"So you're going to have sex with him and poof! All better?"

"Mock if you will—"

"I'm being serious!"

"—but it's what he needs."

"But you don't—you don't like—I mean—oh, fuck."

She laughed. "All those things are true, but exceptions must be made."

"Yeah, but . . . like I said, it's my mess."

"Yes, but you don't want to do it. You never meant to in the first place, and don't want to now, particularly with several people waiting right outside the door—two of them with exceptional hearing—and that's fine." Seeing the look on my face, she softened her tone. "It's all right, Betsy. I truly don't mind. It's nothing to me, and everything to him. Besides . . . aren't you thirsty?"

I was. I hadn't fed yet tonight. Or last night, for that matter. But . . . "Why does it have to be both? Why do we have to drink *and* fuck?"

"*We* don't," she said, "but they do. If we take from them, they need us in the way that they've never needed anyone before. They can't drink, so they go for the next best thing—the best way to affirm life. I guess it's like—like masturbating but not letting yourself reach orgasm. What's the point? It's frustrating and leaves everyone unhappy. We could take and not give ourselves to them in return, but it's a rotten thing to do."

Oh. Well. If you put it that way . . .

"This is very disturbing, and time's a' wasting and my water heater is only so big, so we'd better get cracking, and I *am* thirsty, but if you do this for me I owe you another favor. All right?"

She looked at me, and her little pink tongue came out and tapped one of her canines thoughtfully. "A kissing favor," she said finally.

"Awww, Tina, I told you," I whined, "I don't play that way."

"Not in life, certainly. But vampires have to adjust to many things . . . and quite a few of us find that after death we are—ah—flexible."

That explained a lot. If a strange woman had tried to lay a lip lock on me two weeks ago, I'd have clobbered her with my purse. But here I was, extremely naked, with a gorgeous woman and a guy who wasn't exactly ugly, both of whom would have been thrilled to fuck me, and I was more than a little tempted to be the meat in their sandwich.

It was all very strange. Calgon, take me away!

"Okay," I said with a convincing display of reluctance. "We'll discuss this later."

"Of course," she assured me. "I'd want to wait until we had . . . leisure."

"You know, those pauses you and Sinclair do before you finish a sentence are really terrifying."

"Why do you think we do it? And who do you think taught *him?*" she asked merrily. She rinsed the last of the soap from Nick's body, then beckoned me closer. I ran my hands up his back, then put my hands on his shoulders, leaned in, and bit him. Hot salty life trickled into my mouth and Nick straightened up in a hurry, completely losing the apathy that had cloaked him all night. He tried to turn to face me, but I wouldn't let him.

"Here, to me," Tina said in her sweet, almost musical voice. Nick lunged forward, picked her up, and drove into her. Her back slammed against the tile and her legs were forced up and around his waist. Tina let out a squeak of pain, and Nick started thrusting against her so hard I lost my grip.

"Oh my God, ith he hurting you?" I was horrified. I was ready to pull him off her and put him through the shower door, and never mind that he was the victim.

"Nothing. It's nothing."

It occurred to me that a woman who didn't choose to couple with men was taking a pounding on my behalf, and didn't even have the pleasure of the drink to ease things. Because she wanted *me* to drink. Which I had, like the self-ish cow I was.

It's just . . . I hadn't thought he'd be so rough! So—so brutal and mindless. Of course, he'd tried to be like that with me, but I'd given it right back to him and besides, I liked men. But Tina—

Nick seized her by the thighs and wrenched her further apart; she cried out before she could lock it back.

"Oh, thcrew *thith,*" I said.

I started to pull him off her, but stopped at her sharp, "No! Else it's for nothing!"

So I held her hand instead. She squeezed back, tightening painfully as Nick speeded up toward his climax. Then he was done and collapsing to his knees, already half unconscious, and I caught Tina as she fell forward. "That's it, sweetheart," I told her, brushing damp tendrils of hair out of her eyes. "That's the last pounding you take on my behalf."

"Agreed."

We staggered out of the shower together. I remembered to turn off the water before Nick drowned. But I still felt like putting him through the wall—how's that for irrational?

Chapter 19

"WERE coming, too," Jessica said stubbornly.

"Indeed, no," Sinclair said politely.

"Hey, sidekicks tag along. It's, like, the rule. Besides, I want to watch Vampire 101," Marc gushed.

Dennis and Tina both looked appalled. "It's against all our laws," Tina explained. "And—and—"

"It's completely inappropriate," Dennis said, offended. "We're not circus monkeys. We don't perform for breathers."

"This is a private thing," Tina added. "Between Her Majesty and us."

"About that 'Her Majesty' stuff," Jessica said. "I mean, the girl's something special, no doubt . . . I've always known it."

"Awwwwww," I said.

"Shut up. Anyway, it was more a personality thing than anything else. Why is she the queen? It *can't* be her brains."

"Yeah, that's a very good—oh, thanks, creep."

"Look, honey, you're just not the sharpest knife in the drawer, is all. There's no shame in it."

"Just because I don't have a 142 I.Q. like *some* rich bitches doesn't mean my arms drag on the floor when I walk."

Sinclair was scowling. And so was I! "I can assure you, she wasn't elected. *I* certainly wouldn't have voted for her."

"Did I miss the memo that declared today 'take a big steaming shit on Betsy' day?" I griped.

"S'not my fault you don't check your in-bin," Jessica retorted. "So anyway, Eric, what's the deal with Queenie here?"

"Ugh! Do not even *think* of getting in the habit of calling me that. Seriously."

Sinclair sighed. It was a good effect, since I knew he didn't have to hardly ever exhale. "It's a long story, it's none of your business, she's leaving with us, good night."

At "good night," Marc and Jessica both folded bonelessly to the floor. I leapt aside so as not to be crushed by their falling carcasses. "Hey! Will you stop doing that to my friends? And *how* do you do it? Because I've got Easter dinner coming up with my father and stepmother . . ."

Sinclair actually shuddered when I said Easter—not sure if it was the Jesus angle, or if he was battling some sort of phobia of rabbits—but he quickly recovered. "We will cover that later. Come, Tina. Dennis."

"Good dogs, arf, arf," I muttered.

Sinclair picked up the dozing, dried, and dressed Nick, slung him over one shoulder like a sack of grain, and took him out to the Jaguar. Ignoring my protests, he unceremoniously stuffed him into the trunk, slammed it shut, and got behind the driver's seat. "Coming?" he asked politely, while Tina and Dennis got into the other car, a red Maserati.

"I must be out of my fucking mind," I muttered, climbing into the passenger seat. The neighbor's dog started to run up to the car, tongue already lolling and ready to lick, but I slammed the door in time. "Completely nutso bonkers."

Meanwhile, Sinclair's knees were up to his ears and he

looked decidedly aggrieved as he fumbled for the seat latch. "You have completely destroyed my interior," he complained, fussing with the rearview mirror. "You look tall but you apparently have legs like a platypus."

"Jeez, whine some more. Sue me for wanting to reach the pedals."

He started the engine and jerked in his seat as Rob Zombie's "Living Dead Girl" blared through the speakers.

"This is intolerable," Sinclair shouted in a vain attempt to be heard over the music. He lunged for the volume control, then stabbed irritably at the preset buttons. The car was instantly flooded with—gag!—serene string quartet music.

"Yuck," I commented.

"You took the word right out of my mouth." He rubbed his ear. "For pity's sake, Betsy. You have enhanced hearing. There's no need to turn the music up so loud."

"Are we gonna take Nick home, or are you going to keep bitching?"

"I plan to do both," he said wryly, pulling out of my driveway so sharply I lurched forward.

In no time at all, we were pulling up outside a small ranch house I took to be Nick's. I wasn't about to ask how Sinclair knew where he lived. Some stuff I just didn't want to know. Actually, *most* stuff I just didn't want to know, but people kept telling me anyway.

Sinclair got out, pulled Nick from the trunk, took him inside, did whatever hypnosis trick he had in his pocket for such occasions, and we left Nick dozing.

To my alarm, Tina and Dennis did a fade. "You don't need all three of us to teach you how to hunt," Tina said, waving as Dennis pulled out of Nick's driveway. "Luck!"

"Don't leave me alone with this asshole!" I shouted at the retreating taillights. Then, "Hunt?"

"You did promise," he said silkily. "Come."

"Come. Sit. Stay."

"Oh, if only."

* * *

"VAMPIRES don't exist."

I blinked. "Er . . . sorry, wasn't listening. Did you just say we don't exist?"

"Pay attention. We are myth, legend, folklore."

"Like the Tooth Fairy," I suggested, "with fangs."

"No, not remotely like that, because many children believe in the Tooth Fairy."

"Did you?"

"I was never a child," he said soberly. "Now. Because we don't exist, we are allowed to operate at a level unparalleled anywhere else in the natural world. This is vital, as we—"

"Whoa, whoa. Back up, slick. Never a child?"

"Please, Elizabeth. Try to stay focused. Now, as vampires don't—"

"I *am* focused. Why were you never a child?"

He didn't say anything. We were walking through a nature reserve about seventy miles north of the Twin Cities. I could hear all sorts of life—squirrels, deer, rabbits, bats, bugs, gophers, snakes—rustling and fighting and fucking and eating and dying, all around me. It was interesting, if nerve-wracking. The forest was teeming with life and I could smell it as well as hear it.

"I was never a child," he said at last, "because from the very beginning life was a struggle. I was regularly putting meat on my family's table before I knew the alphabet."

"How?"

"I was too small to use a gun effectively, so I learned how to set traps. Snares, and the like. And I could fish."

"Huh." I had to admit, I was impressed. Even if I absolutely could not see Mr. Slick as a toddler wandering down to the local fishing hole with a pole over one shoulder and a creel over the other. Opie he wasn't. "What'd your parents do?"

"We were farmers."

"No shit!"

"Surprised?"

"Well, yeah. I mean, you're so—" Slick. Refined. Fancy. Rich. Slick. Non-farmeresque. Did I say slick? "You're—uh—"

"Farming," he went on as if I wasn't still stammering, "is back-breaking work. Even now, in this century."

"How d'you know what it's like in this century?"

"I own several local farms."

"Oh. How come? I mean, seems to me like you'd want to get away from it altogether, and—"

"After my parents were killed I couldn't—I did not have the financial resources to—I just wanted to have the farms, and never mind the why of it! Now, back to business. Since vampires don't exist, we are allowed certain freedoms. But access to those freedoms depends entirely on—"

"But we *do* exist," I interrupted. I could take a hint—Sinclair was as rattled as I'd ever seen him, talking about owning *farms*, for goodness sake. So he wanted to get off the subject—I was hip to that. But not if he was going to babble a bunch of fantasy. "Hello? We're walking in the woods, aren't we? Just as undead as hell, right?"

Sinclair sighed. "Lesson one: Vampires don't exist."

"Lesson one blows."

"The point is, we go about our business in secret."

"Why?"

"Because that is the rule."

"But *why* is it the rule?"

He stopped short, exasperated. "Really, Elizabeth, this is not unlike a conversation with a first-grader."

"Oh, blow it out your ass. You can teach Vampire 101—I agreed, and I'm a girl of my word—but you have to make sense. That's *my* rule."

"Yes, and stubborn adherence to *your* rules is why the

most powerful vampire in five hundred years wants your head on a plate."

I made a face and kicked at a pile of leaves on the forest floor. *Know-it-all creep.*

"We. Do not. Exist. We do not seek out our parents. We do not return to our houses. We do not explain to strangers that we are undead."

"Is that why *we* are such total losers?"

"That," he said grimly, "will be taken care of. Now, about stalking—"

"Oh, cripes. Stalking? Do you hear how you sound?"

"How else will you eat?"

"It hasn't been a problem," I replied haughtily.

"Tell that to your policeman friend."

He had me there, the crumb. "So," I said sulkily, "about stalking."

"We don't breathe, our hearts don't beat. Well . . . very often, anyway. And it's surprisingly easy to steal up on someone without their knowing."

"Yeah, the night I woke up in the funeral home—"

"A story you simply must tell me someday," he interrupted smoothly. "As I was saying, if you focus, and practice, you can slip up on anyone—even another vampire."

That was a cheerful thought. Maybe, if I got good enough, I could sneak up on Sinclair and give him a well-deserved wedgie. "So, how do we do it?"

"Do you see the deer?"

As a matter of fact, I did. There was a doe and a yearling, about twenty yards ahead. If I'd been alive I'd never have heard or seen them—it was dark out, for one thing, and they were pretty well hidden back in the woods, for another.

"Yup."

"Let's try to walk up on them. Try to touch the doe before she knows you're there."

"And give her a heart attack? Jeez, she's a mom! Heartless creep."

"The fawn, then," he said impatiently.

"Scare *Bambi?* Sinclair, I swear, if you weren't a vampire, you'd be burning in hell."

He put a hand over his eyes and was silent for a long moment, his lips pressed tightly together. I knew the look. It was one I'd gotten from my father, various teachers, and bosses over the years. He was probably concentrating very hard on not strangling me. Hey, I am what I am. He'd better get used to it.

"Besides," I added, "somebody's coming." A whole herd of somebodies, sounded like. The sound of leaves crunching was very loud; I wanted to clap my hands over my ears. It sounded like a giant chewing Rice Krispies. And their breathing sounded like a winded rhino. I watched fearfully, waiting for the hideous creature to emerge.

"Howdy there, folks. Lost?"

The hideous creature was the game warden, a man in his late forties. He was about my height, with thinning blond hair and watery blue eyes. He was sporting a pretty good tan for April, and wearing a brown uniform with patches bearing the logo of the Minnesota Game and Fish Commission.

"We were just taking a walk," Sinclair said smoothly, shaking his head a little as we heard the doe and her fawn bound away. "Young lovers, you know." He slung an arm around my shoulders and hauled me up against him.

"Ugh!" I said. "I mean, yeah. Young lovers."

"Well, I'm gonna have to ask you to leave," he told us sternly. "We're doing some checking—there's word that one or two of the deer in here might have CWD."

"Chronic Wasting Disease?" Sinclair asked. "Are you certain?"

"No, that's why we're checking. Go on, now," he added kindly.

"Good evening."

"Okay, bye," I said, struggling to remove Sinclair's arm

from my shoulders without being too obvious. It was like trying to dislodge a tree limb.

When we were out of earshot I pulled away. "Chronic Wasting Disease? Isn't that like mad cow disease for deer?"

"Yes."

"Ewwww! And you were gonna have us stalk mad deer!"

"Per the WHO, there is no evidence that CWD can infect humans, much less vampires."

I wasn't about to ask who the hell WHO was. "Nice going, Stalker Boy! Sucking the blood and getting mad vampire disease . . . so *not* on my to do list for the week! Not that any of this bullshit is," I added in a mutter.

"Suck their blood?" Sinclair sounded appalled. "Absolutely not."

"Oh, they were good enough to sneak up on and scare the crap out of, but not good enough to eat?"

He was actually shuddering. I didn't think he could! "No. No. The animals were just practice. And don't ask why; you know why."

"Uh, no, I don't." *Guess I'm not as bright as he thought. Dammit!* "Why not drink from animals? It's got to be easier, not to mention less traumatic. For all of us!"

"Have you not noticed the . . . effect . . . your mouth has on men?"

The effect my mouth . . . oh. Oh! If it was that sensual, that much of a turn-on, then if I tried to bite Bambi, the poor little deer would likely be climbing all over—"Oh."

"Indeed."

"Ugh.

"Yes."

"So only people, huh?" I sighed.

"Yes. But never children."

"Well, *duh.*"

"As long as we're clear. What seems patently obvious to me often seems to take you quite by surprise."

"Look, if you think I'm a dumbass, why don't you just say it instead of pussyfooting around all the—"

"I think you are a dumbass."

"You *what?*" The nerve! "Jeez, you can't even pretend to be nice for five seconds?"

"Whenever I try to be—ah—nice, I get a broken rib for my pains." He patted his left side.

"You deserved that, throwing down a lip lock on me without permission. And after being with *them.*"

"I disagree. I was simply being a good host."

I sputtered while he laughed at me. "Sinclair, you're the worst—the—oh, cripes, I can't think of anything bad enough."

"Public education?" he asked sympathetically.

"Probably better than yours, farmer boy," I snapped back. "Where the hell is the car? I've had about enough of tromping around in the woods with you."

"It's up ahead. Now, you understand very clearly what I meant about taking blood?"

"Yeah, yeah, no need to whip out the hand puppets, I got it." I spotted the car as we emerged from the woods. "Well, it's not like I have to worry about it every night or anything." I cheered up. "Not even the next couple of nights."

Sinclair shook his head. "Truly amazing."

I preened.

"And entirely without precedence. Or merit."

"Cut it out, you're just jealous. Hey, can I drive back?"

"Absolutely not."

"Jeez, am I the Queen or not?"

"Queen you may be, but I draw the line at letting you behind the wheel again."

"Men and their toys . . ."

I climbed in and sulked all the way back to his place.

Chapter 20

WHEN I woke up next to Sinclair, I was the most shocked person on earth. Plus, to increase the creep factor, he was lying on his side, head propped on his chin, watching me. His chest was covered with a mat of crisp black hair, and his—

"Jesus!" I sat bolt upright and grabbed myself. I was, thank goodness, fully clothed. "Don't *do* that! What am I doing here on hell's satin acre?" I started groping my way toward the edge. We were in the middle of his gigantic bed and, I was happy to see, the sheets had been changed. They were such a light gray they were almost silver.

"And good evening to you, too." He watched as I clambered off his bed with all the grace of a laboring hippo. "How is it that you weren't burned to a crisp this morning?"

"What, you're asking *me*? How the hell should I know?"

The sun had caught up with us as we raced to Sinclair's. I didn't think much of it—hadn't I been sleeping in my bed with the curtains open this whole week, and didn't my room face east? But Sinclair flipped out when I opened my car door.

"How was I supposed to know you had an underground route to your place?" I grumbled, squinting at myself in the mirror and combing my fingers through my hair. Did my hair grow now? Would I ever need to worry about booking Simone at Le Kindest Kut? My roots didn't seem to be getting darker. Of course, I'd have to see if that was the case two months from now . . .

"Betsy?"

"What?" Now, if I wanted to try red highlights again—they'd been in and out and now they were trendy again—would it take? Shoulder-length hair was classically trendy, but what if it went out someday? Horrible thought! Locked into an unfashionable hairstyle . . . for eternity! It'd be as bad as being turned into a vampire in the 1960s, stuck with the Mary Tyler Moore look. Ugh! I'd prefer to be staked, quite honestly.

"Elizabeth."

"What?"

"We were discussing why you weren't immolated last night; *try* to stay focused."

"Calm down before you have a stroke. What's the big deal? I figured sunlight didn't bother you any more than it did me."

"Thank you for clarifying. Now back up. Sunlight does not bother you?"

"You were in my room, Sinclair. Remember, it faces east? And my curtains are white and filmy?"

"I assumed you had been resting in the basement." He was looking at me with such intensity I nearly squirmed. "Remarkable. Truly remarkable!"

"Well, yes. Anyway." I coughed modestly. "When you stopped the car, I assumed it was time to get out, not time to wait for the entrance to open for the bat-cave."

Sinclair held up his arm. It was an angry red, almost the

color of a cooked lobster. When he'd reached out, grabbed me, and pulled me back into the car he'd given himself a hell of a burn. "Obviously, you were mistaken."

I shuddered at the memory. It was really embarrassing. There I'd stood, blinking in the sunlight and yawning. Then Sinclair, more white-faced than usual, was reaching for me, his arm coming out of the dark car like a hairy life preserver. "Oh, right," I'd said slowly, stupidly. Had I ever been so tired? "The sun, it burns, oh, the agony . . . oh, cruel rays of zzzzzzzz."

Sinclair cleared his throat, a harsh bark that jerked me back to the present. "Well," I said, staring at his burn. "I'm sorry about that. I didn't mean for you to get hurt. You know, none of this would have happened if you'd let me drive."

"Second-degree burns are a small price to pay, then."

"I would have jumped back in the car myself, but it was hard to think. I was *so* tired."

"And you *so* almost got me fried alive, as you would put it. How could you not have known this would happen to you?" His tone was equal parts impatience and admiration.

"I didn't know I'd pretty much pass out as soon as dawn hit," I griped. "I'm usually in bed before the sun comes up. And the next thing I know, poof—I'm wide awake and it's a brand new night."

"This is an excellent time for your lessons to resume."

"Why?"

"Because you promised."

"No, I mean, why do you care? Why do you want to teach me?"

"Because," he said simply, standing in one fluid movement (I was relieved to see navy boxer shorts), "if you are to be an effective queen, you must know the terms of the society you will rule."

"Oh, come on. You don't really believe all that Book of the Dead stuff, do you? Because you don't treat me like a revered monarch. Not that it would kill you to try," I added.

"If I hadn't known your true rank before last night, I would have when I saw you standing in sunlight and yawning, instead of doing what an ordinary vampire would have done, which is burst into flames."

"Aw, it was nothing," I said with totally fake modesty. "But why did you stick me in your bed? Don't tell me this place doesn't have about a hundred extra bedrooms."

He gave me a slow smile. It was like watching the moon come up. "Host's privilege."

"Pervert." But I was rattled. He really was yummy, dammit. Absolutely gorgeous—and a good boy, when he wanted to be. He certainly could have taken a few liberties. But he hadn't.

And why the hell hadn't he? As if any member of his harem was prettier—or had better toned thighs—than *me*. He could do a hell of a lot worse than the Queen of All Undead, thank you very much! What, royalty wasn't good enough for him? The former Miss Congeniality *and* Miss Burnsville? He didn't like ex-cheerleaders? Every man in America lusted after cheerleaders. And I hadn't been some squad bunny, either; I'd been the choreographer.

"Betsy, are you all right? You've got the oddest look on your face. Even for you."

I shoved the thoughts away. "Why were you awake before me? For that matter, why didn't you fall asleep in the car? We left the woods so late . . ."

"I wasn't worried about the time, provided we were under cover before the sun rose—"

"But why did *I* fall asleep? And why did you wake up before me?"

"I heard those questions the first time. If you'll let me finish . . ." He trailed off and raised his eyebrows. I glared. ". . . ah, compliance. Such a pleasant, early evening surprise." He must have heard my teeth gnashing together, because he added, "The plain truth is, I'm quite a bit older than you are. I don't have to rest all day if I don't wish."

"Oh. So that's one of those things that will eventually happen for me?"

He looked me over critically. I self-consciously straightened out my bangs. "Not all. Some must rest all day. Nostro, for example."

"No need to sound so smug," I said. Because he sure did. I could tell he was loving the fact that, although I could gargle with holy water, I couldn't stay up as late as he could. "So, back to our lessons, then. Yawn."

"But first . . ." Sinclair's grin was almost catlike in its insolence. "There's the little matter of what I told you at the diner a few nights ago."

I had a nasty suspicion, but was ready for him. I wandered toward the chest of drawers by the window. It was taller than I was. "What are you talking about?"

He stalked after me. "I told you there would come a time when you needed my help, and I would give it, provided you put something of mine in your mouth." His hands reached for my shoulders and gently turned me to face him. "Lady's choice, of course, but I do hope you'll—what's that?"

"One of your handkerchiefs," I said, pulling it out of the top drawer. I stuffed it into my mouth, chewed, and swallowed. "Where's the bathroom?" I asked thickly. "I'm going to be sick."

He stared at me for a long moment, then started to laugh. He was laughing so hard he could barely point to the bathroom, and I almost didn't make it in time.

WHILE Sinclair showered, I decided I wanted a cup of tea. Useless, really . . . it sure wouldn't quench my thirst. But I hated waking up in strange places, with strange vampires, with no access to eye liner, and a nice cuppa was just what I needed to soothe my jangled undead nerves.

Problem was, Sinclair's abode was about the size of the White House. I tried to follow my nose and ended up in a spa . . . one that used green tea in the whirlpool to rid the body of antioxidants. Argh!

I went back into the hallway and nearly ran over another woman. "Sorry," I said automatically. I recognized her, which was pretty amazing because the last time I'd seen her she'd been naked and sweaty and having entirely too much fun with Sinclair.

"Oh," I added lamely. I wasn't sure I wanted her to know if I recognized her or not. "Um, hi." I mean, *I* wouldn't have wanted to be recognized. But I was kind of a prude about cheating on taxes, group sex, murder, and stuff.

She sized me up. You can always tell when a woman does it as opposed to a man. A woman checks your hair, your makeup job, your clothes, your shoes. If you're bare-legged she checks to see if you've got alligator skin or if you are acquainted with moisturizer. Basically, she's seeing whether you're a player or not.

A man checks your tits, then your face. It's annoying, but much more straightforward.

"Huh," she said, blowing out her breath in what I assumed was disgust. That was it, just, "huh," and a snort. Nice! She didn't even know me! Usually people have two or three conversations with me before they blow me off.

She was handsome rather than conventionally pretty, with high cheekbones, a wide forehead, strong nose, and deep-set black eyes. They were so dark that, like Sinclair's, I couldn't see her irises. On him it was scary, like you could fall into them. On her it was just weird, like Keanu Reeves's eyes. She was a good two or three inches taller than me, which meant she was one of the tallest women I'd ever seen. She was wearing a red bathrobe and not much else, and was sorely in need of a pedicure.

"Say, I wonder if you could tell me where the kitchen is," I said, when she appeared to be finished, both with the sizing-up and the conversation. "I'm trying like heck to find it in this place, but—"

Her nostrils flared. Since she had a—shall we say—
heroic nose, the effect was startling. I nearly took a step
back. When she spoke, her voice was surprisingly deep and
throaty. "Oh, so because I'm a sister I know where the
kitchen is?"

"I thought—"

"You thought because I'm a black woman in my
bathrobe at eight o'clock at night, I must be kitchen help?
Because you've got that all wrong. For your information, I
don't know a frying pan from my own ass."

"Er—I'm sorry to hear that?"

"I'm not *the help*. I'm the boss's right-hand lady, and I
know you know *that* shit, because I know you watched us
and got your jollies."

I was flabbergasted. I don't think I'd ever been accused
of prejudice before. I mean, everybody who knows me
knows Jessica's my best friend. And anybody who knows
Jessica knows she's smarter, prettier, thinner, and richer
than I am. There's just no comparison. If anything, I tended
to assume blacks ("*Never* African Americans," Jessica had
schooled me. "Shit, my grandparents were from Jamaica.")
were smarter and more successful than I was. Because the
ones I knew *were*.

Having verbally ripped me a new asshole, my nice new
friend was turning away. She stopped when I spoke.

"First of all," I said, and I was *very* angry, so I kept my
tone light, "I thought you might know where the kitchen is
because you appear to live here. Unless bathrobes are suddenly considered trendy evening wear, which I doubt,
because there wasn't a whisper of it in this month's
Vogue."

She opened her mouth but I plunged ahead. "Number
two, watching you guys explore each other's naughty
places wasn't *my* idea. Not that I care what you do with
Sinclair, but bragging about it is just gauche. I mean, like
it's an accomplishment he's jumped your bones? I'm sure

he's got a *rigorous* application process," I added sarcastically. "You have tits, so I guess you pass."

"Don't you talk to me like that," she said sullenly, fingering the belt of her robe.

"Don't *you* talk to *me* like that. I asked you a perfectly nice question and you went off. Maybe if you kept your legs closed once in a while, you could find time to brush up on your manners."

Her arm came up to hit me—not an open-handed slap, I noticed with alarm, but a closed fist. Of course, I was dead and she was human, so to me it looked like she was trying to slug me underwater, but it was alarming just the same.

"Don't you dare!" I snapped. I batted her hand away like it was a pesky fly. Unfortunately, this knocked her back about three feet. Oops. "If you don't want to hear nasty things, don't start. And another thing. If you ever— *ever*—accuse me of being prejudiced again, I will knock you on your fat ass. If you've got a problem with someone who treated you wrong, go take it out on *them*."

I swept past her and marched down the hall. I was always up for a good catfight, provided I had the right ammo. But dammit! I still didn't know where the kitchen was, and now I was thirstier than ever. Should have chomped on what's-her-face, see how she liked *that*.

I turned the corner and heard slow, measured clapping. There was another of Sinclair's harem, standing in the doorway to another bedroom. She was dressed, at least. "Oh, really excellent," she said in a perfect British accent. I loved to listen to Brits talk. "Mitzi's been needing someone to do that for quite a while."

"That Amazon's name is Mitzi?"

She gave me a sly smile. She was a real cutie; short, blond hair in a pixie cut, sky blue eyes, and a teeny dimpled chin. She was wearing a pink T-shirt that did fabulous things for her complexion, and white clamdiggers. Her toes were painted shell pink. They looked like little mother-of-pearls. "You should talk . . . Betsy."

"Fair enough. Say, *you* don't know where the kitchen is, do you? And this isn't a slur on your ethnicity in any way . . ."

"Come along, then." She bebopped down the hall and I practically had to run to keep up with her.

"Is it a race?" I asked.

"Oh, sorry." She slowed her pace a fraction.

"So you guys—you live here?"

"Mm-hmm."

"Do you like it?"

She looked at me, surprised. "What's not to like? You *have* seen Eric Sinclair, right?"

"Uh, yeah." Sure, he was handsome . . . but wasn't he one of the monsters? Wasn't I? Why would she want to be his hors d'oeuvre? "Not that I make snap judgments based on appearances—much—but you don't strike me as the type to enjoy being—um—well—"

She smiled, and the corners of her eyes crinkled in a friendly way. "A raging slut, one of a harem, his breakfast, lunch, and dinner?"

"Well. Yeah."

"Eric Sinclair saved me. I know I don't look it, but he found me on the streets. I was turning tricks on my knees in back alleys. He came up with a much better solution."

"Oh. Oh!" If I'd been alive, my face would be beet red by now. "You don't look—I mean, you're so—"

"My mum had a saying: 'It takes all types to make a world.'"

I'd never talked to a former prostitute before. Oh, the questions I had! How was the money? Were the pimps as bad as they seemed in the movies? Was there a dental plan? Could she tell a cop from a john? Did she ever Do It for fun, or was it all work, work, work? Was pregnancy considered an on-the-job hazard by OSHA?

I jerked myself back to the conversation. "My mom says that, too. Well, I guess the only thing that matters is if you're happy here. That, and if the food's decent. The rest is nobody's business."

She laughed. "The food is wonderful. And it's not exactly a burden, keeping Sinclair well-fed."

We were going downstairs now, but these weren't the front stairs I'd seen before. "Yeah, yeah, so he's not exactly hard to look at. Big deal. And by the way, is there somewhere I can buy a map to this place?"

She laughed again. "You'll get used to it."

"Christ, I hope not."

She quit laughing. The sound snapped off like she was a radio and somebody hit her switch. "You—I thought you were a vampire."

"I am."

"Say Christ again."

"Christ."

"Say, 'Jesus meek and mild.' "

"Jesus meek and mild."

"Recite the Lord's prayer, if you please."

"Only if you give me a cookie when I'm done. 'Our Father, who art in Heaven, hallowed be Thy name; Thy kingdom come; Thy will—' "

"Stop it!" Dennis came rocketing up the stairs, meeting us halfway. His feet seemed to barely touch the floor, he was moving so quickly. His hands were clapped firmly over his ears. His eyes were rolling like a rabid dog's. "Stop it, Karen! I can't get my work done when you're doing that. *Stop making that fucking noise!*"

"It's not me, Dennis," she who I took to be Karen replied, shrinking back against the wall. She jerked a thumb in my direction. "It's her."

"Oh." Dennis slowly lowered his hands. I noticed he was nattily attired in dark chinos, black socks, and a crisp white Oxford shirt. No tie, but he buttoned it all the way up to his neck anyway. "Oh, it's you."

"Sorry about that," I said.

"You needn't apologize to *me,* Majesty."

"I think I do. You looked like you were going to stroke out." *Or wet your pants. Possibly simultaneously.* "Sorry again."

"I'm sorry, too," Karen said quickly. "I didn't think she'd do it. I didn't think she could." She turned to me. "But you're a vampire!"

"That's what they keep telling me. So, about that trip to the kitchen . . ."

"Right, right." She shook herself like a terrier. "This way, then."

Dennis slunk off after a final mistrustful glance over one shoulder. "I really am sorry," Karen said in a low voice. "I mean, I'd never have asked a regular person to do that. Not here, of all places."

"Does it hurt them?" I kept my voice low, too, knowing too well how good vampire hearing was.

"Tina told me it's like hearing metal nails being dragged down a chalkboard, times a thousand. And they hear it in their head, so plugging their ears doesn't do any good—not that they don't try."

"Ouch!"

"But how can you—how can you even say the words? How can you even think them? And what d'you mean, 'Does it hurt them'? *You're* them."

"It's a mystery, all right," I said, a little proudly. Hey, why not? I was a mystery wrapped in an enigma and drenched with Big Mac secret sauce. "Sinclair's trying to figure it out. That's why he's teaching me how to be a vampire."

"Seems like you're the one who could be doing the teaching," Karen said, and then blushed to her hairline. "You didn't hear that, right?"

"Hear what?"

"Thank you."

We went down a couple more hallways and through a swinging door, and lo! Unto us a kitchen appeared. "Jeez, finally," I complained. "If I were still alive, I'd have died of thirst by now."

Karen cleared her throat. "About that. Um. Do you need—I mean, should I get someone?"

"Sweetie, the only thing I need you to get me is a teapot."

She jumped toward a tower of cabinets, rooted around in one, and emerged with a bright red pot, the kind that shrieked bloody murder when the water boiled.

"Thanks." I walked twenty feet to the sink—Sinclair's kitchen was bigger than my dad's entire ground floor—and filled it. "Want some?"

"Let me see . . ." She rooted through another cupboard. "Yes, I think. They have leaves, not bags, today."

"What's wrong with bags? Oh, right, you're a Brit. You're picky about your boiled leaves." I snickered.

"Well, I am! The stuff in teabags is undrinkable. That's the leftovers, you know. They take the good leaves and put them in tins, and the dust that's leftover they stuff into little bags!"

"Calm down before you need your blood pressure checked. I don't care either way. Tell you what, though, I hate those little leaves floating in my tea. Some of them always escape the tea ball. What if they make me throw up?" I added anxiously.

"Throw up?"

I nodded glumly and took a seat at a counter that was long enough to slaughter a couple of cows on. "Yeah, if I try to eat solid food, I puke. Not a pretty sight." I buried my head in my hands. "I just realized! Desserts! No more crème brulée, chocolate cake, ice cream. Ixnay on zabaglione with raspberries, chocolate chip cookies, French silk pie! Oh, I'm gonna cry right now."

"Please don't," Karen said anxiously. She took the teapot from me, which I'd been swinging around in my agitation, and went to the smallest stove—the one with only eight burners. She pressed a button and blue flame popped to life. "Forgive me, but . . . you're only thinking of this now?"

"Give me a break! I've only been dead—er, what day is it? I died late last week."

There was a clang and a slosh as she dropped the pot. "You're—you're newly risen?" Was she . . .? She was! She was actually backing away from me. "But you're not—you should be all over me. I—I can't stay in here with you, I'm sorry, you seem rather nice but I—"

"Quit it!" I snapped. "All that Hugh Grantesque stammering is making me nervous. I'm not going to bite you. I'm not thirsty. Okay, well, I am, but I can control it. Really, I can. Otherwise I would have jumped Mitzi in the hall, right?"

Karen was squished up against the far wall. I could barely see her. Stupid industrial-sized kitchen. "Well . . . I suppose . . . and you *are* interesting." She forced a smile. "And me without my crucifix."

"It wouldn't do any good," I said apologetically. "I can touch them. I can probably *eat* them. No problem. Shoot, I'm wearing one right now."

That got her out of her corner. "Really? You can control your thirst and touch crosses?"

"Haven't we gone over this already? Your attention span is as tiny as your feet. What can I say? I'm an enigma, wrapped in a riddle, drenched with—"

"None of that. Who *are* you?" She was very close now—crossed the kitchen floor pretty quick!—and staring into my face.

I shrugged. "I'm just . . . me, I guess. Just Betsy. At least, that's who I always was."

"Hmm. Well, I don't believe we've been properly introduced. I'm Karen Helmbolt." She gingerly offered me a hand, doubtless expecting me to bite it. Instead I shook it briefly.

"Nice to meet you."

"Likewise . . . I guess."

While I laughed at that, she bent, picked up the pot, refilled it, and walked back to put it on the stove. Then she found a towel and wiped up the water on the floor, keeping more than a casual eye on me the entire time. "Well, it's certainly been interesting meeting you. It's been awfully quiet around here lately. You're the most unique thing to happen around here in—er—" She trailed off.

"Pretty quiet place to live, huh?"

"Oh, yes. Thank God," she added solemnly. Then she flinched. "Sorry about that. Oh! Sorry about *that*. I forgot you didn't—"

"Jeez, get a grip, willya? I thought Brits were laid-back and cool all the time."

"Not on days like today," she said dryly.

Chapter 21

𝘈𝘍𝘛𝘌𝘙 tea, I asked Karen to show me to the library. Color me geek, but I wanted to see the sorts of books Sinclair had lying around. And if he had any history books, I wanted to see if I could find him, or Tina, or Dennis in them. Or even Nostro. Know your enemy and all that, even if your enemy was a pathetic drama queen with a beer belly. Or would that be a blood belly?

Surprise, surprise, the library was right out of a nineteenth-century catalog. Dark walls, lush wine-colored carpet which I sunk into up to my ankles, mahogany furniture, and shelves of books. The desk was big enough for three people to work at comfortably without their ever brushing elbows. Ridiculous! If I didn't know for a fact that Sinclair didn't have to compensate for a darned thing, I'd sure have wondered.

On the wall behind the desk was a framed photo. It was sepia-toned and looked very old. The two men in the photo both had Sinclair's fathomless eyes, except one was a teenager and the other a man in his fifties. The women were petite, dainty, with dark hair and tip-tilted eyes . . . since the photo was black and white, I couldn't tell what color. Only the girl was smiling. She looked about thirteen. *That's his family,* I thought. *His folks and his sister. All dead, now. I wonder if he thought he'd still be around in the twenty-first century when they took this little snapshot?*

It was the only photo in the room.

I started thumbing through the books on the shelves. Shakespeare, no surprise there. The entire James Herriot collection, which *was* a surprise. I hadn't pegged Sinclair as the type to curl up with a book about a Yorkshire veterinarian. On the other hand, he *had* lived on a farm.

The entire wall behind the desk was wall-to-floor CDs. I didn't bother to look at any of them—there was no hope, based on last night's car ride.

I turned to the books. There was a set of leather-bound encyclopedias that smelled terrific, from aardvark to zymogen. Atlases. *The Geography of the World* in thirty-two volumes . . . copyright 1922. A globe in the corner by the window . . . I wondered if it was the hokey type my dad had, the kind that opened to reveal a wet bar. *The Canterbury Tales,* uck . . . even Sinclair wasn't *that* old. Dante's *Inferno* . . . big shocker.

And what were these? The middle shelf had its own unique genre: *Back from Death; Vampires of Historic Note; Walking with the Undead; The Vampire's Guide to Man; The Church and the Undead: A History; Living Dead and Living Well.* Who were these people?

I pulled *Vampires of Historic Note* off the shelf and immediately saw it was well used. It fell open to a heavily marked page, and I saw a bad picture of Nostro scowling up at me. I nearly dropped it.

Nostrodamus, formerly known as Frederick O'Neill.
DOB: February 14, 1627. POB: London, England.
DOD: December 26, 1656.

Awwww! Old Noseo was a Valentine baby. How cute.
Born on Valentine's, dead the day after Christmas. Ick. His
name was Fred? Ha, I knew it! No wonder he changed it as
fast as he could. And what had happened to his British
accent? Maybe he lost it after living in America for two
hundred years.

The book weighed a ton, and it was at least six inches
thick. I shifted my weight and began to read.

Little is known of Nostrodamus in life because of poor
recordkeeping and his reclusive nature.
   In death, however, his exploits are worth noting, to wit:
   The Undead Uprising of 1658. While eventually
defeated, this is a significant event, as Nostrodamus was
able to rally six thousand vampires in a very short time. If
not for the intervention and eventual aid of the Catholic
Church, the Undead may well have taken London.

He'd been dead for two years before leading an uprising?
Ambitious little fucker.

The Maypole Massacre of 1660. Again, Nostrodamus
was eventually defeated by the Church, but only after
egregious loss of life, and this case proves he learned
from his earlier errors. In a stroke of cunning, Nostro-
damus took the town's children and—

I turned the page. No thanks. Did not want to know.

The Plymouth Uprising, 1700. After journeying to the
New World via the cargo compartment of the HRH

Queen Elizabeth I, *Nostrodamus quickly established a foothold in the Massachusetts Bay Colony. This time, he was able to keep control of the town for fifty-six years, before being driven out by settlers and Native Americans, who set fire to Plymouth during daylight hours and staked all who were left alive that night.*

This is the first known record of Native Americans and colonists uniting against vampires. Nostrodamus sacrificed most of his followers to ensure his escape. Many of them were left behind for the townspeople to—

I slammed the book shut, appalled. Cripes, the guy never gave up. Just attack after attack, and he didn't care who got hurt and who got dead. He'd do anything to hold onto his territory.

But he moved. And kept moving . . . sure, after every defeat. Now he was entrenched, and likely wouldn't want to skulk away and pick up the pieces somewhere else. Too bad for us.

And now he was mad at *me*. For what? All I did was laugh at him. And not die a hideous death. And insult him in front of his followers. And get away.

"Fascinating reading, yes?"

I nearly dropped the book on my foot. Sinclair was standing in the doorway, looking like a million bucks in black slacks, a midnight blue shirt, and black shoes. His hair was still damp from the shower, and he smelled vaguely of fresh blood. At my stare, he said easily, "I ran into Mitzi after my shower. And you ran into her, so I hear."

"Yeah, you've got a real sweetheart in that one. Don't let her get away."

"She's quite terrified, you know," he said, sounding amused. "She had no idea who you were when she challenged you. I had my hands full trying to end her hysterics."

I dismissed this absurdity. "Nothing scares her. Where

do all these books come from? I've never heard of some of them."

"Well," he said, straight-faced, "Shakespeare was a famous writer who was born—"

"I know *him,* dolt. I mean these Vampire 101 texts."

"You think once we die, we lose our creativity, or thirst for knowledge?"

"No. I guess not. So there are vamp publishing houses?" I chuckled.

"Yes."

I stopped laughing. "Oh. Listen, can I borrow some of these? All my other research sources have been the fiction section of the library, and the movie theater."

He visibly shuddered. "Please. Help yourself. I insist."

"Great." I started grabbing books. "And I think I'm going."

"You gave your—"

"I *know*. Stop nagging. But last night we covered stalk-ing—"

"Hardly."

"And now I've got all this homework. C'mon, let me get this reading done. I'll come back tomorrow night and you can quiz me."

"Really? What are the penalties for missed questions?"

"Um . . ."

"Kisses?"

"In a pig's eye."

"There's no accounting for taste."

"Have I mentioned I hate banter? I'm going," I said shortly, stomping across the floor and shouldering past him. The stubborn cuss didn't budge, not even when I shoved my body weight against his side. So I had to grunt and wiggle my way past, all the while knowing he was smiling.

"Oh, and I'll need to borrow a car," I called over my shoulder, and was gratified to see the grin drop off his face.

* * *

I downshifted, but not by much, and took the turn in third gear. The car fishtailed behind me and I wrestled with the wheel until it straightened out. The roar of the engine—actually, the car was so pricey it was more a purr than a roar—was music to my ears.

Ah, sweet freedom! So long, Sinclair. See ya, Tina. Bye-bye, Dennis and Mitzi and Karen. Well, maybe not Karen.

I had one hand on the steering wheel, and the other was buried in the CD holder up to the elbow. I groped, felt, and pulled. Soundtrack from *Amadeus*. Nope. I took my hand off the wheel long enough to hit the power button for the window, and out into the night air ole Wolfgang went.

Beethoven: Violin Concerto. Pass. I tossed it. *Sentimento,* Andrea Bocelli. Who the hell was she? Toss. *Mahler: Symphony Number Five*. It probably wasn't any better than symphonies one through four . . . buh-bye. *Chopin: 24 Études*. Et tu, Chopin? Kiss pavement.

Who did I have to bite to find something decent to listen to? And why did I pick the car that had a state-of-the-art CD stereo system but *no damned radio?* Stupid Sinclair. Even if he wasn't an arrogant cuss, I felt like giving him a kick for his musical taste alone.

The flashing red lights in my rearview reminded me that there were worse problems than being trapped in Sinclair's shiny Mercedes with a bunch of his lousy CDs. For example, there was being pulled over at 9:30 at night in a car that wasn't mine, when I didn't have my driver's license.

I pulled over as safely and slowly as I could—a good trick, as I'd been going ninety—and frantically straightened out my bangs while the Bear approached. The Minnesota governor kept slashing the state budget, but there always seemed to be plenty of state troopers around to torment me. They were firing VA nurses left and right, but kept plenty of cops on the road . . . tell me *that's* fair.

More nurses, less tickets. That's my motto.

He stopped just outside my door, and bent down a bit to

look in. I gave him a big smile. Here it came: dumbass question number one.

"Good evening, ma'am. Do you know how fast you were going?"

Nope. Even though I was driving, and I'm the only one in the car, and the speedometer is translucent amber, I have no idea. Twenty-five miles an hour? Thirty?

"I'm sorry, Officer. I'm in a hurry to get home. I guess I wasn't paying attention." Blink, blink. The oops, silly me, but I'm not in the habit of breaking the law so how about you let me off, you big strong sweetie? routine had a sixty-seven percent success rate, particularly when I was wearing my suede miniskirt.

He was still bending down, still staring at me. I took the plunge to head off dumbass question number two. "I'm afraid I don't have my license—I left it at home. And I don't have the registration. This isn't my car, it belongs to—" To whom? My friendly enemy? Nemesis? Local jerk? Undead tormenter? Creep with lousy taste in music? "—um, I borrowed it."

The trooper gave me a sweet, goofy grin. "You're pretty."

Yes! Make that a one-hundred-percent success rate, now that I was postmortem.

For the first time, I had a real glimpse of the possibilities. There had to be a tradeoff if I was expected to give up chocolate. Never again would I be a slave to the speed limit!

"Pretty," the trooper said again, in case I missed it the first time. Like I would! "You're so so pretty. Ummmm."

"Thanks. Is it okay if I go?"

"Uh-huh."

"Okay."

He didn't move. I was afraid I'd run over his toes, so I ordered, "Step back. Get into your car. Don't set any more speed traps tonight."

Worked like a charm.

Chapter 22

ℒ staggered into my empty house. It's not that I wasn't strong enough to easily carry the books, but they were an awkward bundle, and I could barely see over them.

I let the books tumble to my coffee table. The flimsy structure shuddered but, fortunately, maintained its integrity. Then I went to the kitchen.

Time for more tea to distract myself from my raging thirst. I could ignore it a lot of the time, but it was getting harder and harder. When had I fed last? It had been at least two full nights, that was for sure. I'd have to give in and chomp eventually. Maybe when it got really late I'd take a stroll and let myself get mugged.

There was a note on the fridge, scribbled on a prescription sheet and smeared with marinara sauce—Marc simply would *not* use a napkin. It was unbelievable—he looked neat as a pin and was a total slob. I didn't think gays were allowed to be messy.

I came closer and read:

Hello oh vampire queen. Hope lessons with what's-his-face went okay. If he gives you any shit, lemmee at him. Jessica's working late at the Foot tonight and I've got the midnight shift this week. Don't bother looking in the fridge, we drank all the milk. I might bring some patient files home for you to look over. Hungry?

—M.

Oh, he was a sly one. He hadn't let go of his undead vigilante plan. And, if I was going to be honest with myself, as far as plans went, it wasn't such a bad one. If I could get past the whole felonious assault thing. And the fact that, if I fed on them and left them, there was a chance they'd waste away and die.

And what the hell did he mean, they drank all the milk? Dammit! I hated tea without milk, or at least cream.

I was drinking my third cup of milkless tea and deeply engrossed in *The Church and the Undead: A History* when Jessica walked in. She immediately burst out laughing, which wasn't unusual. I was sprawled across the couch in my sushi pajamas and slippers that looked like monster paws. The coffee table groaned under the weight of the books and I had *Gone with the Wind* playing on the DVD player. Best movie *ever*.

"Comfy?" she asked, grinning. She tossed her keys in the dish by the phone nook and dropped her briefcase in the corner where, tomorrow morning, she would spend half an hour looking for it.

"Homework," I said gloomily. "If I wasn't dead, I'd have a splitting headache by now."

"What the hell are you reading?"

"Listen to this: *By definition, the church and the*

Undead are doomed to be enemies. See index vii, xxiii, and xvii. I spend so much time looking up the damn footnotes I have no idea what the hell I'm reading."

She walked over and stared at the volumes. "Jeez," she said, sounding impressed, which was a rare and wonderful thing with her. "What are these?"

"Supersecret vamp stuff. Apparently there's undead artists, writers, bankers, valets . . . blah-blah. And they keep producing stuff like this after they're dead. Wonder if there's an undead best-seller list?"

"How long you been at it?"

"Half an hour! It's been endless. I'm so ready for a break."

"Well, good, because I had regular coffee instead of decaf and I'm wide awake. Let's go do something."

I shrugged. I really wasn't a late-night party girl. Although maybe now that would change.

"Aw, c'mon!" Jessica was begging. "We haven't done something fun, just us, since you—well, you know."

Since I died. Right. "Fair enough." I tossed the book aside, wincing as it slammed into the carpet. "Is there anything good playing at the Hype?"

The Hyperion was an open-all-night movie theater that showed cheapie movies. You could see a movie for two bucks, but it was a movie that opened eight months ago. Usually they got movies right around the time the video store did. And it was always funny to see previews for movies that had been out for three months. Still, two bucks!

Jessica smirked at me. She was looking efficient and businesslike in her gray Armani suit, black hose, and black pumps, but the smirky grin sort of ruined the effect and made her look like a smug first-grader. "You'll never guess."

"Probably not, so why don't you tell me? And don't smile like that, it gives you crow's feet."

"Does not. Go on, guess."

"Uh . . . *Gone with the Wind?*"

The smirk vanished. "Shit, no! Why would I want to watch a movie that glorifies—"

"Oh, here we go."

"—slavery while elevating the rich plantation creeps to the status of demigods?"

"First of all, they're not demigods. They're as flawed as people can be—the heroine's a jerk, for God's sake. Margaret Mitchell makes no secret of the fact that Scarlett O'Hara is vain, willful, obstinate, selfish . . ."

"Oppressive."

"Yes, yes, all right. But Mitchell also points out that Scarlett treats her servants—"

"Slaves."

"Not after the Civil War ended, they're weren't. She treated them better than all the white people, even her own husband! Husbands."

"Yeah, but—"

"*And* the hero was a womanizing, cruel gambler who raped his wife when he got drunk. I mean, hello? These are flawed people. The slaves and servants, on the other hand, are almost universally good, long-suffering, and devoted to their families. The whole point of the book was that there was *plenty* of bad stuff perpetrated by the North. I mean, how many of the freed slaves really *did* get forty acres and a mule?"

This was an old and well-loved discussion. I think Jessica secretly liked the book—I'd found my copy in her room more than once—she just liked to argue about it. And most whites wouldn't dare defend it to her. Me, I had no shame. Also, she was wrong.

"It's a book that glorifies white people at the expense of blacks."

"The vain white people who ended up alone and unhappy, or the white people who got the shit kicked out of them by the Union Army? Or the white people who starved to death during Reconstruction? Or—"

"All *right*."

"You know, for somebody who could buy London, you're awfully touchy about slavery. I mean, no one in your family was ever a slave."

She sniffed. "You can never know my pain."

"The pain of being the first kid on the block to have her own Patek Philippe watch? You poor oppressed creature."

She giggled. "Thank God you understand. This is, of course, why I tolerate your bigotry and snobbishness."

I threw a sofa pillow at her. We had done this part of the dance, too, but with my undead reflexes she had no time to duck. The pillow hit her square in the face and knocked her back two steps.

"Help, help!" she said. "I'm being oppressed!"

"Thief! You stole that line from Monty Python."

"Now *there's* a movie. God, that was quick. I didn't even see your arm move."

"Sorry," I said, and I meant it. I could tell she was a little rattled. "I'll try to slow down a little."

"Don't," she said shortly. "I'll get used to it. C'mon, let's go."

"What *is* playing? You never told me."

"You'll like it. Come on. More research."

SHE was right. I liked it. But I wasn't about to give her the satisfaction of knowing she was right—she got that too often at the Foot and from the horde of adoring boyfriends.

"You know I don't like movies that have Roman numerals after the titles," I whined.

"Shut up. Those are the best ones. Besides, you're out a whole two bucks."

"Plus nine," I said, holding up my 7-Up, which was the size of a gallon ice cream container. I sipped contentedly while the opening credits for *Blade V: Return of the Vampire King's Nephew* scrolled down the screen. I tried to ignore the fact that my feet were sticking to the floor.

I'm afraid I laughed through most of the movie. In particular, when the hero leapt over a moody crowd of bad guys, had a sword fight in midair with the villain, and landed lightly on his feet all the way across the room just in time to prevent the heroine from falling to her death. Then he caught his sunglasses, which had been flying toward him (contemptuously tossed by the villain's henchman) in slow motion, and popped them on his head while the heroine gazed up at him adoringly. Shyeah! All he needed was a halo.

"Will you quit it?" Jessica hissed, elbowing me for the tenth time. "You used to think this stuff was scary."

"Well, now I think it's funny. Oh, look! Even though he emptied his pockets in the earlier scene, now they're bulging with extra bullets. How handy! It's *Treasure Island* all over again. Somebody shoot the head writer."

"Someone's gonna shoot *you*, you don't shut up."

"Hey, even better! Even though he parked miles away, now his car is waiting for him right outside the bad guy's lair. What, is it like the Batmobile? Does it come when it's called?"

"Go get another drink, why don't you?"

"I drink anymore I'll burst. As it is, I might actually have to use the bathroom."

The end came to a predictable, yet satisfying, conclusion, with plenty of room left for yet another sequel. I steered Jessica toward the back door exit.

"Why are we going out here?"

"I need to get some air." Which was a lie, but no need to scare her just yet.

"So, I guess you liked it. I mean, you laughed enough."

"It was great! I should do more research. Rent a bunch of old movies. You know, like classics. *Nosferatu. Dracula. Fright Night. Dracula*—the one with Gary Oldman running around in that little old lady hairdo. I don't know what was creepier, the way he licked blood off razors or the way he wore his long white hair in a bun."

Jessica cracked up. "Like Gary Oldman isn't scary enough!"

"Exactly. And what's that one with Eddie Murphy and Angela Bassett? Oooh, and *Vampires* with James Woods."

"I thought you wanted to watch classics."

"Those are. They're all from the last century, aren't they? And *Dracula 2000*. And—"

"I am *so* glad the millennium thing finally happened. I was getting really sick of movies sticking the number two thousand at the end of every damn title."

"Grump, grump, grump. Let's go down this alley."

"*Where* are we going?"

"I thought we'd take a short cut." The streetlights down in this neck of the woods were few and far between. Really perfect.

Come on, guys, what do you want, a welcoming blare of trumpets?

"Oh. Are you—uh—hunting?"

"No."

"Aren't you thirsty?"

"Yep."

"Why haven't you—uh—"

"Because it's gross," I said irritably, kicking an empty Budweiser can out of my way. It flew down the alley and smashed up against the far wall. "Look: I know I have to get used to it and I should just suck it up, no pun intended, but even though it feels really, really, really good—"

"It does?"

"Best sex you've ever had, times ten."

"Best sex I've ever had, or you've ever had?"

"Har-har."

"Well, there's a pretty big difference."

"Shut up! Besides, it doesn't matter. I still don't like the idea of it. Drinking someone's blood . . . ech."

"I don't blame you, Bets, but you have to," she said earnestly. "What if you get sick?"

"I don't think I can. But I can't put it off much longer, either. I haven't fed in a while. I'm unbelievably thirsty." My tongue felt like a little dry lump in my mouth. "You wouldn't believe how thirsty."

She shied away from me like a nervous horse. "Forget it! I'll kick ass for you, I'll throw money at you, I'll fight creditors for you, I'll buy your house to keep it away from the Ant, I'll help you defeat the forces of evil, but I'm not lunch!"

"Calm down before you have a stroke. I was thinking about the two guys who are following us."

"What two guys?" She started to crane her neck.

"Don't look, for God's sake. You'll tip them off."

"What two guys?" she asked, looking exaggeratedly casual.

"The two who followed us into the movie theater, loitered near the snack stand, then followed us into the movie, and were right behind us when we left."

"Wow. You saw all that?"

"More like smelled."

"Maybe they just want to pick us up. You know, for a date or something."

I snorted.

"It's not outside the realm of possibility," she said dryly. "I mean, people do go on dates. Besides you, I mean."

"I know, but these two smell like dried semen and pancakes. I'm pretty sure they're looking for trouble."

"Did the dried jizz tip you off, or the pancakes?" She was trying to joke, but her voice cracked on pancakes. "Should I call nine-one-one?" she asked, digging into her purse for her cell phone.

"No. Don't worry, Jess. I'd never let anyone hurt you. Especially not these two pukes. Just a minute." I swung around to face them. They probably thought they'd been moving quietly. "Back off, boys. We're in no mood."

"Give us the purses, bitch."

"Jeez, can't you count? She's the only one carrying a purse. And technically it's not a purse, it's a handbag."

"What's the difference?" Jessica asked curiously. I could tell she was taking heart at my complete lack of fear. Either that, or she was easily distracted. No, that was me.

"Well, a purse is more like a bag, and a handbag usually doesn't have a handle. I know it seems complicated, but it's really—"

"Bitches, gimmee your shit *now*."

I scowled at the interruption. Muggers were so rude! "No."

They both blinked at me. They were roughly the same height, a couple inches taller than me, and much broader through the shoulders. Neither of them had made acquaintance with soap nor razor in the past few days, and they reeked of desperation and trapped anger. And they were hungry. Starving, actually. Well, I could relate.

Jessica was unconsciously clutching her handbag—not her purse—to her chest and was watching the three of us like a spectator at a sporting event. She hadn't backed up, though—she was glued to my side. If I hadn't adored her before, I would have now. She was frightened, but she wouldn't run.

"Why don't you guys get lost?" I suggested, while they were still pondering my refusal. Clearly this was the point where the woman in question handed everything over and then submitted to rape. They weren't sure how else to proceed. "You don't want to mess with us."

"Yeah," Jessica echoed loyally. "You don't want to mess with us."

"I mean, we'll fight, you'll lose, and then I'll have to eat you, which sucks because you're both just filthy. I mean, ech! It's called deodorant, gentlemen. It's not hard to find."

That was the end of the chitchat as they both charged me at once. I heard Jessica squeak and jump out of the way, which was smart, because the fur was about to fly. I was still reluctant to—er—what was the military term? Engage? But now it was out of my hands.

I was pretty nonconfrontational in life. I never liked to fight, unless it was a good old-fashioned catfight with lots of insulting nicknames. I certainly wasn't used to getting physical. But it was time to try to get over that, as well as my weird (for a vampire) aversion to drinking blood. If not for my sake, then for my friend's.

I'm sure they were moving very fast, but to me it looked like they were charging me through knee-deep molasses. I caught the wrist of the smellier one and yanked him past me, hard. He smacked into the alley wall and crumpled to a heap on the filthy floor. The other one I caught by the neck, shook like a terrier shakes a rat, then briskly bonked his forehead with mine. He sagged in my grip, unconscious. Thank goodness! The last thing I needed was this guy trying to hump me while I drank.

"Don't look, ith groth," I told Jessica, and then I sank my fangs into his neck.

He was gross, he was disgusting, he reeked, and it was just fine. His blood wasn't gross. His blood was like sweetly potent burgundy. His whiskers rasped against my cheek as I drank my fill. It was over in less than a minute.

I let go of him right about the time Jessica stopped throwing up. "I told you not to look," I said, hurrying over to her, licking the blood off my rapidly retracting fangs. I pulled her away from the wall she'd leaned against—yuck. It was so slimy, it shined. "Why'd you look?"

"It wasn't that. I mean, I looked, but it wasn't bad. There was hardly any blood. You know, because you drank—" She made a "hurp-hurp" sound and I stepped back in case she wasn't done barfing.

"I'm sorry," I said miserably. "I shouldn't have fed in front of you."

She straightened up and said with a familiar snap, "Don't

be sorry. It was just that it was so fast." She looked up at me, her forehead shiny with sweat. "I mean, my adrenaline barely had time to get moving and it was scary but you weren't scared and then one of them was flying through the air and then it was over. I think it was more that than anything else."

"Oh. Are you all right?"

"I'm fine." She straightened up and added firmly, "Too much bad movie popcorn."

"I know it was stale," I said dryly, "but it wasn't that bad."

"I'm used to gourmet popcorn."

I laughed. "Jess, you're one in a billion."

"Fucking A right. Keep it in mind." She shoved her hand in mine as we stepped around our would-be assailants. Her palm was almost as cold as mine, and sweaty. I squeezed, and she squeezed back.

"Um, Betsy, is that guy going to end up like Nick?"

Good question. I thought about it. "I don't know. I don't think so. I mean, Nick liked me before. So the feeding— me biting him—meant more than it did . . . or should have, I guess is the way to say it. And it didn't seem to affect Marc. But this guy is a stranger."

"You're talking through your ass. You have no idea."

"None," I said glumly. "Thus Vampire 101 with Sinclair." We went home.

Chapter 23

"HERE I am, just wandering down a deserted street in the middle of the night. I hope I don't run into any trouble. Goodness, that would just ruin my whole evening." I strolled and hummed, trying to project Innocent Victim. I was certainly dressed for it—red linen A-line skirt, white blouse, red Ferragamos. Last year's, but it was dark in the alley—who'd know?

Five minutes went by, and my feet were killing me. "This is stupid!" I yelled to the shadows where Sinclair was lurking. "I'm not a goddamned worm on a hook. I gave up watching *Seinfeld* reruns for this? It's—aaiigh!"

Someone threw a brick wall on top of me—at least, that's what it felt like—and we hit the dirt—literally! Stupid Lake Street . . . filthy even after it rains. I smacked whoever it was on the side of the head and my hand instantly went numb. It was like slapping a brick. A dirty brick. I felt him slam my shoulders into the ground, and then I saw a flash of—fangs?

I shrieked like a fire alarm. Stupid Sinclair and his stupid Vamp 101! His big plan was to teach me more stalking, but I bet he didn't expect a vampire to grab me.

I articulated this stream of consciousness with, "Stupid!"

"Pretty," the thing that needed mouthwash crooned. "Don't scream anymore."

"Ha! I haven't even gotten warmed up! And cripes, do you need a bath." His mouth flashed down and I managed to get my arm up in time. He bit me anyway and I yowled. "Stop it stop it stop it!"

He licked his lips thoughtfully and stared down at me. He had shoulder-length hair that had last been washed when Bush was president . . . the *other* Bush. His eyes were the color of dirt, his cheeks were scattered with pockmarks, and his denim shirt had holes in the breast pockets. Still, that was no reason to let yourself go.

"What, Laundromats aren't open at night?" I griped.

"Who are you?" he asked at last, looking vaguely puzzled. "You're delicious, and fast, but you're not a vamp—"

He quit talking as he was jerked off me. I looked up to see Sinclair holding him off the ground by the scruff of the neck. I half expected him to start scolding my attacker. Bad undead nightstalker! Naughty!

I climbed painfully to my feet. "Finally," I said. "What were you waiting for, violins?"

The guy who'd jumped me was scary, but Sinclair was all towering fury in his black overcoat with flashing eyes. He swung, and the vampire went sailing into the nearest brick wall.

Quick as thought, Sinclair was there, picking him up off the ground and shaking him like a rat, then swinging again. He flew through the air with the greatest of ease and smashed into a Dumpster.

Sinclair picked him up *again*—I could barely follow this, he was moving so quickly—and again there was a *whoosh,* and a *thud.*

"This is the queen."

Whoosh! Smack!

"*My* queen."

Whoosh! Smash!

"Never touch her."

Whoosh! It was like being in a twisted Batman rerun. Blam! Smash!

"*Never* touch her."

"Okay, that's enough!" I yelled. My would-be blood-sucker was a huddled, bloody, garbage-y mess. The last toss had thrown him inside the Dumpster, and I jumped in front of it. Sinclair grabbed my shoulders and pushed me aside, but I clung like a limpet. "All right, okay, ease up. He made a mistake, let's not spread him into the road like undead jelly."

"He hurt you," Sinclair snarled. Literally snarled—his upper lip lifted away from his teeth and everything. "He bit you without permission."

"Hello, whose bright idea was this, anyway? And it's not like I'm walking around wearing a crown. He had no idea who I was." Shit, *I* had no idea who I was. "Just . . . calm down, okay? Take a breath. Take ten. You're really freaking me out."

He stared down at me. "You need to rid yourself of this tender heart."

"Hey, I'm hard as nails, chum. I just don't like the *noise,* is all." Not to mention the *thud-squish* every time the vamp hit something solid.

"He hurt you," Sinclair repeated stonily.

I held up my arm. "Oh, barely, you big mommy. See? It's practically all healed anyway. Having to smell him was a lot more traumatic. Did you *see* the state of his shirt? Yech."

He stared at the chubby flesh of the underside of my arm (note to self: do more curls), then gently took it in his big hands. He held my arm thoughtfully for a moment, then pressed his lips to the wound.

"Uh." Why did I feel that tickling touch between my legs? He was nowhere near my legs.

He lapped up the fast-drying blood, then pressed a kiss to the rapidly healing wound.

"Er." I realized I was leaning closer to him, when I should have been throwing him into the Dumpster with the other one. His dark head was bent over my arm and I itched to run my fingers through his hair. "Sinclair. Could you. Uh. Not do that?"

He was pulling me closer to him.

"Please?"

He was bending his head over mine, and I could see the savage flash of his fangs in the lone streetlight.

"Pretty please with blood on top?"

He kissed me so hard I was pulled up to my tiptoes, forced to cling to his shoulders for balance. This hurt (stupid pumps!), but I didn't care. His tongue swept into my mouth and I tasted my own blood. This was as provocative as if Sinclair had suddenly stripped down to his privates in the alley.

I had fistfuls of his coat and was kissing him back. I could feel my mouth get crowded and knew my fangs had come out . . . in response to my own blood, how fucked up was that?

Kissing Sinclair was like making out with a sexy timber wolf—he was licking my fangs and nipping me lightly and growling under his breath and it was . . . oh, it was really something.

Why wasn't I scared? I was in an alley with two vampires, making out with a very bad man who was a lot bigger and stronger than I was. Someone who hadn't exactly asked for this kiss—just took what he liked. What was the matter with me? Why was I still kissing him? And why was I still having this internal monologue?

Sinclair had left my mouth, which felt rudely swollen, and was trailing kisses down the side of my neck. I could hear myself gasping—a good trick, since I hardly ever had to breathe.

He was cuddling me into his chest and kissing my neck and stroking my back, and I was loving every second of it. There was a split-second pause and then Sinclair moved in for a bite.

Luckily, half a second was all I needed. I let go of his coat and staggered backward, and when he reached for me, I grabbed his hand and pulled him past me, hard. He smacked into the wall behind us, bounced off, and whirled to face me.

"Making out ith one thing," I tried not to gasp, "but none of that thtuff."

"Mmmmm." He touched his mouth, bemused. His fangs were gone. Damn it! How'd he do that? "What's wrong with your voice?"

"Nothing." Let's—no. What can I say without s's? "I want to go home now," I said carefully. "I have had enough for one night."

"You didn't learn much," he pointed out.

Just that you're about the best kisser in the world.

"More than you think," I replied.

Chapter 24

$\mathcal{I}$ woke (*rose?*) to see Sinclair standing over me. This was not the best way for me to start the day, which I believe I put across by screaming like a girl in the third grade.

"And a fine evening it is," he said by way of reply. He was splendidly dressed in black pants, a black mock turtleneck, and a black jacket. He was holding a glass of plum wine in one hand, and had his other hand buried in his pocket up to the wrist. He was *muy* suave, damn him, and I had the fleeting thought that he looked like a vampiric James Bond.

On Nostro and his minions, the all-black thing looked like a cliché. But Sinclair made it seem as though he was the one who started the trend, so on him it looked good.

It wasn't fair. I had to die to meet someone really fabulous, and it was someone I couldn't stand. I had no idea if I didn't like him because I wanted to jump his bones, or because he was an arrogant snot. Or both.

"You've gotta stop hovering over me when I wake up," I groaned, throwing back the covers and standing. His eyebrows arched at my pajamas—cream, with a pattern of salmon sushi and tuna rolls—but, thankfully, he didn't comment. "Seriously. You're gonna give me a heart attack one of these days."

"You slept well?"

"Like the dead," I chortled.

He leaned in close. This was extremely disturbing. What was more disturbing was how I wanted to grab him by the ears and plant one on that sinful mouth.

"Could you not crowd me the second I get up?" I bitched.

He ignored me. "I quite enjoyed our little . . . interlude last night."

"You would. Can you please do me a favor and at least ask before we lock lips?"

"No," he said carelessly.

I ground my teeth and shoved past him. He trailed after me like a big, muscular puppy. "Why in the world are you going into the bathroom?"

"Habit," I said, and shut the door in his face. Then locked it for good measure.

After my early evening ablutions, such as they were, I walked into the kitchen to see Sinclair listening politely to Marc, who was explaining how he'd saved dozens of lives in one measly ER shift.

"—and then all the other docs were like, 'no way, man, it can't be done,' and I'm all 'dudes, step back, I'll do it and damn the consequences,' and they're all, 'we're getting the hospital administrator, man,' and I'm all 'dammit, dudes, this boy will die without my help,' and they're all—"

"I thought you were doing paperwork last night," I said. "You know, catching up on your charts. Filing. Stuff like that."

Marc gave me a good glare for interrupting the fantasy. "This happened after I got caught up," he said stiffly.

"Sure it did. Why are you here?" I asked Sinclair.

"Who cares?" Marc asked. "Stay as long as you want."

"That was *not* an official invitation," I said quickly.

"Tina and Dennis and I require your services. Things are escalating with . . . a certain other party."

"You mean old Noseo is finally making a move?"

Sinclair also glared, clearly not caring for the way I blurted out vampire biz to mere mortals. "In a word, yes. We can discuss the subject further en route."

"Oh, come on, Sinclair," I whined, "why do I have to get involved? I just got up and now I have to rush off to the mansion of sin? Besides, I've got stuff to do today. Tonight, I mean."

"Stuff?"

"Yeah. I haven't been to the bookstore all week—the one time I got near it I got snatched away to that creepy mausoleum—*and* I need a pedicure. And I have to get some new clothes, because I don't have a lot of evening wear and these days I'm all about evening wear. Plus, it's practically summer and I haven't even *looked* at bathing suits. What's the matter?"

Sinclair had been rubbing his forehead, as if a killer migraine had just sunk its claws into his brain. "Elizabeth, Elizabeth. You are so young you make me tired."

Marc laughed.

"Uh . . . thank you? Anyway, I've got places to go, and your house is nowhere on the list."

"I must insist."

"Oh, jeez!"

"Probably vamp politics take precedence over a foot massage," Marc said between gulps of coffee.

"Oh, as if *you* know. Stay out of this."

Sinclair cleared his throat before Marc and I started throwing things at each other. "Your friend is correct."

"Dammit, dammit! Like I have any interest in this at all," I griped. "Because to be brutally honest—"

"Which you never are," Sinclair interrupted.

"—it's all so damned dumb. It is! I bet you think so, too, but you'll never admit it."

"No, never," he agreed.

"I can't think of a more annoying way to spend the evening," I griped. I hated, hated, *hated* having a plan for the evening only to find it completely trashed by someone else's stupid agenda. *Hated*. "I really can't!"

"Neither can I," Sinclair said dryly.

"You hush up. Do I at least have time for some juice?"

"If you hadn't taken five minutes to complain, we might have."

"*Fine.*" I resisted the urge to kick one of the table legs. "Guess we'd better get going, get this over with. I—wait." I cocked my head toward the front door and saw Sinclair was doing the same thing.

"Cut that out," Marc ordered. "You guys are giving me the creeps. You look like a pair of golden retrievers."

"Someone is coming."

"It's—I think—" A tentative rap on my front door. I hurried over to open it. My father stood on the front step. "It's my dad!" I said aloud, both for Sinclair and Marc's benefit, and because I was *very* surprised.

"Hello, Betsy." He tried a smile. It didn't quite fit. "All right if I come in?"

I stepped back, pleased to see him while cursing his timing. He'd had all week to visit, and he picked now?

"Sure, come on in. Dad, this is my roommate, Marc, and this is my—uh—my—"

"Eric Sinclair," he said, extending a hand to be shaken. "A great pleasure."

"Meetcha," my dad mumbled, shaking Sinclair's hand as quickly as he could and then dropping it like a trout. "Um, Betsy, could we—?" He motioned toward the back of the house.

"Oh, sure. Guys, we'll be right back."

"Nice to meet you," Marc said.

"Time is our enemy," Sinclair added. Like any woman who'd hit the big three-oh didn't know *that*.

Back in my bedroom, I shoved my dry cleaning pile on the floor, clearing a space for my father to sit down. But he remained standing. He didn't look so good, either. He'd always been a handsome guy, and now that his thinning dark brown hair was liberally flecked with salt and pepper, he was right out of central casting for Distinguished Gentlemen. The Armani didn't hurt, either. But it didn't hide the crow's feet, nor did it cover up the red-rimmed eyes and lines of exhaustion around his mouth.

"What's up, Dad?" I sat down on my bed and rubbed my hands together. I could count on one hand how often he'd visited me. This did not bode well. "Everything all right at home?"

"Well, no. That's why I—your stepmother and I—well, I needed to talk to you."

"About?"

He blinked at me, and then burst out, "What do you think? You're dead, Betsy. We were at the funeral."

"No you weren't," I said automatically, trying to figure out where he was going with this. "It was canceled because I'd gone on walkabout."

"I know," he said bitterly.

"Really? Because it seems like a few of the details have slipped your mind."

He shook his head hard, like there was a fly buzzing around his ear. "You look like my daughter, and you've got her smart mouth, but Elizabeth is dead. My daughter is dead."

"Dad, I'm *right here.*"

"And we have to move on," he continued stubbornly. "With our lives and—and things. So stay away, Betsy. Go be dead."

He started to walk to the door, but I was off the bed in a flash, had crossed the room and clapped my hand on his shoulder and pulled him away from the door in about half a second. I shoved him toward the chair, ignoring his frightened gasp.

"You've had your say—such as it is. Now it's your turn to listen to me." Had I ever been so mad? Right now, it was hard to remember. I shoved my hands into my pockets. I didn't trust them. They wanted to fly to my father's face and pull the skin off in strips. They wanted to grab his throat and tear it open. "I always knew, deep down, you were a coward. You're famous for taking the easy way instead of the right way. At work, at home, with your wives—you always avoided conflict and took the low road. Well, I managed to love you anyway. But I'm not letting you do this."

"Elizabeth—please—" He was cringing away from me. I realized I was looming over him like a blond bird of prey, and backed up.

"I'm going to be at your place for Easter dinner. As scheduled. It's been like that for years, remember? *You* set it up. Mom got me for New Year's; you got me for Easter; Mom got me for Memorial Day weekend; you got me for the Fourth of July. Just because I was too stubborn to stay dead doesn't mean your wife is getting out of baking a ham this year. Assuming she can find the fucking stove."

I jerked him out of the chair and propelled him toward the door. "I'll see you on Easter, Dad. And don't lock me out, either. Trust me on this." I hissed the last bit directly in his ear. "You wouldn't like it."

I knew I sounded mean and tough, and I was glad, but I wanted to burst into tears. I always knew he was weak, but I assumed he'd at least be happy I wasn't dead.

Sinclair was still on his feet when I hauled my dad into the kitchen. "Ah, Mr. Taylor," he said politely, as if his damned supervamp hearing hadn't picked up every word. "Allow me to see you out." He seized my father by the collar, crossed the room, and tossed him out the door like a naughty puppy. Then he shut the door with a satisfying bang.

Marc was staring at me. "What's wrong with your eyes?"

"What are you talking about?" I asked irritably.

"They're . . . they're all red. The whites are blood red."

"My contacts are bothering me," I snapped.

"But you don't wear—"

Sinclair had come close and was also peering into my face. "Hmm."

"Oh, cut that out," I snapped. "God, I am *so* pissed off right now!" I felt like I could pick up the entire house and throw it down the block. Or wear knockoffs! No, that was just my rage talking.

Marc was leaning as far away from me as he could. I had the impression it was completely unconscious. "You're upset? How come?" he asked innocently.

"Give me a break. I know you must have heard."

"Well . . . it was kind of loud . . ." He smiled sympathetically. "What are you going to do?"

"Worry about it later. Are we going, or what?" I practically yelled at Sinclair.

"We are."

"Good night, Marc, you eavesdropping floozy."

"Knock 'em dead, Oh Majestic Queen of the Narcissistic Undead."

"As far as royal titles go," I said, following Sinclair out the door, "that one stinks."

On the way to the car, Sinclair tried. He really did. "Ah, Elizabeth, do you wish—?"

"I wish not to talk about it is what I wish, and I *really* wish you hadn't heard the whole damned thing."

"I apologize."

I waved a hand irritably and climbed into the passenger seat. "It's nothing new. You know? This behavior of his? Absolutely typical." I flipped the mirror down. My eyes were their usual blue-green. Marc must be snorting coffee grounds again. "I guess I never outgrew waiting for him to be a better man."

"Perhaps if you give him some time . . ."

"He's got two weeks. Then it's Easter. But for now, I guess we have bigger fish to fry."

He looked at me for a long moment, then smiled. "Yes, we do. But for now, I think you're remarkably brave."

"Oh, don't start with me. I could not be less in the mood."

But his comment cheered me up a little.

"I *won't*."

"But you must."

"No!"

"Are you so anxious for Nostro to gain more power?"

"Why does this have anything to do with me?"

"You know why. We've risked ourselves for you, Majesty, many times."

"Thanks, but nobody asked you to. *I* didn't ask you to."

"You were foretold."

"Enough with that!" I was close to panic. I had thought this would be more Vamp 101, but instead it was an advanced course: "Why Betsy Has to Help Us Overthrow the Most Obnoxious Vampire in Four Centuries."

That's why they were so interested in me. Not just because I was the Queen, but because I was the Queen who brought all the tribes together, who ruled them as one. Like the speaker of the House, only way more bloodthirsty. More Book of the Dead crap, which Tina had been reading to me all night. It was like attending Bible school in hell.

I should have known not feeding with them would be a mistake. It was all very casual . . . in addition to Sinclair's harem, several "friends" lived at the mansion: women for him and Tina, men for Dennis. Any one of them (or any three of them) would have jumped at the chance to be my dinner, but the whole group-meal thing freaked me out. As did the blood-sucking thing, frankly.

Unfortunately, they were mighty impressed when I passed up the chance to feed. Too impressed. Between that and not burning to death the other day, everyone in the house was convinced I was the Queen. Except the Queen herself, of course.

"Elizabeth." I blinked and noticed Sinclair was snapping his fingers in front of my face. "I've been calling your name for thirty seconds. Did you have some sort of attention disorder before you rose? You seem to have a difficult time paying attention."

I batted his hand away. "Never mind. Not only am I not El Vampiro Chosen One, or whatever, but I'm barely a vampire."

"You should probably make that feminine," Tina suggested gently. "La Vampira."

"This is no time for a language lesson," I said irritably. "Anyway, whoever you guys think I am—"

"Whomever," Sinclair said with a smirk.

"—I'm not her."

"She's got us there," Dennis said apologetically. "She really is a terrible vampire. Too dumb to go up in flames in sunlight, and not nearly ruthless enough."

"Shut up, Dennis. Although you've got a point," I added grudgingly.

We were in one of Sinclair's living rooms. He had three that I knew of. And probably his very own morgue in the basement. It was late—close to midnight. So, lunchtime, in vampire time. Tina, Dennis, and Sinclair had been taking turns explaining how the four of us were going to knock Nostro's block off. I wasn't buying it.

"Look, you guys. I'm a secretary." Whose father preferred her to stay dead. *Oh, stop that. Stay focused.* "If you need me to type a bunch of memos calling for Noseo's resignation, I'm your girl. You got a stack of filing you need taken care of before we can kick ass, bring it on. You want some office supplies? I'll fill out the paperwork in triplicate. But I'm not a kingmaker."

"You—" Tina began, but I cut her off.

"Shit, I'm a little new to the game to be choosing sides and overthrowing tyrants. A week ago I was still installing Netscape Navigator!"

"This pains me as much as it does you, Elizabeth," Sinclair said, picking up his wineglass and taking a distracted sip. "A woman of your erratic temperament would not have been my first choice. More damning, you are young—young when you died, and as a vampire you're a positive infant. But how much more do you need to see to believe?"

I sniffed. "Quite a bit more, actually."

He pointed to the Book of the Dead, which had its own nifty little cherry wood stand next to the fireplace. I'd been tempted to boot it into the flames more than once this evening. "Our book—our Bible, if you will—tells of a female vampire who will not be burned by the sun, who can control her thirst, who has dominion over beasts—"

"They're just dumb dogs!"

"—who is still beloved by God—which is why you can wear a cross around your neck."

"Still not buyin' it," I said stubbornly. "Coincidence."

"You can do all these things, Elizabeth. And what's more, you are yourself—I don't doubt that the woman before me is much the same as the twit who breathed a month ago."

"Hey!"

"You're vain, you think constantly of your own pleasure, you like your pretty things, you're fond of your creature comforts . . ."

"Oh, you're one to talk, Satin Sheet Boy!"

He remained unruffled, though Dennis had to force his laugh into a cough. "You have remained *you*. This is the most definitive proof . . . you can think of others—friends and strangers alike—before your own needs. Most vampires would drink from their own grandmothers if thirsty enough. Plus, people react to your charisma."

Tina and Dennis nodded, and I blurted, "But I don't have any char—"

"Do you really think if Dr. Marc had met just any vampire, he would have allowed her to feed from him, taken a meal with her, then moved into her home and done everything to help her?"

"That's different, that's—"

"Different, yes, but more than you know. He instantly wanted to be with you, and never mind the fact that he is not oriented to your sex."

"Oriented to my—now you're just getting weird."

"Your friend Jessica never once was frightened of you—correct? Not only did the book foretell your unique abilities, not only do we vampires know who you truly are, but ordinary people feel it, too."

"Marc's a nice guy who wanted to hang out with me, is all," I said defensively. "And Jessica's like a sister to me—of course she wouldn't be scared." But even as I said it, it didn't ring true. My own father was afraid of me—but not Jessica. Marc was ready to throw himself to a messy death—and now he was plotting with Jessica on ways to make me help the world. In the space of a week. *Less* than a week.

"Elizabeth, as difficult as you are finding this to believe, you were meant to help us destroy Nostro. To bring peace. That will benefit all of us, vampires and humans alike."

"But—"

"Your friends *and* your parents. If you are the queen," he added slyly, "you can be sure no one will turn your mother into a midnight snack."

I jumped up. "Is that a threat?"

"Of course not. Even now, Nostro could be sending the Fiends to your mother's house. He's very, very angry with you. Of course," he added, no doubt guessing I was ready to bolt from the room and put Mom up in a Super 8, "I made arrangements for her to leave the state yesterday."

"You . . . how?"

"I was very persuasive," he said, and smiled. It wasn't one of his sneaky nasty smiles, either, but a sunny grin that made him look years younger. "Never fear, she who bore you is safe. And quite a fascinating woman, I might add— she instantly guessed I was a vampire and, for a refreshing change, didn't scream the house down. She did, however, threaten to brain me with a gold-plated candelabra if I 'tried any funny stuff.' " He turned to Tina. "By the way, I promised her you would come by for tea some night . . . she has several questions about the war."

"Oh, the war," Tina said, rolling her eyes. She was sitting cross-legged by the fireplace and looked just as cute as a bug in a pink blouse and white capri pants. "That's all academics ever want to talk about. 'What was the Civil War *really* like? What did you think of General Grant? Did the slaves really want to be freed?' Ugh. Not to mention, I'm too young to remember! But no one listens."

I relaxed slightly. As much as I could ever relax in this place, anyway. I believed Sinclair. Don't ask me how I knew, but it was plain he was telling the truth. (Also, I wanted to go along on that tea party . . . I had a few questions myself.)

Mom was safe. But for how long?

And it was nice of him not to bring up my father with the others. It was embarrassing enough that Marc and Sinclair knew my dad didn't want me around. Which is why this whole queen thing was so *weird*. I mean, my *father* doesn't want me, but eighty zillion vampires do? Give me a break.

It wasn't fair. I didn't ask for this, and I didn't deserve it, either. But I didn't say so out loud. Nobody promised fair. I knew that by the time I was in junior high.

They were all staring at me like undead cats, so I

cleared my throat and asked a question. "Does—does Nostro think I'm the Queen?"

"No. He thinks you are a rare vampire, the kind born strong, but he discounts all things in the Book of the Dead—he must, else he'd have to believe in his own downfall."

"So, why does he care?"

"Oh, he wants you," Tina put in quickly. "You think vampires are born strong every day? You think vampires *rise* every day?"

"Good point," I said. "I haven't the faintest idea how to make a vampire. It's probably not very easy."

All three nodded, and the effect was so compelling I almost nodded myself. Tina continued, "Nostro is a huge believer in population control, because it's a lot easier to control the vampires who are already here. Which reminds me, Betsy . . . why *are* you here?"

"Well, Sinclair showed up at my house—uninvited, as usual—and we—"

"No," Dennis interrupted. "Who turned you? What happened? We've all been wondering."

"We understand if it's a delicate subject," Tina added sympathetically. "Getting murdered isn't much fun."

"Oh, that. I wasn't murdered. I got run over by a car."

"An Aztek," Sinclair said, looking amused.

"Yeah. How'd you know? Never mind. Anyway, I woke up dead. But I was attacked a few months ago—I think by the Fiends."

Dead silence (really!) while they digested this. "So . . . the Fiends attacked you—were set on you, maybe? But you didn't die. Then, months later, you *do* die . . . but not by vampire. And now you're . . ." She trailed off.

"Has any vampire ever risen who wasn't turned first?" I forced a laugh. "I mean, it can't be *that* unusual . . . right?"

Another silence.

"Uh . . . guys?"

"How is it that the Fiends didn't kill you?" Sinclair asked.

"Beats me! They all swoooped down on me like rabid flying squirrels, and I beat them off with my purse and yelled myself hoarse."

Tina hid a smile, but Sinclair was all Mr. Interrogator. "Where were you?"

"Outside Khan's. You know that Mongolian barbecue place?" Mmm . . . Mongolian barbecue. When I'd been alive, I would have killed for a plate of sautéed beef and noodles, with extra garlic sauce. "It's on 494, right across—"

"Mongolian barbecue?" Dennis asked.

"Garlic," Sinclair said.

"Of course!" This from Tina. "Did you like garlic in life, Majesty?"

"What's not to like?"

"Well, that explains it."

"Not to *me*."

"Some of the legends are true," Sinclair said. "We're actually allergic to garlic. It acts as a blood coagulant."

I must have looked as blank as I felt, because Dennis elaborated. "Tough to suck someone's blood if it's all clotted."

"Yuck!"

"Sorry," Sinclair said, sounding anything but. "I imagine you stepped from the restaurant, positively reeking of the stinking rose, and they couldn't bear it. But that doesn't explain . . ."

"Maybe the Book of the Dead . . ." Tina began.

Sinclair shook his head. "There isn't time. But it's interesting, isn't it?"

"Quite."

"What?" I said. "I figure, I was in the wrong place at the wrong time . . . twice."

"Or the right time," Sinclair said quietly.

"Cut it out, Mr. Mysterious, you're creeping me out. Let's talk about the Fiends. What is their deal? Are they rabid vampires or overgrown bats or what?"

"It's an . . . experiment, I guess you could say," Dennis said reluctantly. I saw Sinclair's lips go thin with distaste as Dennis continued. "Nostro's experiment. No one is quite sure what the purpose is. I'd say the kindest thing to do would be to stake the lot of them."

"Agreed," Sinclair said firmly.

"Whoa, wait!" I held my hands up like a referee. "It's probably not their fault. That crummy Nostro probably made them that way. Maybe they can be fixed."

"Again with that tender heart," Sinclair observed.

"Again, blow me. That's not it. I just—uh—think they might be good minions. That's all." Plus, they were just so pitiful. I should have hated them for landing me in this mess, but mostly I felt sorry for them. Poor ugly smelly things. Give them a bath, cut their hair, let them gambol in the park like undead puppies (on leashes, of course), who knew?

"We do need to get moving on this," Tina said, doing me the courtesy of ignoring my lameass minion excuse. "Nostro's given us a deadline."

"I still don't know why he cares so much," I grumbled.

"It's all about pride, Elizabeth. And an ego that monstrous won't face possible defeat . . . from any quarter."

Oh, yeah, *Nostro's* ego was huge. "Look, we can't just storm the castle, right? He's got a zillion followers."

"Cut off the head," Tina said coolly, "and the body will die. Better yet, the body will throw its allegiance to you."

I grimaced. "Swell."

"Majes—Betsy, I know this must be difficult." Tina gave me a warm, understanding smile, which instantly put me on my guard. "As you said, you've only been one of us for not quite a week. You should be adjusting to your new life, not plotting to overthrow despots."

"Yeah, exactly! *Thank* you!"

"But time is running out," she went on implacably. "We need your assistance on this as soon as possible."

"Why? What's the rush? He's been around for a few hundred years, but you guys have to kick him off the anthill this week?"

Tina and Sinclair exchanged a glance. "We just do," Sinclair said smoothly. "We'd like you to co-op—"

"Whoa, hold up there, Dr. Deception! What's going on? What haven't you triad of retards told me?"

"Oh, now, *that* was uncalled for," Dennis sniffed.

"Ah . . ." Tina looked at Sinclair again, who shrugged. "Well, Majesty, when I was at Nostro's—when I gave you the locket and we left his territory without permission—"

"Permission?" I practically shrieked. "He threw us in the pit to murder us!"

". . . that was essentially an act of war. And Nostro has given us until tonight to bring you back."

"Or?"

"Slaughter."

"We think he's getting ready to go to war anyway," Sinclair added. "You're his excuse. He has been growing steadily more unstable over the centuries. He came so close, so many times. If you read the books, you know."

Skimmed the books was more like it. But yes, I knew.

Sinclair was still droning away. "He is all bottomless ambition and cruelty. Now that he finally has a kingdom, he is wildly paranoid of anything that might take his power. You frightened him badly when you couldn't be hurt by holy water, and more than anything, he can't let anyone see his fear."

Well, that made a lot of sense. The biggest bullies in the world were the ones who were scared to death of losing their power base—like my former boss. And Saddam Hussein. And Nostro.

Still, I wasn't sure what I could do to help them. I mean, I wanted to help. I'm pretty sure I wanted to help. But what could somebody like me do? Sure, these days I could take on a couple of would-be rapists, but a horde of evil vampires loyal to Nostro? Only if I could bring along a flamethrower.

I slowly tuned back in. Sinclair was *still* talking!

"I've tolerated him because, until now, we kept out of each other's way. I overlooked his misdeeds and he overlooked my freedom."

"That was swell of both of you."

"But your presence changes things. Complicates them, too. The time for apathy is done."

The time for what is what? Oh, who cared. "I don't know about all that, but I'll tell you what—I never thought I'd be scared of a bald guy in a bad tux. I mean, he's sincerely crazy. It's not just the numbers he controls and the bad clothes and the bald spot . . . he's creepy."

Tina nodded. "Probably a sociopath in life. Either that, or he went mad after he died."

"Yuck-o. And his history! Cripes, it's enough to give a troll nightmares. He doesn't care who gets hurt or killed as long as he can be the boss. He started trying shit when he was barely dead, you believe that? I'd never trust him to do the right thing on his own—and I sure don't trust him to do right by the vampires he forced to be on his side."

Sinclair nodded. Tina looked relieved and I could practically read her mind: *By jove, I think she's finally getting it!*

"He's always regretted letting me go," Sinclair explained. "Knowing me and mine aren't under his control eats at him. One day we'll come downstairs and find two hundred vampires waiting for us. I would prefer," he added dryly, "to be proactive."

"Yeah, but shouldn't we . . . I dunno . . . spy out the land, or something? I mean, we can't just go charging over there. Right? Hello? Anybody? Right?"

Tina spread her hands. "We're out of time."

"Oh, this is crazy! You guys are sincerely nuts, you know that?"

Sinclair cleared his throat. "Dennis?"

Instantly Dennis jumped to his feet, hurried out, and a moment later returned carrying four plain white shoeboxes stacked in his arms like a little column. He set the boxes down, then left again, and came back with six more. He spread them out in front of me and began flipping the tops off the lids.

I screamed. With joy. Flip! A pair of lavender Manolo Blahniks with the dearest three-quarter-inch heel was revealed. Flip! A pair of Beverly Feldman sandals in butter-cup yellow. Flip! An ice-blue pair of L'Autre Chose sling-backs. Flip, flip! *Two* pairs of Manolo Blahniks, one black lace, one red leather. Gold Salvatore Ferragamo heels . . .

I moaned and pounced on them. They were all in my size! I tugged off my tennis shoes, yanked so hard my socks went flying over my shoulder, and slipped into the yellow sandals. Bliss!

"Mirror!"

"I can't believe we're bribing our future queen with designer shoes," Tina muttered.

"Mirror!"

"Over there," Sinclair said, and pointed. There was a mir-ror above the fireplace. I dragged a chair over, plucked the mirror from the wall, hopped down, and leaned it against the far wall. I peered at the reflection of my feet. I felt like Dorothy in the ruby slippers. Like Princess Di during her coronation! Like—like a vampire queen with a truly out-standing shoe collection.

"I have *never* looked more amazing."

Tina made gagging noises, which I, being a well-shod lady, ignored. I twirled in front of the mirror. "These are wonderful! How did you do it?"

"I saw your shoe collection when we were at the house the other night, and had my ladyfriends do some shopping while we slept. Mitzi sends her regards."

I made a mental note to check the rest of the shoes for scorpions. "These are so, so pretty! Amazing!"

"What a pity you can't keep them." Sinclair sighed theatrically and motioned to Dennis, who started putting the lids back on the boxes.

I nearly wept. "What? Why?"

"Well . . . you're so adamant about not helping us. Not being a kingmaker, as you put it. Very wise and practical, but of course useless for our purposes. Thus, Plan B must be put into effect. Perhaps Nostro will accept these as a token of peace."

Nostro? Nostro putting his nasty clammy fingers all over the buttery soft suede, the delicate embroidery? Giving them to Shanara? Using them for the Fiends to play fetch? Never, never, never!

"Don't touch! Bad vampire!" I snapped, and Dennis froze in mid-reach. "I'll help you. *And* I get to keep the shoes."

"Done and done," Sinclair said, his lips twitching as he tried not to smirk. I'm sure he thought I was vain and weak-willed and a complete idiot. Who cared? I was a vain weak-willed idiot with the season's coolest shoes.

I jumped off the chair, flung my arms around Sinclair, and kissed him full on the mouth. He was so surprised I nearly toppled him over. "Do I get a bonus pair if we settle Noseo's hash tonight?" I asked, peeking up into his dark, dark eyes.

"Kiss me like that again, and I'll buy you a baker's dozen."

I let go of him like he was hot—which he totally was, I mean, oofta!—and not without regret. Hugging Sinclair was like hugging a great smelling rock. I was willing to bet even the guy's earlobes were well-defined. "Better not tempt me. Okay, so, let's go get the bad guy."

"It's that simple?" Tina asked. She shook her head at us, grinning as Sinclair, with a bemused expression, touched his mouth.

"A deal's a deal," I said, admiring my pretty feet. Of

course, we all knew it wasn't just about the shoes. At least, not entirely. Probably not entirely. But Sinclair was no fool—this was all the excuse I needed to do what seemed more and more like the right thing.

Plus, it made me feel loads better. Dad didn't want me around, but these guys needed me. Maybe I was worth something after all.

"YOU'RE going to help them overthrow Nostro, then." Dennis effortlessly lifted a full case of wine up onto the bar. I'd asked for more plum wine, and Tina and Sinclair were downstairs plotting strategy.

I had no interest in the gory details . . . I suspected they wanted me along more for the power of my pseudostatus ("We've got the queen on our side . . . surrender!") than any actual fighting or tactical skill I'd bring. At least I hoped so.

"Sure. Look: It's not that I want Nostro to stay in charge, because I don't. He's a crazy creep and he treats his Fiends badly and all the other vampires are scared shitless of him, except maybe for Sinclair. I mean, when the monsters are scared of somebody, they should probably get rid of that person, right?"

"Right . . ."

"I mean, did you read that book about him? Cripes, it read like a history text from hell. You read it, right?"

"Many times."

"Right. Yuck. Anyway, I was just hoping to stay out of vamp politics. But if they can use me to kick him off the mountain . . ." (and if I can increase my shoe collection by eighty percent) ". . . it seems like the thing to do." Hearing it out loud, I was actually more than half convinced. Okay, a quarter convinced. But progress was being made.

"What if you change your mind?"

I caught on. Dennis was leery about my one-eighty. Didn't want me chickening out when it got nasty, and leaving his friends high and dry. Completely understandable. I rushed to put him at ease. "Don't worry. I won't. Besides, I owe that creep for siccing Shanara on my friends. *And* for throwing me in the pit with the Fiends. And for the Maypole Massacre of sixteen-whatever."

"But you weren't even alive then."

"So? You *did* say you read the book, right? I almost threw up reading about that little dosey-do-and-swing-your-partners. Creep."

"He is a temperamental man."

"Yeah, like a rabid wolverine is temperamental. And frankly, I'm sick of worrying about running into some of his tribe, sick of being dragged to his various hideouts . . . yuck! This week would have been hard enough without being caught up in Nostro's war." Reciting his sins against me was getting me worked up. I vibrated with righteous indignation. This was starting to seem like a really good idea, and never mind the shoes.

"So your mind's definitely made up?"

"One . . . hundred . . . percent," I said emphatically. "You don't have to worry."

"Actually," he sighed, "now's when I have to *start* worrying."

I had just enough time to wonder why he was swinging a case full of wine bottles at my head when everything went bright white, then dead black.

Chapter 25

WHEN I woke up I was horribly thirsty. I knew why. Dennis, that traitor schmuck asshole, had hit me so hard if I'd been alive it would have killed me. At the least, he probably shattered my skull.

While I was dead to the world my body healed itself, and now I was unbelievably thirsty. I cursed myself for turning down Sinclair's offer to share dinner. It had seemed so morally upright at the time, and now it was probably going to get me really dead.

I opened my eyes. I was in a windowless, cellar-like room. Cement walls and floors. Chilly as hell. Smelled like mud.

"Asshole," I croaked. I cleared my throat and tried again. "Asshole, you there?"

"Yes," Dennis said, with the nerve to sound apologetic. He straightened up from whatever he'd been doing and gave the chains around my ankles an experimental tug. "Sorry about that. For what it's worth, this is really for the best."

"Oh, okay, then I'll just stop worrying. Jackass. Just tell me *why*, you jerk. Sinclair takes good care of you. He's the good guy. I heard you and Tina have been with him for, like, forty or fifty years. So why the double cross? Were you always an asshole, or is it, like, a recent development?"

"Nostro is my sire." Dennis said that with a simple dignity that made me want to kick him. "Everything I am is because of him. When he asked me, years ago, to go to his enemy, how could I refuse?"

I tugged at my wrists. Nope. Don't know what I was chained up with—titanium? cold silly putty?—but it wasn't budging. Wrists above my head, ankles spread wide . . . and this slab was really cold.

"Let me get this straight, jackass. Nostro ripped you open like a trout and drank from you like a fountain while you were alive, and from that you've inferred that you *owe* him?"

"It wasn't like that. He released me. He freed me."

"He turned you into a Happy Meal, and you were dumb enough to think it was a favor."

Dennis slammed the knife I hadn't noticed he was holding into my upper thigh. Yow! There was a 'chunk!' as the tip embedded itself in the slab of stone I was chained to. It stung like crazy, but I wouldn't give him the satisfaction of yelling.

"Ow!"

Okay, I'd give him a little satisfaction.

"I've been stabbed before," I sneered. "Barely a week ago, in fact. *And* I've been audited, *and* I come from a broken home. In short—no offense, shorty—you don't scare me." I wriggled again . . . no go. In addition to the indignity of being clobbered with a case of plum wine, dragged to the bad guy's hideout, and chained to a stone altar (did Nostro keep a hack scriptwriter on the payroll to feed him clichés?), my clothes were in tatters. Dennis had been busy with the knife before I woke up. "You'll have to do a lot better than that."

Dennis bent close to me, so close I could see the candlelight gleaming off the gel he used in his hair. It occurred to me for the first time that he looked like an egret. "I threw all your new shoes into the fire," he whispered in my ear.

I howled in agony and thrashed ineffectually. "Bastard!" I wept. "You'll pay for that."

He straightened up, lips tightening with disgust. "You make my gorge rise."

"I bet you say that to all the girls, you overly moussed nancy boy."

"You care more about your pretty fripperies than anything else."

Fripperies? That was a new one. And it was tough to argue, so I kept my mouth shut.

"*You,* the queen? Never. Not while I'm around to serve my master."

"I agree with you! Hey, I never asked to be the queen, jerkweed. It wasn't exactly on my top-ten list of things I'd like to do after I die. I'll renounce the throne, okay? I never wanted it anyway. And I'm pretty sure it's not mine."

"It won't work. They'll never let you alone." He sighed. We both knew "they" meant Sinclair and Nostro. "It doesn't matter now. You'll die. You'll never rule."

"Let me get this straight. You believe I'm the queen, even though your master doesn't. And the Book of the Dead was right, but you just don't like it? Not *too* pathetic."

I wriggled again, and again to no avail. I tried to ignore the image of lavender Blahniks roasting in the fire, turning black, the room filling with the stench of burning leather . . .

He snapped his fingers before my eyes. "Pay attention!"

"Whaaaaaaat?" I whined.

"Yes, you're right. I tolerated your presence when you had no intention of helping Eric Sinclair. When you were a cute young vamp for him to coax to his bed."

"Ewwww! Fat chance, shiny head!"

"What a liar you are! The entire staff knew you slept together."

"Yeah, but we just slept together. We didn't—you know. *Sleep* together."

He shook himself, as if the effort of talking to me was tiring him out. "However. The moment you changed your mind about joining with them to overthrow my sire—"

"It was clobberin' time. Yeah, I got that part. Listen, answer a question—how the hell do you kill a vampire? Specifically, how will you kill *me*? You can't toss me into the Pit this time, because the Fiends are scared of me. And you can't lock me in a room facing east and wait for the sun to do your dirty work. A holy water facial won't do it, either. Not that I would mind a facial, so if you think it'll work, go right ahead. Just go easy on the exfoliants; I have combination skin."

Dennis's brow wrinkled and he looked worried for a brief moment. Then he shrugged. He gestured to his left, and I looked where he was pointing. There were several swords propped in the corner. "Cutting off your pretty little head should do the job nicely."

I grimaced. Yeah, I didn't really see any way around that one. "You know something? I'm actually kind of glad it's come to this. Me or Nostro. Because I am sick to *death* of this shit—the kidnappings and the treachery and whose side are you on . . . it's so fucking childish. How can any of you stand it?"

"We know our place." He jerked the knife out of my thigh. "A pity you never did."

"Nobody tells me my place, needle dick." Hey, maybe I was the queen! At the least, I wasn't in a hurry to get on my knees for Nostro *or* Sinclair. Bully for me. "Well, chatting's been fun, but we should probably get to it, right?"

He blinked down at me. "You *want* to have your head cut off?"

"Anything's better than lying here freezing my ass off

and smelling your mousse. Suave is all wrong for your hair type, by the way. It's so fine and girly, you should use Aveda products."

He smoothed his sleek head and glared. "Never mind your silly jokes."

"I never joke about hair. Say, where *is* your psycho boss, anyway? I would've expected him to be in here with forty or fifty of his closest underlings, gloating nonstop and looking like a designer's bad dream."

Dennis grimaced. He probably thought it was a smile. My, my, he was getting good and pissed. Excellent. "He's killing Eric and Tina. But he'll be right along."

I quit smirking. Part of the reason I'd been so flip, other than the complete absurdity of my situation—I mean, come on, half naked and chained to a stone slab?—was because I'd been expecting Sinclair and Tina to rescue me.

"The day Nostro gets the drop on Eric Sinclair is the day I . . ." I couldn't think of anything absurd enough.

". . . get your head cut off," Dennis finished helpfully.

"Hmm."

"I signaled my tribemates, of course, as soon as I had you. Some of us brought you here, and the rest set fire to Sinclair's mansion. We had the place surrounded, and anyone who made it out would have gotten a holy water shower. Not that anyone made it out, I'm sure. Vampires are incredibly flammable."

I thrashed ineffectually. That gorgeous Victorian, crammed with priceless antiques. And my new shoes! And Sinclair and Tina, and their ladyfriends, and the guys who were in Dennis's harem! *And my new shoes!*

And it was all my fault. Sinclair and Nostro had been at war for years and years, but it was my presence that escalated the situation. They might have stayed at an impasse for another five hundred years. But for me. It was all my fault. And I'd never get the chance to make up for it.

"You fucker," I said helplessly.

"All's fair in love and etcetera," he said lightly. "I'm afraid I can't wait much longer for Nostro. Best to dispatch you and commence celebrating. Also—aaagggkkk!"

I stared. There was a long metal blade sticking out of the side of his neck. Just as my eyes had adjusted to what they were seeing, Tina wrenched the sword out of Dennis's neck and swung again. He ducked away from her. She instantly turned and smashed the sword down on the chains between my ankles. And again. And—

"Watch it!"

She spun and ducked, and Dennis's blade went whistling over her head. I kicked and wrenched as hard as I could. She'd weakened the chains, and if I could just—

I kicked free of the chains and flipped my feet over my head, quickly, to gain momentum. Now I was standing behind where my head and shoulders had just been. The chains were biting into my wrists, which probably would have broken if I'd tried this last week, but I ignored the pain. I braced my weight against the altar and pulled as hard as I could. There was a tearing—both of my flesh and the chains—and then I was free.

"Oh you fucker," I said breathlessly, turning. Seeing Tina alive helped me focus my anger on the lost shoes. Mighty would be my wrath! "Now you're gonna get—yuck!"

Tina was kneeling before me, holding Dennis's head by the hair and very plainly—yeerrgh!—trying to hand it to me.

"Majesty, I beg your forgiveness for the indignity you suffered and offer you the head of our enemy as—"

"Put that thing down," I said impatiently. "I can't talk to you when you're shaking his head like a damned maraca."

"At once, Majesty."

She dropped his head and I yanked her to her feet and gave her a hearty smack on the mouth. "That's for that whole nick-of-time thing you seem to have going on." I kissed her again. "And that's for cutting off the bad guy's head." *Mwah!*

"And that's for being so cute." *Mwah!* "And that's for not being dead."

"Sure," she said, fending me off with an elbow. "You're all affectionate *now,* when there's no time. Let's go."

"Where's Sinclair?"

"We split up to find you. Since that honor was mine, I imagine he ran across Nostro instead. Now I have to show you to your people."

"My—" She tossed me a sword, then grabbed my arm and pulled me along so fast I stumbled to keep up. "My people?" I glanced back, more than happy to be leaving the cheerless little room I had wondered if I would die (again) in. Dennis's headless body was twitching all over, then shuddered and went still. It didn't turn into dust and whirl away, just lay there like a puppet with its strings cut. And its head missing. Another gross-out in a week filled with indignities.

"The only reason I got back here in time to help you was because I told Nostro's people you were the foretold queen."

"Yeah, but how'd you avoid being barbecued? Dennis seemed pretty sure you guys were ashes."

"The underground tunnel, of course," she said with bare impatience. She was still hauling me along like a sack of feed. "They blocked it, but poorly. Under normal circumstances they might have succeeded, but Sinclair was so angry you'd been taken—I've never seen him like that." She shivered a little. But maybe it was just the chilly room temperature.

"That Sinclair. A big mushy pussycat at heart. So everyone got out okay? That's so great! I mean, I thought you guys were all toast. Literally toast."

"Ah . . ."

"I was so bummed when he told me you were all dead! But I kept talking and stalling anyway, you know, like they do in the movies. It was all I could think of to do. And look how great it worked out!"

Tina looked at me for a moment that probably seemed longer than it was. "Karen's dead, Betsy."

I stopped short. Karen, burnt up? Burnt to *death?* And for what? Status and territory. Boys and their toys, fighting over *land*. Even though this city was plenty big enough for two head vamps.

What a fucking waste.

"I'm sorry," Tina continued when I didn't say anything. "I know you liked her. If it helps, the feeling was definitely mutual. You were all she could talk about the last couple days."

"I—I didn't know her. She made me tea, is all. But she was nice. I thought she was really nice." I was too numb from all the rapid events to say much more, but beneath the numbness I could feel anger stirring. It reminded me of black water moving under ice in January. When I stopped feeling numb, someone was going to pay through the nose.

"So . . . so you guys got out and came here. Piece of cake, right?"

Tina snorted. "Dennis left too quickly with you—a rather large error of judgment, which I'm happy to say cost him his head. Eric and I got out and came straight here, yes. I was prepared to fight my way in, but instead told everyone I ran across that I was there for their salvation and our queen. And, for a wonder, no one tried to stop me. That tells me they might be ready. If I show you to them, they may yet turn on him."

"Think so?"

"No," she said grimly, hauling me up a flight of stairs, "they're too frightened. To stop me, but also to help me. Though I've noticed that when we put you into the equation, interesting things happen. So we'll try. And if I see Nostro I'm going to have his balls for breakfast."

"Thanks for the visual."

"There!" She pointed; there was one hell of a brawl going on in the ballroom. At least thirty people were fighting and kicking and punching and clawing at each other. Nostro and Sinclair were probably in the middle of it.

Tina dropped my hand and waded in. I turned and ran. Past the ballroom, past the swimming pool, all the way outside. I knew what I wanted—now how to find it?

I stared in confusion at the grounds—just my luck, Nostro lived on a damn half acre. Where the hell were the . . .?

A teeny, red-haired vamp scuttled around the corner right into me, clearly having no interest in joining the fight. When I seized her arm, she squeaked and shrank away from me.

"Where are the Fiends?"

"Please—don't—don't hurt me—"

"The Fiends, twit! Where does your boss keep them? I know they're locked up around here somewhere."

She blinked up at me and when I got a good look at her I felt sick. She couldn't have been more than fourteen when she died. She weighed, at rough guess, about eighty pounds. Scrawny as hell and with the biggest brown eyes I'd seen outside of a pet shop. A teenager forever. Perpetually in the throes of adolescence . . . I couldn't think of a worse fate. Sinclair was a pig, but he wasn't killing teenage girls. If I hadn't already made up my made to fight Nostro until he was in little pieces on the ground, I would have done it in that instant.

"Their cage is behind the barn," she said in a small voice. "I can show you just pleasedonthurtme."

"Relax, cutie. This is shaping up to be your lucky day. You'd better stick with me. It's dangerous in there."

"Oh, dangerous? Tell me! I thought the Korean War was bad." She relaxed a little as she realized I wasn't going to use my sword to cut off her head. "I'm—I'm Alice, by the way."

"I'm the queen, Alice." Korean War, let's see, that made her—forty? Fifty? I'd never get used to this. "It's nice to meet you, now come on."

The Fiends sent up an ungodly racket when they saw

me. I groped and was relieved to find Dennis hadn't relieved me of my cross . . . he probably hadn't been able to touch it, or had forgotten about it. I flashed the Fiends and they went into their abject cringing routine.

Was I really going to do this? It could backfire and then I'd be fucked.

Well, I was fucked anyway. I took a deep breath, smashed the locks on their cage with a few punches—it hurt, but nothing compared to what it felt like when I tore my wrists free of the chains—and stepped inside.

"Uh . . . your—uh—your queenness . . . majesty or whatever . . . I wouldn't . . ."

"It's okay." At least, I hoped it was okay. If not, I wouldn't have long to regret my actions. About five seconds, tops. "I think I've got their number." I held out my torn, bleeding wrists. I could still bleed from a pulse point, it seemed, just not as well as when I was alive, and not as hot. The flow was thick and sluggish, and such a dark red it was almost black. It made me feel slightly sick to look at it.

The Fiends crawled toward me, sniffed me up and down, then lapped from my wrists. Their breath was cold. Their smell was indescribably bad.

"What are these things?"

"They're vampires who weren't allowed to feed when they rose." Alice was clutching the bars and watching us with big scared eyes. "They become animals when that happens . . . they lose their sense of self. All they know is hunger."

"Huh." I felt sorrier than ever for them—they'd once been *people!* Even if they were the authors of my new existence, I still felt bad. "Is it fixable?"

Long pause. "I . . . I don't know. No one has ever been able to—I mean, my lord Nostro wouldn't—"

"Say no more. And stop calling him lord. Alice, this appears to be working. So I'm gonna try something and probably I won't get killed. But I might. Hey, it wouldn't be the first time. Anyway, are you with me or against me? It's okay if you want to stay out here."

"Stay out here? And let you go in alone?" She looked woefully tempted for a moment, then shook herself like a dog. "I think—I think I'm with you." She stared at me through the bars, then lowered her gaze to my cross, which was still giving off its brave little light. It reminded me of the Snoopy nightlight I'd had as a kid.

She looked away, then looked back, as if drawn. She brought one hand up to cover her eyes, but it stopped halfway to her face. "You're so brave and . . . and strong. And it must be right, for how can you—"

"Today, Alice, could you answer my question today? I still have to save my new friends, kill Nostro, and get home in time to set the VCR to tape Martha Stewart."

"I'm your servant," she said softly. She squeezed the bars so hard I heard metal groan. "Forever and ever. Because you were nice and because you would have let me stay outside. Even if I won't. Stay outside, I mean."

"Swell. I think." Would I ever get used to people instantly throwing me their allegiance? Lord, I hoped not. "Here's the plan."

Chapter 26

W ITH Alice and the Fiends hot on my heels, we charged back up to the house and ran into the ballroom. The Fiends appeared willing to follow wherever I led, which was a huge relief—I didn't relish trying to keep them all on leashes. And they hadn't tried to devour me, which was a big plus.

Nostro and Sinclair were still going at it so fast I couldn't see a thing. Just blurs of fists and the thuds of blows landing. For a wonder, no one else was fighting; most of the others were up against the far wall listening to Tina. Everybody looked scared.

"—not interfere! Whoever wins this will be our new lord and you *cannot* interfere! That was our law when mortals were still cringing in caves!"

Cringing in caves? Oh, very nice. Trust Tina to leave us all with a disturbing mental image.

"*I'm* going to interfere," I said hotly. Behind me, the Fiends were crowding me and rubbing against my legs. It was comforting, if unbelievably creepy. I pointed to the blur that was Nostro and Sinclair. "Sic him!"

Yowling and snarling, the Fiends rushed forward. So did I—in time to grab Sinclair and pull him out of the way. As quick as I was, a Fiend still knocked us sprawling and I caught a blow from Nostro that made my ears ring. I shook it off and rolled over on my back to watch.

You know in cartoon fights how all you can see is smoke and whirling limbs and stars and birds and stuff? That's what it was like. The Fiends were snarling, Nostro was screaming, and we were all staring. Then the Fiends started making wet noises, Nostro was gurgling, and then the wet noises continued. But Nostro wasn't making any more noise. Tough to do, when you're in pieces.

Dead silence, broken by me whispering, "That was for Karen, you piece of shit."

Nobody said anything. Thirty vampires were staring at me, and the triumph on Tina's face was almost too much to bear. Her face was like a beacon, beautiful and terrible at once. She didn't look like a preppy cheerleader just then, but like a warrior claiming victory.

I turned to Sinclair, sure one of his coolly sarcastic remarks would break the tension, and then I screamed and scrambled to my feet and tried not to puke, all at the same time.

Sinclair was horribly burned. Most of his left side was a blackened mess. All his hair was gone. His eyelids were gone. I could see the veins in the skin of his left arm as they tried to sluggishly move blood through his dead system.

Incredibly, he was *smiling*. His cracked lips pulled back and his teeth looked even whiter and longer against his burned flesh. I should have been terrified, but this was someone I knew, even if it was someone I didn't like. Much. I think.

"Victory," he whispered.

I burst into tears. Well, as much as I could, now that I couldn't cry real tears. Sure, victory, but at what cost? And what happened next? He was burned because of me, he'd lost his home—and most of his flesh!—because of me. Karen was dead because of me. And instead of recovering or feeding to get better or staying the hell out of the fight, he'd come running to my rescue.

"Sinclair—Eric—what—"

"He needs to feed," Tina said as Sinclair put a hand out and steadied himself by clutching her arm. "From you. Your blood will heal him quicker than anything else."

"It's a queen thing?"

She nodded, but she wasn't looking at me. Her eyes were big and sad as she stared at Eric. "Water will help—it facilitates the healing process. Then—"

"Right, right, you can explain later." I remembered them dumping Detective Nick into the shower. At the time I thought it was to get him clean. Now I wondered.

I gingerly grabbed Eric's right hand and pulled him over my back, fireman style.

"Oh, now I must object to this," he said to the back of my thigh.

"Shut up, Eric. It'll feel better soon . . . you must be in agony . . ."

"The lengths I must go to so you'll call me by my first name."

I made a sound, a cross between a laugh and a sob. Sinclair was an unwieldly package, but, thanks to my vamp strength, light as a page of paper. "Shut up, you jerk. This is no time for your nasty sarcasm."

"You must tell me how you turned the Fiends's loyalty from Nostro," he said conversationally, upside down. God, this was the weirdest day ever! "Such a thing has never been done before."

"You're always so nosy."

"You're always so intriguing."

I carried him to the pool room, then stood him up and steadied him.

"Really, this is all so unnecess—"

"Take a breath," I said, standing so close to the edge my toes dangled over.

"Why?" Sinclair asked, reasonably enough. Then we plunged into the deep end.

I had time to think, *oh, shit, the chlorine's going to sting him like hell*, but from the look of relief on his face, that wasn't the case at all.

I wondered why water helped. Was it because we were technically dehydrated? We didn't sweat or pee or cry, but dump us into a pool and everything got better? Weird. Maybe there was an explanation in one of those giant boring books I'd borrowed.

Sinclair pulled me to him gently and I went willingly enough. He was a blackened husk because of me; the least I could do was let him regain strength from my blood. I only hoped I had enough to do him any good. Was drinking from a vampire—from me?—so very different from drinking from someone who was still alive? Tina seemed to think so, and that was good enough for me.

I shivered as his teeth broke the flesh of my throat. It was like losing my vamp virginity. The water was deliciously cool as we floated near the bottom of the deep end. It was odd and delightful to be completely comfortable underwater and not have to worry about coming up for air.

I had my hands on his shoulders and, while he drank from me, I could feel the skin on his back knitting together, reforming from nothing, could feel him regaining strength and vitality. He stroked my back as he fed, which was lovely—soothing and sweet and comfortable. *Being* lunch felt as good as *drinking* lunch. This was the pleasure of being taken, of being held by a creature much larger and stronger, a creature who could break you if he chose, but wouldn't. (Probably.) It was the pure pleasure of surrender.

Eric pulled back and smiled with a look of pure uncomplicated happiness. His face healed itself while I watched in shocked amazement. So fast, it was happening so fast! Then he was whole, perfect—a completely gorgeous male specimen. With really big canines. It had taken less than five minutes.

I laughed underwater and nearly choked. He pulled me to him again, not nearly so gently this time, and then his mouth was covering mine, his tongue was rubbing against mine, and his arms were around me, pressing me against him.

We kissed for an hour . . . or so it felt. He pulled me free of my rags and I helped him out of the burned tatters he'd barely been wearing. Mindful that he couldn't bear the cross, I took it off and let it float away, making a mental note to retrieve it later. When I touched his throbbing, firm length I was glad I was floating and not standing—I doubt I'd have been able to keep my feet. He was huge and beautiful and I wanted every inch inside me.

I was tired of fighting my attraction to him, tired of pretending I didn't feel it in my stomach every time he smiled. Love? I didn't know. I'd never known anyone like Eric Sinclair, who thought I was a hopeless twit but had fought for me, lost everything for me, and secured a throne for me.

His lips closed over one of my nipples and he suckled gently. Then his tongue rasped across the firm peak and I had to remind myself not to gasp underwater. His hands were everywhere, kneading and stroking my back, my buttocks, my thighs. Then he released me and dove.

My back arched as I felt him part me with his thumbs, as I felt his tongue burrowing inside me. I stared blindly toward the pool's surface while his tongue stroked and teased and licked and stabbed, while his fingers restlessly kneaded my thighs.

I wrapped my legs around his head and seized a fistful of his hair, fairly grinding his face into me. The sensations from his lips and tongue, coupled with the sensual feeling of the water caressing every inch of me, were putting me into ecstatic overdrive.

Then I felt his fangs pierce me, felt him suck gently, drinking from the very center of me, and I spun away into orgasm. Spun? No, was shoved, *thrust* into orgasm, and I screamed silently, staring at the gorgeous light on the surface.

He reached up, found my waist, and pulled me down to him, kissing me every inch of the way until his mouth was covering mine again.

She's so beautiful she feels so good ah I can't I can't hold back I have to have her have to be inside her oh Elizabeth my darling my own oh oh oh . . .

I froze. I was hearing thoughts, but they sure weren't mine. And it wasn't like he was taking over my brain, it was more like I was . . . eavesdropping. Since when could I read his mind? Anyone's mind? Could he hear me?

Eric, I have a galloping case of VD, that's not going to be a problem, is it?

Nothing; he kept kissing me and was now sucking my lower lip into his mouth. I reached for him, found his enormous length, and stroked gently.

Now I have to now take her touch her now have her now oh please don't let me hurt her oh Elizabeth my luminous queen I'd die for you . . .

He pressed forward. I looped my legs around his waist—we were now drifting upside down—and slowly impaled myself on his length. It was tight—it was unbelievably tight—and splendid and amazing and wonderful.

I felt his hand in my hair, forcing my head up, and he watched my face as he came into me, inch by inch by inch.

Don't stop, I mouthed at him.

Ah sweetheart as if I could . . .

And still he came forward, kept pushing into me. He buried his face in my throat as he forced himself to enter with excruciating slowness, forced himself to hold back for fear of hurting me.

Which was all very nice, except I wanted to come again. Wanted to feel him all the way up inside me. Wanted to feel him in my *throat,* wanted to ride him until I was screaming and clawing, wanted to see his eyes roll up and feel him spasm against me. I wriggled closer and he shuddered; I bit him on the throat and he shoved, seating himself within me with one thrust.

I squirmed against him, enjoying the sensation of being pinned, impaled. Fucked.

No oh no don't don't I'll hurt hurt I'll hurt her ah ah AH AH ELIZABETH YOU FEEL SO GOOD . . .

I locked my ankles behind his back, dug my nails into his shoulders, and shoved back at him. I bit him again, on the other side, and he writhed against me. We thrust against each other . . .

Can't stop can't stop can't can't Elizabeth oh Elizabeth you feel alive to me you feel like no one else to me Elizabeth

. . . almost battling beneath the water, surging and thrusting and writhing against each other; his mouth found mine again and he kissed me so hard one of his canines pierced my lower lip.

MORE MORE MORE MORE MORE MORE MORE

I came so hard I saw spots—or maybe that was the pattern on the pool vent—came so hard I could feel myself clenching around him . . .

ELIZABETH! ELIZABETH! ELIZABETH!

. . . felt him shudder as he found his own release. It was—it was like being alive again!

His grip tightened, his tongue thrust even deeper into my mouth, and then he was relaxing, relaxing and slipping out of me, smaller and softer, but still formidable.

I started to pull away—float away, actually—but he grabbed me back and held me for a long moment while we drifted toward the surface. I couldn't hear him in my head anymore, which made me sad.

Love? I had no idea. But it had sure been something.

Chapter 27

$\mathcal{I}$ nearly yelled as my head broke the surface. The pool room was filled with dozens of vampires, all waiting patiently. I dove back down, swam around for a few minutes, found Sinclair's sister's cross—easier than I would have believed!—and put it back on. I lurked on the bottom of the pool for another minute, then gathered up my courage and swam back to the surface.

Yep, they were all still there. Nuts. I treaded water and tried to think about where I'd get some clothes. And about what they must have seen. They were all staring down at me and were completely expressionless. God knew what they were thinking. First dead, then a vampire, then a queen, now a whore. What a week!

Tina knelt by the pool and held up a robe. I swam to her and got out, let her help me into the robe—ewww, a polyester-cotton blend, but I was in no position to be picky—and got it belted in about half a nanosecond.

Sinclair, that shameless hussy, had no problems with

modesty. He simply lifted himself from the pool and stood before our audience, splendidly naked. While I stared, the teethmarks on his throat and shoulders healed. Nothing else happened, but I still stared.

"Behold," Tina said loudly, "your Queen and her consort!"

The assembled vampires cheered, but it was a subdued hoo-rah. More like a communal "Mm-hmm." They probably thought the new boss was the same as the old boss.

It was so obvious they were still afraid. I felt bad for them, but what could I do but try to prove I wasn't a balding sociopath? Maybe after they got to know me they wouldn't be scared anymore. And—wait a minute.

"Uh . . ." I raised a finger.

"Nostro is no more," Sinclair said sternly (and nudely). "The Fiends are under my Queen's command. As are all of you."

"Uh . . . Eric?"

"Any who do not wish to swear allegiance may leave now, tonight. We will not force your hand; you are free to come and go as you wish. Those dark days are over. But any who remain, and swear loyalty to her Majesty the Queen, will be under our protection so long as we live."

Consort?

"Consort?" I asked. I was having a hard time catching Tina's eye, all of a sudden, and why should that be? "Tina? Consort? What?"

Vampires all over the room were kneeling, were brushing their foreheads against the tile, but I had no eyes for them. And still, Tina wasn't looking at me. *"What's going on?"*

A few of the closer vamps cringed away from me—a good trick in mid-kneel—and Tina coughed, while Sinclair turned to give me a thoughtful look. Then he smiled at me. Why should his smile be scary now, of all times?

"Hello? Am I in the room? Is someone gonna answer me? Consort? What's going on?"

Tina coughed again. "We—ah—didn't get a chance to finish explaining the prophesies from the Book of the Dead. Because Dennis—and we just didn't."

"Soooooooo?"

"But you were foretold, and Nostro's downfall was foretold, and Eric being—uh—being your King was also—"

"What?" I could actually feel my eyes bulge. "What did you say?"

"She said Eric being your King was also," Alice piped up helpfully from somewhere behind me.

"Quiet, you. Tina, explain. *Now.*"

" *'And the first who shall noe the Queen as a husband noes his Wyfe after the fall of the usurper shall be the Queen's Consort and shall rule at her side for a thousand yeares.'* At least," she added, "that's as close as I can recall. It goes on in the same vein for quite a bit, no pun intended. I'll show you the appropriate passage when we get back."

"What?" I actually swayed on my feet. Sinclair steadied me. I yanked my arm away and nearly fell back into the pool. "I'm the queen and Sink Lair is the king? Since fucking when?"

"Since fucking," Sinclair said helpfully.

"Why didn't either of you tell me? Why didn't you warn me? For a thousand years? What?"

"Well," he who was on my permanent shit list said reasonably, "if I said, 'Elizabeth, dear heart, I want to make love to you, but just so you know, I'll come to the crown right after I come in you,' then I wouldn't have gotten to see you naked."

Tina accurately read the look on my face, because she quickly stepped in front of Sinclair and spread her arms protectively in front of him. The jerk just looked amused, and stared at me over the top of her head.

"That's not why, Majesty. You've touched him deeply, which is why he's being flip." Then, under her breath to Sinclair, "Cut it *out.*" She gave me a big, fake smile. "It was foretold, that's all. Just like your ascension to the throne. There's nothing any of us can do about it."

"Want to bet?"

Sinclair spread his arms wide. "Sweetest, you sound so cross. We have a coronation to plan, so put on a smile. Also, as soon as I rebuild my home, you'll move in, of course."

"Want to bet?"

"Well, perhaps later, then. After the . . . er . . . happy surprise has worn off."

"You said!" I jabbed a finger toward Tina's chest. She flinched, but held her ground. "You said if I became Queen I could get rid of Sinclair!"

"You wanted to get rid of me?" The asshole had the audacity to sound hurt.

"I didn't think Sinclair would end up being your consort," she said weakly, but I knew she was lying. She might consider me her queen, but Eric was her sun and moon, closer than any brother. What he wanted, she would get for him. She revered me, but she loved him. "But now—the book was right. It's been right about everything. And—and we just have to accept it, is all."

"Accept my ass!"

"Well, if you—" Sinclair began.

"You shut up. I'm going home!" I said loudly. I tightened the robe's belt. How was I going to do that? I had no keys, no car, no driver's license, and no underpants. Fortunately, I was too furious to care. "Both of you stay the hell away from me—*I mean it!"*

Tina bit her lip and stared at the floor, but Finklair smiled at me. "Impossible, my Queen. You and I have a kingdom to run."

Epilogue

So, I'm the queen of the dead. As if it's not hard enough adjusting to the fact that I killed the bad guy—and I'm not the only one amazed, believe me—now I'm a dead monarch. And the lout I'm hopelessly attracted to, yet despise, is my king. For all intents and purposes, we're stuck for the next thousand years. A thousand fucking years! We'll be running longer than *The Simpsons!* Every time I think about it I want to shove somebody—a specific somebody—through a wall.

A week ago my biggest problem had been losing my job. Ah, for the sweet freedom of those days. Now I had to worry about running a kingdom of vampires, keeping my hands off Sinclair (because, oh God, I still wanted him, would do just about anything to feel his hands and—other things—again), giving Tina the cold shoulder until I decided to forgive her, keeping Jessica and Marc from starting their new crime fighting business (HELP, Inc.), and helping thousands of vampires adjust to being in charge of their own destiny.

I also had to find time to rebuild my relationship—such as it was—with my father and the Ant. While it was convenient that they were pretending I wasn't an ambulatory dead girl, I couldn't let things go on like that. If I had to get used to my father's trophy wife, he could get used to my return from the dead.

Not to mention finding permanent suck buddies and a paying job—I was undead and unemployed, and couldn't live off Jessica's charity forever. The very idea was ridiculous. But convincing her of that was likely to be the most difficult task of all.

I put Alice in charge of the Fiends . . . they were still at Nostro's place, but they had more room to run, and hopefully some genius vamp would be able to fix them. I was resisting pressure from almost everyone to have them staked. It was tough saying no—it was tough getting used to the idea that I was in charge. I was the youngest vampire by several decades, and it was just too weird.

I'd insisted on giving Karen a proper funeral, which apparently went against all vamp rules. Like I gave a fuck. But I put my foot down, and it was surprisingly well attended. Not bad for a midnight service.

I didn't speak to Sinclair or Tina during the service, but took the urn home. It's sitting on my mantel right this minute. A reminder to me that collateral damage is never acceptable.

My mom was also at the service. She was completely taken with Sinclair. He really swept her off her feet when he swooped in like a dark angel to whisk her out of harm's way. She thinks the fact that Sinclair is the king is just dandy. I tried to explain his trickery, sneakiness, and out-and-out dishonesty—without actually mentioning the pool boinking—but it fell on totally deaf ears. "You know, Betsy, just because you're undead doesn't mean you have to be unwed."

Yeah, sure. I planned to *stay* unwed, for a thousand years to be exact. Having that wretch Sinclair as a consort was bad enough; I wasn't about to become the little undead woman.

I'd also run into Nick recently, in one of those funny coincidences that often happen in the suburbs—we both happened to be grocery shopping at the same Rainbow Foods.

He had looked a little better, and seemed only mildly surprised to see me in the fresh-squeezed juice department. He had no memory of reading about my death, or of our time together. So that was one worry off my list.

Now if I could just get Sinclair to quit dropping off pairs of designer shoes. In his last card he said he would drop off a pair a day until I forgave him. I'm up to fourteen pairs of Pradas, eight pairs of Manolos, and six Ferragamos.

Maybe I'll forgive him . . . eventually.

I'm still waiting for this season's red Jimmy Choo slides.

SOOKIE STACKHOUSE SHOULD HAVE KNOWN
THAT GETTING INTIMATELY INVOLVED WITH
A VAMPIRE WASN'T A GOOD IDEA . . .

Dead to the World

TURN THE PAGE AND TAKE A BITE OUT OF
THE LATEST BOOK IN CHARLAINE HARRIS'S
ACCLAIMED SOUTHERN VAMPIRE SERIES,
AND FIND OUT WHY THIS SEXY MYSTERY IS
GOING TO KNOCK 'EM DEAD. OR UNDEAD,
AS THE CASE MAY BE . . .

AVAILABLE IN HARDCOVER
FROM ACE BOOKS IN MAY 2004!

THE New Year's Eve party at Merlotte's Bar and Grill was finally, finally, over. Though the bar owner, Sam Merlotte, had asked all his staff to work that night, Holly, Arlene, and I were the only ones who'd responded. Charlsie Tooten had said she was too old to put up with the mess we had to endure on New Year's Eve, Danielle had long-standing plans to attend a fancy party with her steady boyfriend, and a new woman couldn't start for two days. I guess Arlene and Holly and I needed the money more than we needed a good time.

And I hadn't had any invitations to do anything else. At least when I'm working at Merlotte's, I'm a part of the scenery. That's a kind of acceptance.

I was sweeping up the shredded paper, and I reminded myself again not to comment to Sam on what a poor idea the bags of confetti had been, and even good-natured Sam was showing signs of wear and tear. It didn't seem fair to leave it all for Terry Bellefleur to clean, though sweeping and mopping the floors was his job.

Sam was counting the till money and bagging it up so he could go by the night deposit at the bank. He looked tired but pleased.

He flicked open his cell phone. "Kenya? You ready to take me to the bank? Okay, see you in a minute at the back door." Kenya, a police officer, often escorted Sam to the night deposit, especially after a big take like tonight's.

I was pleased with my money take, too. I had earned a lot in tips. I thought I might have gotten three hundred dollars or more—and I needed every penny. I would have enjoyed the prospect of totting up the money when I got home, if I'd been sure I had enough brains left to do it. The noise and chaos of the party, the constant runs to and from the bar and the serving hatch, the tremendous mess we'd had to clean up, the steady cacophony of all those brains . . . it had combined to exhaust me. Toward the end I'd been too tired to keep my poor mind protected, and lots of thoughts leaked through.

It's not easy being telepathic. Most often, it's not fun.

This evening had been worse than most. Not only had the bar patrons, almost all known to me for many years, been in uninhibited moods, but there'd been some news that lots of people were just dying to tell me.

"I hear yore boyfriend done gone to South America," a car salesman, Chuck Beecham, had said, malice gleaming in his eyes. "You gonna get mighty lonely out to your place without him."

"You offering to take his place, Chuck?" the man beside him at the bar had asked, and they both had a we're-men-together guffaw.

"Naw, Terrell," said the salesman. "I don't care for vampire leavings."

"You be polite, or you go out the door," I said steadily. I felt warmth at my back, and I knew my boss, Sam Merlotte, was looking at them over my shoulder.

"Trouble?" he asked.

"They were just about to apologize," I said, looking Chuck and Terrell in the eyes. They looked down at their beers.

"Sorry, Sookie," Chuck mumbled, and Terrell bobbed his head in agreement. I nodded, and turned to take care of another order. But they'd succeeded in hurting me.

Which was their goal.

I had an ache around my heart.

I was sure the general populace of Bon Temps, Louisiana, didn't know about our estrangement. Bill sure wasn't in the habit of blabbing his personal business around, and neither was I. Arlene and Tara knew a little about it, of course, since you have to tell your best friends when you've broken up with your guy, even if you have to leave out all the interesting details. (Like the fact that you'd killed the woman he left you for. Which I couldn't help. Really.) So anyone who told me Bill had gone out of the country, assuming I didn't know it yet, was just being malicious.

Arlene has often told me I am too nice for my own good, though I assure her I am not. (Tara never says that; maybe she knows me better?) I realized glumly that, sometime during this hectic evening, Arlene would hear about Bill's departure. Sure enough, within twenty minutes, she made her way through the crowd to pat me on the back. "You didn't need that cold bastard anyway," she said. "What did he ever do for you?"

I nodded weakly at her, to show how much I appreciated her support. But then a table called for two whiskey sours, two beers, and a gin and tonic, and I had to hustle, which was actually a welcome distraction. When I dropped off their drinks, I asked myself the same question. What had Bill ever done for me?

I delivered pitchers of beer to two tables before I could add it all up.

He'd introduced me to sex, which I really enjoyed.

Introduced me to a lot of other vampires, which I didn't. Saved my life, though when you thought about it, it wouldn't have been in danger if I hadn't been dating him in the first place. But I'd saved his back once or twice, so that debt was canceled. He'd called me "sweetheart," and at the time he'd meant it.

"Nothing," I muttered, as I mopped up a spilled piña colada, and handed one of our last clean bar towels to the woman who'd knocked it over, since a lot of it was still in her skirt. "He didn't do a thing for me." She smiled and nodded, obviously thinking I was commiserating with her. The place was too noisy to hear anything, anyway, which was lucky for me.

But I'd be glad when Bill got back. After all, he was my nearest neighbor. The community's older cemetery separated our properties, which lay along a parish road south of Bon Temps. I was out there all by myself, without Bill.

"Peru, I hear," my brother Jason said. He had his arm around his girl of the evening, a short, thin, dark twenty-one-year-old from somewhere way out in the sticks. (I'd carded her.) I gave her a close look. Jason didn't know it, but she was a shape-shifter of some kind. They're easy to spot. She was an attractive girl, but she changed into something with feathers or fur when the moon was full. I noticed Sam give her a hard glare when Jason's back was turned, to remind her to behave herself in his territory. She returned the glare, with interest. I had the feeling she didn't become a kitten, or a squirrel.

I thought of latching on to her brain and trying to read it, but shifter heads aren't easy. Shifter thoughts are kind of snarly and red, though every now and then you can get a good picture of emotions. Same with Weres.

Sam himself turns into a collie when the moon is bright and round. Sometimes he trots all the way over to my house, and I feed him a bowl of scraps and let him nap on my back porch, if the weather's good, or my living room, if the weather's poor. I don't let him in the bedroom anymore, because he wakes up naked—in which state he looks *very* nice, but I just don't need to be tempted by my boss.

The moon wasn't full tonight, so Jason would be safe. I decided not to say anything to him about his date. Everyone's got a secret or two. Her secret was just a little more colorful.

Besides my brother's date, and Sam of course, there were two other supernatural creatures in Merlotte's Bar that New Year's Eve. One was a magnificent woman at least six feet tall, with long rippling dark hair. Dressed to kill in a skin-tight, long-sleeved orange dress, she'd come in by herself, and she was in the process of meeting every guy in the bar. I didn't know what she was, but I knew from her brain pattern that she was not human. The other creature was a vampire, who'd come in with a group of young people, mostly in their early twenties. I didn't know any of them. Only a sideways glance by a few other revelers marked the presence of a vampire. It just went to show the change in attitude in the few years since the Great Revelation.

Almost three years ago, on the night of the Great Revelation, the vampires had gone on TV in every nation to announce their existence. It had been a night in which many of the world's assumptions had been knocked sideways and rearranged for good.

This coming-out party had been prompted by the Japanese development of a synthetic blood that can keep vamps satisfied nutritionally. Since the Great Revelation, the United States has undergone numerous political and social upheavals in the bumpy process of accommodating our newest citizens, who just happen to be dead. The vampires have a public face and a public explanation for their condition—they claim an allergy to sunlight and garlic causes severe metabolic changes—but I've seen the other side of the vampire world. My eyes now see a lot of things most human beings don't ever see. Ask me if this knowledge has made me happy.

No.

But I have to admit; the world is a more interesting place to me now. I'm by myself a lot (since I'm not exactly Norma Normal), so the extra food for thought has been welcome. The fear and danger haven't. I've seen the private face of vampires, and I've learned about Weres and shifters and other stuff. Weres and shifters prefer to stay in the shadows—for now—until they see how going public works out for the vamps.

See, I had all this to mull over while collecting tray after tray of glasses and mugs, and unloading and loading the dishwasher to help Tack, the new cook. (His real name is Alphonse Petacki. Can you be surprised he likes "Tack" better?) When our part of the cleanup was just about finished, and this long evening was finally over, I hugged Arlene and wished her a happy New Year, and she hugged me back. Holly's boyfriend was waiting for her at the employees' entrance at the back of the building, and Holly waved to us as she pulled on her coat and hurried out.

"What're your hopes for the New Year, ladies?" Sam asked. By that time, Kenya was leaning against the bar, waiting for him, her face calm and alert. Kenya ate lunch here pretty regularly with her partner, Kevin, who was as pale and thin as she was dark and rounded. Sam was putting the chairs up on the tables so Terry Bellefleur, who came in very early in the morning, could mop the floor.

"Good health and the right man," Arlene said dramatically, her hands fluttering over her heart, and we laughed. Arlene has found many men—and she's been married four times—but she's still looking for Mr. Right. I could "hear" Arlene thinking that Tack might be the one. I was startled; I hadn't even known she'd looked at him.

The surprise showed on my face, and in an uncertain voice Arlene said, "You think I should give up?"

"Hell, no," I said promptly, chiding myself for not guarding my expression better. It was just that I was so tired. "It'll be this year, for sure, Arlene." I smiled at Bon Temps's only black female police officer. "You have to have a wish for the New Year, Kenya. Or a resolution."

"I always wish for peace between men and women," Kenya said. "Make my job a lot easier. And my resolution is to bench-press one-forty."

"Wow," said Arlene. Her dyed red hair contrasted violently with Sam's natural curly red-gold as she gave him a quick hug. He wasn't much taller than Arlene—though she's at least five foot eight, herself, two inches taller than me. "I'm going to lose ten pounds, that's my resolution." We all laughed. That had been Arlene's resolution for the past four years. "What about you, Sam? Wishes and resolutions?" she asked.

"I have everything I need," he said, and I felt the blue wave of sincerity coming from him. "I resolve to stay on this course. The bar is doing great, I like living in my double-wide, and the people here are as good as people anywhere."

I turned to conceal my smile. That had been a pretty ambiguous statement. The people of Bon Temps were, indeed, as good as people anywhere.

"And you, Sookie?" he asked. Arlene, Kenya, and Sam were all looking at me. I hugged Arlene again, because I like to. I'm ten years younger—maybe more, though, since Arlene says she's thirty-six and I have my doubts—but we've been friends ever since we started working at Merlotte's together after Sam bought the bar, maybe five years now.

"Come on," Arlene said, coaxing me. Sam put his arm around me. Kenya smiled, but drifted away into the kitchen to have a few words with Tack.

Acting on impulse, I shared my wish. "I just hope to not be beaten up," I said, my weariness and the hour combining in a disastrous burst of honesty. "I don't want to go to the hospital. I don't want to see a doctor." I didn't want to have to ingest any vampire blood, either, which would cure you in a hurry but had various side effects. "So my resolution is to stay out of trouble," I said firmly.

Arlene looked pretty startled, and Sam looked—well, I couldn't tell about Sam. But since I'd hugged Arlene, I gave him a big hug, too, and felt the strength and warmth in his body. You think Sam's slight until you see him shirtless unloading boxes of supplies. He is really strong and built really smooth, and he has a high natural body temperature. I felt him kiss my hair, and then we were all saying good night to each other and walking out the back door. Sam's truck was parked in front of his trailer, which is set up behind Merlotte's Bar but at a right angle to it, but he climbed in Kenya's patrol car to ride to the bank. She'd bring him home, and then Sam would collapse. He'd been on his feet for hours, as had we all.

As Arlene and I unlocked our cars, I noticed Tack was waiting in his old pickup; I was willing to bet he was going to follow Arlene home.

With a last "Good night!" called through the chilly silence of the Louisiana night, we separated to begin our new years.

I turned off onto Hummingbird Road to go out to my place, which is about three miles southeast of the bar. The relief of finally being alone was immense, and I began to relax mentally. My headlights flashed past the close-packed trunks of the pines that formed the backbone of the lumber industry hereabouts.

The night was extremely dark and cold. There are no streetlights way out on the parish roads, of course. Creatures were not stirring, not by any means. Though I kept telling myself to be alert for deer crossing the road, I was driving on autopilot. My simple thoughts were filled with the plan of scrubbing my face and pulling on my warmest nightgown and climbing into my bed.

Something white appeared in the headlights of my old car.

I gasped, jolted out of my drowsy anticipation of warmth and silence.

A running man: At three in the morning on January first, he was running down the parish road, apparently running for his life.

I slowed down, trying to figure out a course of action. I was a lone unarmed woman. If something awful was pursuing him, it might get me, too. On the other hand, I couldn't let someone suffer if I could help. I had a moment to notice that the man was tall, blond, and clad only in blue jeans, before I pulled up by him. I put the car into park and leaned over to roll down the window on the passenger's side.

"Can I help you?" I called. He gave me a panicked glance and kept on running.

But in that moment I realized who he was. I leaped out of the car and took off after him.

"Eric!" I yelled. "It's me!"

He wheeled around then, hissing, his fangs fully out. I stopped so abruptly I swayed where I stood, my hands out in front of me in a gesture of peace. Of course, if Eric decided to attack, I was a dead woman. So much for being a Good Samaritan.

Why didn't Eric recognize me? I'd known him for many months. He was Bill's boss, in the complicated vampire hierarchy that I was beginning to learn. Eric was the sheriff of Area Five, and he was a vampire on the rise. He was also gorgeous and could kiss like a house afire, but that was not the most pertinent side of him right at the moment. Fangs and strong hands curved into claws were what I was seeing. Eric was in full alarm mode, but he seemed just as scared of me as I was of him. He didn't leap to attack.

"Stay back, woman," he warned me. His voice sounded like his throat was sore, raspy and raw.

"What are you doing out here?"

"Who are you?"

"You known darn good and well who I am. What's up with you? Why are you out here without your car?" Eric drove a sleek Corvette, which was simply Eric.

"You know me? Who am I?"

Well, that knocked me for a loop. He sure didn't sound like he was joking. I said cautiously, "Of course I know you, Eric. Unless you have an identical twin. You don't, right?"

"I don't know." His arms dropped, his fangs seemed to be retracting, and he straightened from his crouch, so I felt there'd been a definite improvement in the atmosphere of our encounter.

"You don't know if you have a brother?" I was pretty much at sea.

"No. I don't know. Eric is my name?" In the glare of my headlights, he looked just plain pitiful.

"Wow." I couldn't think of anything more helpful to say. "Eric Northman is the name you go by these days. Why are you out here?"

"I don't know that, either."

I was sensing a theme here. "For real? You don't remember anything?" I tried to get past being sure that at any second he'd grin down at me and explain everything and laugh, embroiling me in some trouble that would end in me . . . getting beaten up.

"For real." He took a step closer, and his bare white chest made me shiver with sympathetic goose bumps. I also realized (now that I wasn't terrified) how forlorn he looked. It was an expression I'd never seen on the confident Eric's face before, and it made me feel unaccountably sad.

"You know you're a vampire, right?"

"Yes." He seemed surprised that I asked. "And you are not."

"No, I'm real human, and I have to know you won't hurt me. Though you could have by now. But believe me, even if you don't remember it, we're sort of friends."

"I won't hurt you."

I reminded myself that probably hundreds and thousands of people had heard those very words before Eric ripped their throats out. But the fact is, vampires don't have to kill once they're past their first year. A sip here, a sip there, that's the norm. When he looked so lost, it was hard to remember he could dismember me with his bare hands.

I'd told Bill one time that the smart thing for aliens to do (when they invaded Earth) would be to arrive in the guise of lop-eared bunnies.

"Come get in my car before you freeze," I said. I was having that I'm-getting-sucked-in feeling again, but I didn't know what else to do.

"I do know you?" he said, as though he were hesitant about getting in a car with someone as formidable as a woman ten inches shorter, many pounds lighter, and a few centuries younger.

"Yes," I said, not able to restrain an edge of impatience. I wasn't too happy with myself, because I still half suspected I was being tricked for some unfathomable reason. "Now come on, Eric. I'm freezing, and so are you." Not that vampires seemed to feel temperature extremes, as a rule; but even Eric's skin looked goosey. The dead can freeze, of course. They'll survive it—they survive almost everything—but I understand it's pretty painful. "Oh my God, Eric, you're barefoot." I'd just noticed.

I took his hand; he let me get close enough for that. He let me lead him back to the car and stow him in the passenger seat. I told him to roll up the window as I went around to my side, and after a long minute of studying the mechanism, he did.

I reached in the backseat for an old afghan I keep there in the winter (for football games, etc.) and wrapped it around him. He wasn't shivering, of course, because he was a vampire—but I just couldn't stand to look at all that bare flesh in this temperature. I turned the heater on full blast (which, in my old car, isn't saying much).

Eric's exposed skin had never made me feel cold before—when I'd seen this much of Eric before, I'd felt anything *but*. I was giddy enough by now to laugh out loud, before I could censor my own thoughts.

He was startled, and looked at me sideways.

"You're the last person I expected to see," I said. "Were you coming out this way to see Bill? Because he's gone."

"Bill?"

"The vampire who lives out here? My ex-boyfriend?"

He shook his head. He was back to being absolutely terrified.

"You don't know how you came to be here?"

He shook his head again.

I was making a big effort to think hard; but it was just that, an effort. I was worn out. Though I'd had a rush of adrenaline when I'd spotted the figure running down the dark road, that rush was wearing off fast. I reached the turnoff to my house, winding through the black and silent woods on my nice, level driveway—that, in fact, Eric had had re-graveled for me.

And that was why Eric was sitting in my car right now, instead of running through the night like a giant white rabbit. He'd had the intelligence to give me what I really wanted. (Of course, he'd also wanted me to go to bed with him for months. But he'd given me the driveway because I needed it.)

"Here we are," I said, pulling around to the back of my old house. I switched off the car. I'd remembered to leave the outside lights on when I'd left for work that afternoon, thank goodness, so we weren't sitting there in total darkness.

"This is where you live?" He was glancing around the clearing where the old house stood, seemingly nervous about going from the car to the back door.

"Yes," I said, exasperated.

He just gave me a look that showed white all around the blue of his eyes.

"Oh, come on," I said, with no grace at all. I got out of the car and went up the steps to the back porch, which I don't keep locked because, hey, why lock a screened-in back porch? I do lock the inner door, and after a second's fumbling, I had it open so the light I leave on in the kitchen could spill out. "You can come in," I said, so he could cross the threshold. He scuttled in after me, the afghan still clutched around him.

Under the overhead light in the kitchen, Eric looked pretty pitiful. His bare feet were bleeding, which I hadn't noticed before. "Oh, Eric," I said sadly, and got a pan out from the cabinet, and started the hot water running in the sink. He'd heal real quick, like vampires do, but I couldn't help but wash him clean. The blue jeans were filthy around the hem. "Pull 'em off," I said, knowing they'd just get wet if I soaked his feet while he was dressed.

With not a hint of a leer or any other indication that he was enjoying this development, Eric shimmied out of the jeans. I tossed them onto the back porch to wash in the morning, trying not to gape at my guest, who was now clad in underwear that was definitely over-the-top, a bright red bikini style whose stretchy quality was definitely being tested. Okay, another big surprise. I'd only seen Eric's underwear once before—which was once more than I ought to have—and he'd been a silk boxers guy. Did men change styles like that?

Without preening, and without comment, the vampire rewrapped his white body in the afghan. Okay, I was convinced he wasn't himself, as no other evidence could have convinced me. Eric was way over six feet of pure magnificence (if a marble white magnificence) and he well knew it.

I pointed to one of the straight-back chairs at the kitchen table. Obediently, he pulled it out and sat. I crouched to put the pan on the floor, and I gently guided his big feet into the water. Eric groaned as the warmth touched his skin. I guess that even a vampire could feel the contrast. I got a clean rag from under the sink and some liquid soap, and I washed his feet. I took my time, because I was trying to think what to do next.

"You were out in the night," he observed, in a tentative sort of way.

"I was coming home from work, as you can see from my clothes." I was wearing our winter uniform, a long-sleeved, white boat-neck T-shirt with "Merlotte's Bar" embroidered over the left breast and worn tucked into black slacks.

"Women shouldn't be out alone this late at night," he said disapprovingly.

"Tell me about it."

"Well, women are more liable to be overwhelmed by an attack than men, so they should be more protected . . ."

"No, I didn't mean literally. I meant, I agree. You're preaching to the choir. I didn't want to be working this late at night."

"Then why were you out?"

"I need the money," I said, wiping my hand and pulling the roll of bills out of my pocket to drop it on the table while I was thinking about it. "I got this house to maintain, my car is old, and I have taxes and insurance to pay. Like everyone else," I added, in case he thought I was complaining unduly. I hated to poor-mouth, but he'd asked.

"Is there no man in your family?"

Every now and then, their ages do show. "I have a brother. I can't remember if you've ever met Jason." A cut on his left foot looked especially bad. I put some more hot water into the basin to warm the remainder. Then I tried to get all the dirt out. He winced as I gently rubbed the wash-cloth over the margins of the wound. The smaller cuts and bruises seemed to be fading even as I watched. The hot water heater came on behind me, the familiar sound some-how reassuring.

"Your brother permits you to do this working?"

I tried to imagine Jason's face when I told him that I expected him to support me for the rest of my life because I was a woman and shouldn't work outside the home. "Oh, for goodness' sake, Eric." I looked up at him, scowling. "Jason's got his own problems." Like being chronically selfish and a true tomcat.

I eased the pan of water to the side and patted Eric dry with a dishtowel. This vampire now had clean feet. Rather stiffly, I stood. My back hurt. My feet hurt. "Listen, I think what I better do is call Pam. She'll probably know what's going on with you."

"Pam?"

It was like being around a particularly irritating two-year-old.

"Your second-in-command."

He was going to ask another question, I could just tell. I held up a hand. "Just hold on, let me call her and find out what's happening."

"But what if she has turned against me?"

"Then we need to know that, too. The sooner the better."

I'd had my hand on the old phone that hung on the kitchen wall right by the end of the counter. A high stool sat below it. My grandmother had always sat on the stool to conduct her lengthy phone conversations, with a pad and pencil handy. I missed her every day. But at the moment I had no room in my emotional palette for grief, or even nostalgia. I looked in my little address book for the number of Fangtasia, the vampire bar in Shreveport that provided Eric's principal income and served as the base of his operations, which I understood were far wider in scope. I didn't know how wide or what these other moneymaking projects were, and I didn't especially want to know.

I'd seen in the Shreveport paper that Fangtasia, too, had planned a big bash for the evening—"Begin Your New Year with a Bite"—so I knew someone would be there. While the phone was ringing, I swung open the refrigerator and got out a bottle of blood for Eric. I popped it in the microwave and set the timer. He followed my every move with anxious eyes.

"Fangtasia," said an accented male voice.

"Chow?"

"Yes, how may I serve you?" He'd remembered his phone persona of sexy vampire just in the nick of time.

"It's Sookie."

"Oh," he said, in a much more natural voice. "Listen, Happy New Year, Sook, but we're kind of busy here."

"Looking for someone?"

There was a long, charged silence.

"Wait a minute," he said, and then I heard nothing.

"Pam," said Pam. She'd picked up the receiver so silently that I jumped when I heard her voice.

"Do you still have a master?" I didn't know how much I could say over the phone. I wanted to know if she'd been the one who'd put Eric in this state, or if she still owed him loyalty.

"I do," she said steadily, understanding what I wanted to know. "We are under . . . we have some problems."

I mulled that over until I was sure I'd read between the lines. Pam was telling me that she still owed Eric her allegiance, and that Eric's group of followers was under some kind of attack or in some kind of crisis.

I said, "He's here." Pam appreciated brevity.

"Is he alive?"

"Yep."

"Damaged?"

"Mentally."

A *long* pause, this time.

"Will he be a danger to you?"

Not that Pam cared a whole hell of a lot if Eric decided to drain me dry, but I guess she wondered if I would shelter Eric. "I don't think so at the moment," I said. "It seems to be a matter of memory."

"I hate witches. Humans had the right idea, burning them at the stake."

Since the very humans who had burned witches would have been delighted to sink that same stake into vampire hearts, I found that a little amusing—but not very, considering the hour. I immediately forgot what she'd been talking about.

"Tomorrow night, we'll come," she said finally. "Can you keep him this day? Dawn's in less than four hours. Do you have a safe place?"

"Yes. But you get over here at nightfall, you hear me? I don't want to get tangled up in your vampire shit again." Normally, I don't speak so bluntly; but like I say, it was the tail end of a long night.

"We'll be there."

We hung up simultaneously. Eric was watching me with unblinking blue eyes. His hair was a snarly tangled mess of blond waves. His hair is the exact same color as mine, and I have blue eyes, too, but that's the end to the similarities.

I thought of taking a brush to his hair, but I was just too weary.

"Okay, here's the deal," I told him. "You stay here the rest of the night and tomorrow, and then Pam and them'll come get you tomorrow night and let you know what's happening."

"You won't let anyone get in?" he asked. I noticed he'd finished the blood, and he wasn't quite as paper-white as he'd been, which was a relief.

"Eric, I'll do my best to keep you safe," I said, quite gently. I rubbed my face with my hands. I was going to fall asleep on my feet. "Come on," I said, taking his hand. Clutching the afghan with the other hand, he trailed down the hall after me, a snow-white giant in tiny red underwear.

My old house has been added on to over the years, but it hasn't ever been more than a humble farmhouse. A second story was added around the turn of the century, and two more bedrooms and a walk-in attic were upstairs, but I seldom go up there anymore. I keep it shut off, to save money on electricity. There are two bedrooms downstairs, the smaller one I'd used until my grandmother died, and her large one across the hall from it. I'd moved into the large one after her death. But the hidey-hole Bill had built was in the smaller bedroom. I led Eric in there, switched on the light, and made sure the blinds were closed and the curtains drawn across them. Then I opened the door of the closet, removed its few contents, and pulled back the flap of carpet that covered the closet floor, exposing the trapdoor. Underneath was a light-tight space that Bill had built a few months before, so that he could stay over during the day or use it as a hiding place if his own home was unsafe. Bill liked having a bolt-hole, and I was sure he had some that I didn't know about. If I'd been a vampire (God forbid), I would have some myself.

I had to wipe thoughts of Bill out of my head as I showed my reluctant guest how to close the trapdoor on top of him, and that the flap of carpet would fall back into place. "When I get up, I'll put the stuff back in the closet so it'll look natural," I reassured him, and smiled encouragingly.

"Do I have to get in now?" he asked.

Eric, making a request of me: The world was really turned upside-down. "No," I said, trying to sound like I was concerned. All I could think of was my bed. "You don't have to. Just get in before sunrise. There's no way you could miss that, right? I mean, you couldn't fall asleep and wake up in the sun?"

He thought for a moment, and shook his head. "No," he said. "I know that can't happen. Can I stay in the room with you?"

Oh, God, *puppy dog eyes*. From a six-foot-five ancient Viking vampire. It was just too much. I didn't have enough energy to laugh, so I just gave a sad little snigger. "Come on," I said, my voice as limp as my legs. I turned off the light in that room, crossed the hall, and flipped on the one in my own room, yellow and white and clean and warm, and folded down the bedspread and blanket and sheet. While Eric sat forlornly in a slipper chair on the other side of the bed, I pulled off my shoes and socks, got a night-gown out of a drawer, and retreated into the bathroom. I was out in ten minutes, with clean teeth and face and swathed in a very old, very soft flannel nightgown that was cream-colored with blue flowers scattered around. Its ribbons were raveled and the ruffle around the bottom was pretty sad, but it suited me just fine. After I'd switched off the lights, I remembered my hair was still up in its usual ponytail, so I pulled out the band that held it and I shook my head to make it fall loose. Even my scalp seemed to relax, and I sighed with bliss.

As I climbed up into the high old bed, the large fly in my personal ointment did the same. Had I actually told him he could get in bed with me? Well, I decided, as I wriggled down under the soft old sheets and the blanket and the comforter, if Eric had designs on me, I was just too tired to care.

"Woman?"

"Hmmm?"

"What's your name?"

"Sookie. Sookie Stackhouse."

"Thank you, Sookie."

"Welcome, Eric."

Because he sounded so lost—the Eric I knew had never been one to do anything other than assume others should serve him—I patted around under the covers for his hand. When I found it, I slid my own over it. His palm was turned up to meet my palm, and his fingers clasped mine.

And though I would not have thought it was possible to go to sleep holding hands with a vampire, that's exactly what I did.

Coming Soon from Berkley

Undead and Unemployed

HELP WANTED

"Delightful, wicked fun!"
—Christine Feehan

MaryJanice Davidson
Author of *Undead and Unwed*